I0784658

When You *Saved* Me

Brianna Remus

Also by Brianna Remus

Falling for You Trilogy

Dare to Fall

Dare to Need

Dare to Love

Pebble Brook Falls Series

If I Asked You to Stay

If You Loved Me

When You Saved Me

Author Note

This book contains elements that are only suitable for adults over the age of 18. It also contains elements that some readers may find difficult including: fire entrapment on the page, animal in precarious situation (no animals are harmed or abused), discussion of combat trauma, discussion of fire survivors with injuries, description of fire burns.

For the ones who know what it means to have your soul yearn for another.
Only to have that gift ripped away from you by the cruelty of this world.

And for my Papa Roland and all the first responders who showed up valiantly on 9/11.

Prologue

CHARLIE

Everything burns.

Heat from the flames licking up my bedroom walls singes the hairs on my skin as I look around–panicking. There is no way out.

THERE. IS. NO. WAY. OUT.

TRAPPED.

I am trapped in the corner of my room with nothing but a wet towel draped over my head and shoulders to ward off the heat.

There's no use. The water I soaked the towel with is starting to evaporate from the heat. What's left of the water is quickly turning hot, making it nearly impossible to breath under the damp cloth.

Smoke fills my lungs as I try to breathe through the

flimsy white top I put on this morning, completely unaware of what the evening would bring.

Think, Charlie. Just think.

I look around the room through hazy eyes to find anything that might keep the fire at bay and give me some time. I come up short.

Bedding.

Wooden dresser.

Vanity filled with makeup and hair products. Everything is either already engulfed in flames or highly flammable.

I'm going to die here, the thought strikes a blow to my heart, leaving me wracked with fear that feels insurmountable. Every wish I made that never came true flashes through my mind like a whip of lightning. A reminder of all the things I will never get to do as soon as the fire makes its final leap to the far side of my room where I've taken refuge.

My heart races as the anxiety spikes.

What should I do?

Black smoke pummels toward my ceiling as the white frilly comforter and sheets are ignited.

I can't breathe. The heat. The smoke. It all fills my lungs as I pull the small opening of the towel over my face even more.

I don't want to die here.

My heart lurches in my chest as I choke down another lungful of air and out of the corner of my eye I see my window. *Yes!* In all the frantic chaos, I didn't think about it. Slowly, I creep towards the window, only a few feet away from me. Careful to only take in short breaths. It burns so much; I start hacking through the slit of the towel covering my face.

Bright light beams at me as I raise my face over the windowsill and look up and down the street my apartment building is on. To the far left, the front of a red fire truck peeks around the corner of the building. People are gathered all along the street staring up in shock. Gripping the low edge of the window, I dig my fingers under the metal lip of the window, desperate for a single breath of fresh air.

All the way up on the seventh floor, there's no way I can get out, but if someone can see me…maybe they can send help.

A grunt pushes past my lips as the towel slips from my shoulders and I push upward on the window.

It doesn't budge.

Not a single inch.

"*No,*" I whisper through clenched teeth. Giving the window another shove upward, the muscles in my arms and shoulders strain against the friction but the window stays closed.

Heat lashes at the back of my eyes as tears swarm my vision.

"No!" I scream this time, throwing my fists against the glass. Over and over again, I hit the windowpane, raw fear giving me one last burst of adrenaline until the smoke consumes my lungs again, draining every last bit of energy I have from the oxygen being depleted from my muscles.

"Please, someone see me," I say, but my voice is swallowed in the chaos surrounding me. Another wracking cough hits my chest and throat as something across my room cracks loudly in the roaring flames.

Everything is on fire now except for the sliver of floor I have between myself and the outside facing wall. Drawing my feet as close to myself as possible, I strain to cover as much of myself with the towel as I can.

Burning. My entire body is burning.

I blink back the tears and take in a few shallow breaths before I let out another scream, "Help! Please! Help me!"

The only answer is the whipping fire before my vision tunnels, my breath gets lodged in my throat and everything goes dark.

Death is peaceful. It is floating high above my fears of bright red and blue light that burns and takes and devours.

Floating. Yes. I am floating.

Darkness gives way to light, and I see him. Bright green eyes the color of fresh spring look down at me. He is saying something with his beautiful mouth, but I don't hear a word. My heartbeat rushes in my ears.

Alive. Not dead. *Alive.*

I think I smile at him. This beautiful man with bright green eyes and black hair with stubble along his jaw.

How can eyes like his be so vivid and haunted at the same time?

I want to ask him. I want to know what lies behind his eyes. But something above us catches in my vision and then I'm falling.

CRASH!

Air leaves my raw lungs. Pain erupts in the back of my head and little stars dance along my vision.

I look to my left and see him. Those piercing green eyes under worried brows as he reaches for me.

I'm on fire.

I'M ON FIRE!

I want to scream at him to save me. Please! Put the fire out. It burns.

"Stay with me," his voice is weak. It doesn't match him. Not at all. "Keep your eyes on me."

No sound moves past my lips as I try to reach for him, but my arm is stuck. Something is holding me down. I can't…I can't move.

The pain…*the pain*!

A hiss of hot breath rushes into my lungs and darkness takes me once again.

Chapter 1

Seven Years Later

CHARLIE

"Oh my gosh, Casper! Look how cute this town is!"

The white furball chirped with a meow and popped his head up like he knew exactly what I'd just said. Sticking my fingers through the front of his crate, I gave him a scratch under his chin before looking back to the small downtown area we were driving through in our new hometown.

Townsfolk bundled in long coats and scarves walked along the cobblestone sidewalks. Trees were decorated with twinkling lights—remnants from the holiday season that just passed.

There were so many cute shops inside of the old brick buildings. Excitement thrummed through my veins as I wondered what little treasures I might find inside.

As I slowly drove forward, I made a note to come back to Sarah's Bakery. It looked too cute with its pink awning and swirly logo. You could always tell how good a place was by the number of people inside. The small bakery was packed to the brim with patrons. Every single table was occupied and there were several people standing in line.

My new home.

I still couldn't believe it. After years of dreaming, I finally made the decision to pack up my life in Charlotte and move to a small mountain town in Georgia. It would be an adjustment for sure, but I was excited for what was ahead.

About twenty minutes past the downtown area, rolling hills started appearing on both sides of the road with grand mountains in the distance. Even with the gray winter sky, the view was stunning.

Having grown up in Charlotte, North Carolina, I'd been a city girl through and through. The idea of being surrounded by nature and wide-open spaces called to me though, and I was excited to finally be where my heart longed for. I'd needed space and something different for a long while.

"I think this one might be us," I said to Casper. His front paws were tucked underneath himself and his eyes were starting to get droopy like the long ride had finally taken its toll on him.

The GPS cued me to turn left onto what appeared to be a long winding dirt road. Tall brown grass lined both sides for what had to be miles over countless hills. I smiled to myself because this was exactly what I hoped it would be. Not a skyscraper in sight. No trash on sidewalks or lost tourists asking too many questions.

Just pure, untouched beauty.

When I leased Badger Creek Cabin, the landlord reached out to me and told me I should meet him at his house on the property first so he could show me how to get to the cabin since there wasn't a designated road for it.

I was nervous at first. I wasn't exactly the best with directions and if there wasn't even a road leading to my new home, I was likely to get lost on more than one occasion. But the landlord made it seem like it would be a fairly easy drive once I got it down.

Casper's paws stretched through the front grate of his crate a few minutes later when we arrived at my landlord's house.

I pulled up next to a giant truck in the driveway and took a moment to settle in. The main house was also a cabin that appeared to be made of fir wood with a beautiful reddish hue to it that was a stark contrast to the dull grass that surrounded it. With a wraparound porch, it looked exactly like the tiny cabin I was meant to stay in, just on a grander scale.

My heart fluttered with excitement, and I let out a little squeal as I clapped my hands together. "Okay, buddy! We're here!" I popped my head closer to the front of his crate and crooned at him. He purred with appreciation when I ran my fingers between his ears.

Leaving the car running so Casper would stay warm, I hopped out and smiled at the bite of cold air hitting my cheeks. I loved winter. In fact, I loved every season Mother Earth had to offer us. Each one brought something different and beautiful. A new experience every few months always made it feel like life was brimming with energy.

Gravel crunched under my boots as I headed up the walkway. When I got to the front door, I took a deep breath in. This was the start of my brand-new adventure, and I couldn't believe after years of conjuring this moment up in my mind, I was finally here.

I knocked three times before burying my hands in my coat pockets. Footsteps sounded on the other side of the door.

"Eek!" I whispered to myself.

The door swung open to reveal a giant man taking up most of the entrance. My gaze landed at chest height and the first thing I noticed was how his T-shirt laid perfectly over his sculpted pectoral muscles.

Oh! I thought to myself before my eyes skated upward. Black stubble lined his square jaw, making a perfect backdrop for plump lips that seemed almost too soft against his dark features. But his eyes...bright green like a lily pad dancing along the surface of a pristine lake.

His eyes.

I know those eyes.

"You," I said aloud before I had a chance to think about the word I'd just sputtered.

The same realization sparked in those vivid irises as he looked me up and down with fiery indignation.

"No." His voice was gruff and stern before he stepped backward and slammed the door in my face.

I remained standing on his front porch where he left me in utter shock wondering what mystical forces might be at play here. The man who saved me seven years ago was my new landlord and he'd just slammed his front door in my face.

Well, this is off to a great start.

I peeked through the long window that lined the side of his door, but the blinds were closed so tightly, I couldn't see even a sliver of the inside.

The cold was starting to seep its way into my jacket the longer I stood on his front porch. There was no mistaking the recognition in his eyes when he saw me. I just didn't understand why he didn't want to see me. How the recognition turned into…disdain.

Maybe I should have turned away and found a new place to stay. Intruding on his space wasn't my intention and if he didn't want me here then I could respect that. But I'd also fought for this opportunity for years. The least he could do was give me a little more than a *no*.

Raising my closed fist, I went to knock on his door again but didn't get the chance when it flew open, and he stepped through the threshold. I looked to my fist hanging midair and swallowed before it fell to my side.

We were nearly toe-to-toe, and I had to crane my neck to look into his face.

"I'm Deacon Calhoun." He extended his hand out to me.

I looked at it and blinked. No apology. No explanation for why he slammed the door in my face and left me out here in the cold.

Okay, this is how things are going to go then. I can play along with this if it gets me what I want.

Slipping my hand in his, I almost moaned at the warmth

that engulfed my palm. But when I peeked up at his face, I saw a flicker of pain dance across his eyes and his brows pinched together slightly.

"It's nice to formally meet you, Deacon. I'm Charlie Banks."

"Yes, I know."

I supposed he did know. Not just from that fateful day we had together but from my paperwork I submitted for the rental.

If there was ever an awkward moment in my life, this one surely took the cake. I pulled my hand away, severing the connection that seemed to cause him distress.

"Are you still okay with me being here, Deacon?" The cold was biting and all I wanted to do was get situated in my new home and snuggle with Casper after this frigid greeting.

His voice was gruff as he said, "It's fine. Let me show you the way to the cabin."

As he tried to move past me, I grabbed a hold of his wrist, and I swore he stopped breathing. Avoiding my gaze, he kept his eyes locked straight ahead.

"I can leave if this is too uncomfortable for you." Not knowing why he was reacting this way toward me, it was all I could offer. I didn't want to go. But if it was something he needed me to do, I would.

Haunted by some unknown part of our entangled past, his eyes were sullen as they shifted to look at me. "It's fine."

With a deep breath, I let go of his wrist and followed him in silence as he jumped into his truck, and I settled back into the driver seat of my sedan.

Casper let out a little squeak of concern. He always had a way of knowing when I was feeling off.

"Looks like we're in for a bit of a ride with this one, buddy. But I think it'll be okay." The hum of his purr settled my nerves as I shifted gears and followed behind Deacon's truck.

The drive wasn't too long. Maybe a little more than five minutes. When the cabin came into view, my breath hitched, and my heart fluttered.

"Wow," I breathed. "It's so beautiful."

Still behind the wheel of my car, I stared at the tiny cabin before me. Bright fir wood, the same as the main house, was stacked in layers building up the frame of the home. The porch was much smaller than Deacon's, but it was perfect with a rocking chair and side table that had a small pot of primroses. Three hanging pots filled with pansies swung in the gentle breeze along the edge of the overhang.

Picturesque didn't begin to cover it. I was smitten with the cabin and beyond thankful that Deacon decided to let me stay here after his momentary panic…was panic what I saw in his face?

Shaking my head, I let any worries about my new landlord go. The property seemed huge, so I doubted we would run into each other that much anyway.

Deacon appeared from the driver's seat of his lifted truck, so I grabbed Casper's small crate and headed toward the front door.

Butterflies struck my stomach when I heard the sound of rushing water. "Is there a river behind the cabin?" I asked excitedly as I watched him sort through a ring of keys. I didn't miss how large his hands were and blushed when I thought back to how warm he felt when we shook hands earlier.

Deacon grunted his affirmation. "Didn't you see the photos online?"

"Yeah, but I didn't realize the river was right behind it. I thought it was just somewhere on the property."

He settled on one of the keys and pushed it into the lock. "I wouldn't suggest going onto the dock. It needs to be repaired after a big storm blew some of the panels off. I'll be around this weekend to get it back in working order."

"That would be wonderful. Thank you."

Those striking green eyes glanced at me over his shoulder and for a moment I wasn't standing on a charming cabin porch anymore. Heat licked up my ribcage and my lungs burned from smoke inhalation. The only thing keeping me cognizant was the sound of his voice, calling after me. Telling me to stay awake. That he would do anything to get me out.

Meow! Casper let out a whaling note of frustration that broke me away from the glimpse into my past.

Lifting the crate upward, I stroked his paw and told him, "It's okay, buddy. Almost time for you to run free again."

"Is that a cat?"

I looked up at Deacon who seemed to have found an even more disdainful look than the one he gave me when he first saw me at his house.

"Yes, his name is Casper." I lifted the crate so Deacon could see him clearly.

He looked down at Casper. His lips shifted into a tight line before he looked back at me.

I shrugged. "The rental posting said that pets were allowed."

He mumbled something under his breath that sounded a lot like 'I hate cats' before shoving the cabin door open. I brought Casper's carrier closer to my chest and whispered to him, "He didn't mean that."

Casper and I followed Deacon inside and I had to quiet the squeal that built inside my throat. The space was so cute! It was loft style with a pretty decent sized kitchen. White veined quartz sat on top of sage green cabinetry that gave the space an elevated feel from a typical cottage core vibe. A small loveseat took up one corner of the living space with a pine and mahogany wood coffee table in front of it.

Best of all, the bed on the opposite side of the space was king-sized and looked heavenly after the long drive I'd just made. A yawn ached at the back of my throat, but I kept my mouth closed trying to stifle it.

"There's fresh towels and linens in this closet here." He opened a narrow doorway that housed three shelves of every-thing I would need. Then he pointed to the only other door in the space, to the right of the bed. "The bathroom is through that door over there. It's a tight space, but with it only being you it should be fine."

He paused for a moment, his hand lingering over the door handle. "It is *just* you, right?"

I chuckled. "Yes. I'm not sneaking another tenant in here, I promise."

His eyes turned stormy, the bright green darkening a few shades. Then, I realized he wasn't asking about me sneaking in a tenant. He was wondering if I had a man who might be visiting.

I refrained from snorting. After his cold greeting, I was going to keep my extra-curricular activities to myself. He didn't need to know what he didn't need to know.

"Everything looks great, thank you." I changed the subject from my waning love life, then set Casper's crate on the ground so I could let him out to explore. A quick undoing of the latch and he bounded through the opening.

His little whiskers flinched as he sniffed the air of his new home before setting his sights on Deacon. Casper pranced toward him, and I couldn't help but giggle when he started rubbing against Deacon's jean clad legs, winding around and around.

"Um, what's it doing?" For such a large man, Deacon looked genuinely disturbed by my little fluff ball.

I grinned. "He's just saying hello. When he winds through your legs like that, it means he likes you."

Confusion knitted his brows together. "How can he like me? He doesn't even know me."

"I'm not sure." I bent down to pick up Casper. "Maybe it's your winning personality," I snickered. He glowered at me.

Silence filled the small space as we stared at one another, neither one willing to give an inch. That was when I noticed the small ember flakes amongst the pine green of his irises. I'd never seen eyes like his before.

I let myself become entranced by them, noticing all the fine details so I might keep them with me. Not that I would ever need a reason to think about him. Especially not about the small scar that split the cupid's bow of his upper lip. Or what it might feel like to run my palm against the side of his stubbled jaw.

He cleared his throat, snapping me out of my spiraling thoughts. I stumbled back a step, like being too close to him might make me do something stupid. The man clearly loathed my existence for whatever reason. The last thing I needed to do was complicate things in my new home.

"Well, thanks for the tour. I've got it from here."

"Right. Yeah. I, um, left my phone number on the fridge in case anything comes up that you need help with."

I glanced behind me where a sticky note with his phone number was taped onto the fridge door. "Thanks."

Another awkward pause and then, "Okay, I'll get out of your hair."

With that, Deacon walked out my new front door and I was left to wonder what I'd just gotten myself into.

Chapter 2

Charlie

Decor ideas for my new space were already swirling through my mind. Before I knew who my landlord actually was, I'd emailed him asking if it would be okay for me to paint and decorate the cabin to my liking. At the time, he seemed pretty okay with the idea, but I wondered how Deacon felt about it now.

I just won't bring it up to him again, I thought. Do now, ask for forgiveness later. I was pretty sure that was how the saying went.

Most of the night was spent tossing and turning from images of a distant past. There were so many questions I wanted to ask Deacon. Too many unknowns that made my stomach buzz. At the same time, his standoff attitude made me feel thankful for our separation. The last thing I wanted was for his foul mood to put a damper on the excitement I had for my new home.

Taking a deep breath in, I lowered my shoulders and forced a smile onto my face. My mother always taught me that happiness was a smile away and even now, I knew it was true. In my darkest moments, I would push myself to grin and found that within a few seconds my mood would lighten, and the gloom would dissipate.

With a renewed pep in my step, I crouched next to the loveseat where I'd placed Casper's bed and gave him some snuggles. "I'll be back in a little bit, buddy. Hold down the fort for me, will you?" His eyes narrowed into slits; a loud purr vibrated his throat.

Grabbing my keys from the counter, I headed out the door to explore my new hometown.

The back seat of my car was filled with art supplies and various wall paints. A few bottles of red wine were stuffed between everything. I had every intention of breaking in my new little home with some pinot noir, Ludovico Einaudi blasting, and my paintbrush in hand tonight.

But first, I needed sustenance. It probably would have been the wiser decision to stock up on groceries before filling my car to the brim with art supplies, but a girl loves what she loves. Plus, it gave me the perfect excuse to stop by Sarah's Bakery, that I saw on the drive through town.

"This is so cute!" I said to myself as I stood in front of the bakery. White and pink stripes on the awning made it feel like I was transported to a quaint café in Paris. Sweet notes of powdered sugar, fruit, and cinnamon hit my nose when I walked inside.

Dozens of eyes shifted toward me as the door snicked shut behind me. A small smile pulled at the corners of my lips, as I took in the patrons circled around small tables. Children, adults and elders were all gathered together sharing in what appeared to be hot chocolate and delicious pastries.

The scene before me was exactly what I pictured when I set my sights on living in a small town. Kiddos darted from table to table like they knew every person in here and felt safe enough to do so. Adults seemed to be holding multiple conversations at a time, many of them speaking to people at other tables from time to time.

Charlotte was very much a Southern city, but I had often felt lost in the hustle and bustle. People didn't wave to me when I walked on the sidewalk to work. Baristas at my local coffee shop hardly knew my name, even though I'd gone there almost daily for several years. There were almost *too* many people. It was easy to just keep to yourself and not work toward getting to know anyone else.

Pebble Brook Falls was different. Even though I'd only been here a day, the place seemed to warm my heart. I was excited to get to know everyone and for them to get to know me.

When I made my way to the checkout counter, the crowd

went back to their eating and conversations, paying me no more attention.

"Hi!" I said to the young woman behind the counter. Her long brown hair was pulled back in a high ponytail with ringlet curls draping over the side of her shoulder.

"Hi," she beamed at me.

"Can I get a chocolate croissant please?"

"Of course." Tapping the screen in front of her, she entered my order. "Is there anything else I can get you?"

I peeked at the glass display case. "Um...maybe half a dozen of the chocolate muffins. Those look divine."

"They're one of my favorites. You definitely won't be disappointed."

"Awesome! I can't wait to snack on them later."

As she entered the rest of my order, another woman came through what looked to be the back kitchen door. With similar dark brown hair and a button nose, I wondered if the two were related somehow. She peered into the back side of the glass case and took inventory of the treats.

I looked back to the cashier and extended my hand to her. "I'm Charlie by the way. I just moved into town."

Taking my hand and shaking it, she responded, "I'm Stephanie. It's nice to meet you, Charlie."

When our hands parted, she asked, "Where are you moving from?"

"Charlotte, North Carolina. I just got in yesterday."

"Did you buy a house in town?"

"Actually, I'm staying in Badger Creek Cabin. It's a rental out in the country."

The other woman behind the display case popped her head around the corner. "Badger Creek Cabin?"

"Mmhmm." I nodded. "Do you know it?"

Wiping her hands on her apron, she rose to her full height. "I helped the owner renovate it. Deacon's one of my good friends. I didn't realize you had already moved in." She walked up next to Stephanie, and we shook hands. "I'm Sarah, it's nice to meet you, Charlie."

"Sarah, as in *Sarah's Bakery,* Sarah?" My brows shot up.

"Yup! That's me."

"Oh my gosh, well I have to thank you for what looks to be some amazing food I'm about to scarf down."

She giggled. "Don't mention it. Steph, give her this one on the house."

"Oh no." I waved my hands. "You don't have to do that."

Giving me a stern look under her long eyelashes, she said, "If you're staying at Badger Creek Cabin with Deacon Calhoun as your landlord, I insist."

Twisting my lips to the side I couldn't help but wonder what was in store for me if it was known across town how much of a grump Deacon was. I slipped my credit card back into my wallet and slid onto one of the barstools next to the display case.

"I take it I'm not the only one he's grumpy to then?" I asked, partly not wanting to know the answer but also letting my curiosity win over.

"Oh yeah, that's just how he is," Stephanie said with a smirk.

Sarah responded, "He's one of my best friends." Then

she bumped Stephanie with her hip. "But that does not mean I condone his…poor demeanor."

I slipped the chocolate croissant out of the paper bag and took a bite. Eyes rolling into the back of my head, I couldn't help but moan. It was a perfect combination of flakey bread with just the right amount of melted chocolate. "Oh my god," I said around the bite. "I don't think I've ever tasted something this good in my entire life." I picked up the croissant and shook it once to make my point. "And I've had about a dozen of these *in* Paris."

Sarah's face lit up with pride. "Well, I don't think I've ever received such a wonderful compliment. Thank you, Charlie."

"Don't let it go to your head, cousin." Stephanie rolled her eyes playfully.

"Can't make any promises." Sarah winked back.

Cousins. Definitely made sense given how much they looked alike.

"So, you're really best friends with Deacon?"

"Yeah," she drew out the word. "I'm a sucker for the broody ones. Don't let the sourpuss attitude fool you though. He's one of the most loyal and selfless people I know. He'd give the shirt off his back to his enemy if they were in need. I just think he's been through some things in life that created his hard shell. But once you crack the exterior, he's really just made of fluff on the inside."

Stephanie snorted. "Don't let him hear you say that."

"Eh." Sarah shrugged. "I can take him." Then she turned her attention back to me. "Has he given you any trouble?"

My throat went dry. How did I explain that my new land-lord had saved my life when my apartment building went up in flames and when I saw him for the first time since then, he slammed his front door in my face? Sarah was his best friend. I definitely didn't want to make it seem like Deacon was a bad guy to her. The last thing I wanted to do was make enemies in my new hometown. News traveled fast in Southern cities, and I imagined it traveled even quicker in small towns.

So, I settled on, "He was fine. I can tell what you mean by a rough exterior. He hasn't said much to me, but it's almost like I can tell he is thinking a lot about having me stay on his property... Maybe even regretting it."

Sarah slid her eyes to Stephanie. Some secret language passed between them, and I wanted to know what they were thinking, but decided I'd probably already said too much.

"Any thoughts on how I might crack that exterior?" I asked quietly.

Sarah's smile was warm. "I don't know you well, Char-lie, but you seem like a really great woman. Just be yourself and I know he'll come around. He just..." She nodded her head side to side. "Takes a little time to warm up to people. I wouldn't take anything he says or does right now too personal."

I looked down at the croissant in my hand, studying the flakey layers. What Sarah didn't know was that I had a striking feeling the way Deacon acted toward me was incred-ibly personal. While it didn't make sense to me, there was something about the day we first met that he struggled with.

It wasn't normal for someone to have such a striking reaction to the person they saved. Maybe something happened after I passed out from the pain of my burn that I wasn't privy to. Or maybe he was just a grump like Sarah said and he really would come around in time.

Either way, I was going to make it my mission to find out because I knew there was something more than disdain hiding behind those green eyes. Something I couldn't quite pinpoint, but I felt it in my heart when I looked at him. A sensation that only people who were bonded by the same trauma experienced.

I just had to figure out what, exactly, it was.

"I'll definitely do that. I really appreciate you giving me some guidance and it was nice to meet you both." Shoving the rest of the croissant back into the paper bag, I slid off the stool.

"Of course! I'm glad we were able to meet, Charlie. And if you ever need anything, you know where to find me." Sarah gave a little wave before she disappeared through the back door.

"Nice to meet you, Charlie!" Stephanie said as I gathered my food and set toward the exit.

"You too, Stephanie!"

The bell chimed above the door as I swung it open. The temperature had dropped at least a few degrees while I was inside; it was refreshing after feeling stifled from thinking about Deacon and I's past.

Tilting my head back, the gray sky reminded me of darker times. Moments that I had to crawl away from to save myself. Moments that left a mark, but also made me stronger. Deacon might be holding onto something from our past, but that didn't mean I had to let his poor mood impact me. I'd worked too hard to let anything get in the way of my joy, including a devastatingly handsome man who was starting to occupy my thoughts more than I liked to admit.

Chapter 3

Deacon

Not even an entire twenty-four hours passed, and my thoughts were already consumed with a petite redhead who I had thought I would never have to see again.

When Charlie Banks showed up on my front porch, I couldn't help but feel like I was being damned to hell on earth. I ran away from her seven years ago. Leaving everything I knew behind me in Charlotte, only to be tricked by some cruel twist of fate.

Now, she was only a few acres away from me.

It wasn't far enough.

I could still feel her presence like a ghost of memories past coming to haunt me.

Maybe slamming the door in her face had been an asshole move. Admittedly, she scared the fuck out of me and the moment I set my eyes on her, my body just reacted. I had to get away.

After she asked me if I was okay with her staying in my cabin, I should have said no. I was already regretting telling her it was fine.

Sleep evaded me last night and I'd spent the entire day today busying myself with mindless tasks. I checked on my best friend's–Johnny–archery store since he was away on his honeymoon. Then I spent countless hours tinkering around the house trying to find any sort of project that would distract me.

When all the loose cabinet doors and leaky faucets were fixed, I texted Sarah and asked her if I could join her and Ranger for dinner. There was no way in hell I could manage another night alone knowing how close Charlie was to me. I needed a distraction, and fast.

I knocked on the front door of Sarah and Ranger's ranch house and heard barking on the other side. As the door opened, a giant yellow hurricane of fur barreled through and nearly tackled me to the ground.

"Asher!" Sarah scolded. "What have we talked about you jumping on our guests?"

Asher wound through my legs. Bending over, I scratched the top of his head, right behind his ears. Giant golden eyes beamed up at me as his tongue lolled out of the side of his mouth.

"Don't listen to her, buddy. You can tackle me anytime you want."

When I looked up at Sarah, she had her arms crossed over her chest and was shaking her head. "I swear that dog could get away with murder and no one would be upset."

"You're probably right about that." Sarah and Ranger had taken Asher in while our best friends, Johnny and Willow were away on their extended honeymoon. She might have seemed frustrated by Asher's antics, but I knew Sarah loved the dog just as much as his own parents did.

"Alright, let's get you two in the house. It's freezing outside today."

Stuck to my side like glue, Asher and I followed Sarah into the house. Savory notes floated in the air and my stomach grumbled. Forced to distract myself all day, I'd worked around the house right through lunch and was desperate for a home cooked meal.

Sarah led us into the kitchen. I nearly choked on laughter as I saw Ranger at the stove with a pink apron tied around his neck and waist.

"Dude, what the fuck are you wearing?" I chuckled.

Spatula in hand, Ranger turned around and growled, "She"—he pointed at Sarah with the spatula—"made me wear this."

Eyebrows raised, I looked at her.

She shrugged, but the gesture didn't match the shit eating grin on her face. "I just bought him that new button down and didn't want him getting anything on it. Men are so messy. You're all just a bunch of neanderthals in nicer clothing."

Ranger and I scoffed at her.

"Says the woman who put my friend in a frilly pink apron. We might be neanderthals, but you're just cruel, woman."

Ranger leaned over and gave me a fist bump.

"Uh-uh. No way." Sarah scissored her arms back and forth. "There is no way you two are ganging up on me tonight."

Ranger's expression softened before he stepped toward her and planted a kiss on her forehead. I looked away. "I wouldn't dream of ganging up on you, sugar."

"Good," she responded chastely. Then I felt her attention shift back onto me.

Shit. I knew that look and it always meant trouble. Sarah had been the second person in Pebble Brook Falls to become my friend and by friend I meant she essentially forced me to enjoy her company until I actually started to like the idea of having her around.

Ever since I left Charlotte, and my entire life behind, I'd become somewhat of a lone wolf. I'd known Johnny from our time together in the military and when he'd told me about his hometown, it felt like the right move. I had needed to get away from the noise and prying eyes in the city. I had needed....*space* and clarity.

There was no part of me that thought moving to a small town would mean I would find my closest friends. Even if they were a giant pain in my ass sometimes.

"Speaking of ganging up on people, I met your new renter, Deacon." The way her lips tilted upward, and her nose scrunched just a little, I knew I was about to be in trouble for something. But beyond that, my spine stiffened at the mere thought of Charlie.

Fuck. I couldn't even think about the woman without my body reacting. I needed to get my shit together if I was going to survive her living on my property.

"Yeah?" It was the only word I could get out, but I regretted how suspicious it made me sound.

Ranger looked between us like he had no idea what we were talking about but knew I was in the hot seat for something. Like the smart man he was, he let Sarah be while he started to dish out our dinner onto plates.

What I would give to be in his shoes right now.

"Mmhmm." Sarah nodded, crossing her arms. "Why are you torturing the poor girl?"

My mouth gaped and sweat started coating my palms. "What did she say to you?"

Sarah snorted. "Not much, just that you seemed pretty rough around the edges and barely said a word to her."

I let out a quiet breath, hoping that was all Charlie had told Sarah and not that I'd been a complete ass who slammed a door in a woman's face from utter shock.

Just play it off.

"I'd say that's a fairly accurate depiction of how I am with everyone," I said nonchalantly. "You know it's difficult for me to be around new people."

Her eyes narrowed. "It's difficult for you to be around a beautiful redhead? Who I might add was a bright ray of sunshine when she stopped by my bakery earlier today." The right edge of Sarah's lip curled up. "That is the kind of new person you have a difficult time being around?"

Ranger started divvying out our plates in front of the stools around the kitchen island. "Take it easy on the guy, sugar. Maybe it's been a while since Deacon has played ball and this woman makes him a little uneasy."

Sarah turned her burning gaze on Ranger. "A little uneasy isn't how she described her interactions with him, babe. From what she described; he was a total brute!" Completely exasperated with the two of us, Sarah shook her head and rolled her eyes.

"All I'm saying is maybe there's a reason Deacon acted that way," Ranger responded in my defense.

They both looked at me expectantly and I felt my blood heat under the weight of their observation. Discomfort ran through me. They were getting uncomfortably close to the one thing I'd kept hidden from everyone in my life. When I looked down at Asher by my side, even he had a look of curiosity in his eyes.

The truth was so close to the surface, and I wondered what it might be like to share the burden with someone else. To not have to carry its heaviness all alone anymore. But as memories of wild flames, billowing smoke and the screams of a beautiful young woman filled my mind, my throat clamped up with unspoken words.

No one else needed to experience the pain from that day. Certainly not the people I held closest to me. It was mine to shoulder. And I fully intended on keeping it that way.

"I'm just not used to having someone in my space. It's been only me out there for a really long time and it'll take some adjusting. But I'm fine."

Sarah raised her brows at me. She didn't have to say anything for me to know what she was thinking.

I groaned. "And I'll make an effort not to scare her off."

Sarah smiled and Ranger shook his head with a grin on his face. He knew the powers of influence his woman held. I'm sure she used her persuasiveness on him all the time given the pink apron he wore.

"Good," she said with mock sternness. "Now, we can eat."

We all took our places in front of the plates Ranger served. I didn't waste any time digging in. With the day I'd had and Sarah's pestering, my stomach had started eating away at itself.

The first bite of steak had me moaning in gratitude. It didn't take me long to clear the plate and head back to the stovetop for seconds.

Great food and even better company were the perfect distraction as we wound up digging into a fresh wildberry pie Sarah had made earlier that day. Ranger poured me two fingers of bourbon and we sat around their firepit on the back deck.

In the silent moments, it didn't take long for the burning fire in front of me to slowly morph into a scene I tried to bat out of my mind almost every day. It was a constant battle that raged inside of me, and I spent the rest of the night wondering how I was going to win now that I had a reminder of the mistake I made that day living on my property.

Sarah was right. Charlie was a beautiful woman. One I felt drawn to the moment I saw her tiny body curled into a ball in the corner of her demolished bedroom, the threat of death looming over her. The scar I knew she bore—the one that matched my own—had been my fault. And now I was forced to live with that mistake for the rest of my life.

Chapter 4

Charlie

A shrilling ring shattered the silence in my new home. Grabbing my phone from the kitchen counter, I pressed the green button to answer my mom's call and put it on speaker.

"Momma!"

"Sweetheart! I have dad on the call with me. How are you settling into the new place?"

I took a moment to look around the space and felt a sense of peace in my heart. The walls were still barren and the small number of boxes I had were mostly still packed, but it still felt like home.

"It's going really well." I grabbed the rest of my paint brushes and started assigning them to their respective containers. Last night, I started setting up my painting space. It was much smaller than what I had in my last place, but I knew the rich nature that surrounded the cabin would be inspiration enough for me to continue my work with ease.

"I'm almost done setting up my painting area. The landlord even agreed that I could paint some murals on the walls inside the cabin."

"That's wonderful honey." My dad's voice came through the line. "Did you get a chance to meet him in person yet? Do you feel safe?"

A smile pulled at my lips. Always the protective one, my father had the hardest time after the fire. If he had it his way, I would have stayed with my parents indefinitely after I was discharged from the hospital. But he knew that wasn't going to work. I'd always been a free spirit who needed her space. It was part of my creative process.

So, I hid the fact that I had met my landlord years before I moved to Georgia and that he wasn't exactly throwing a welcome party in my honor. My parents didn't need any reason to worry about me. Plus, I could handle Deacon Calhoun. Even if his presence did something funny to my insides and that it was difficult to look at him without wondering how perfection could truly exist in a man as rugged as him.

"He's perfectly fine, Daddy. He should be coming around in the next few days to fix the dock behind the cabin. Did I tell you guys that it's right on the river? I can see the water from my back window!"

"That sounds amazing, Charlie," my mom responded right before my dad said, "Well, don't go on the dock until he fixes it."

I rolled my eyes. "I promise I won't."

Casper jumped on the arm of the sofa next to where I was

still organizing all my brushes and paints. He let out a little squeak that melted my heart.

"Casper says hello."

I could nearly hear my parents smile through the phone when they both responded, "Hello, buddy! We miss you!"

Casper bumped his head into the palm of my hand and flopped over. I stroked his belly. My parents were of those few people who loved animals as much, or maybe even more than they loved humans. They didn't mind that I hadn't given them human grandchildren yet. Both of them were completely content with having Casper to spoil.

And they spoiled him rotten. The fluff ball had an entire section of my tiny closet dedicated to a bin of toys my parents surprised us with before we left for our trip.

I was thankful for it though. My parents supported me in whatever decisions I made for myself. They trusted that I knew what I was doing, and it felt nice knowing I had their approval.

We spent the next hour chatting away on the phone while I organized my art supplies to my liking. They updated me on all the gossip going around Charlotte and we planned for a visit at the end of winter when spring brought the forest back to life.

By the end of our phone call, I stepped back and took in my cultivated space. A blank canvas sat atop my easel next to the open window looking over the rushing water of the river. It was the perfect spot, and I already had butterflies thinking about painting the deep blues of the water and greens from the surrounding pine trees.

"Wanna go for a little adventure, buddy?" Casper perked up when he heard the sound of my voice.

The temperature outside was likely dropping given how low the sun was behind the trees. So, I traded my leggings and sweatshirt for warmer clothes and slipped on my boots and beanie hat before I put Casper's booties on his paws. When I strapped the last one onto his back paw, he stared up at me, unmoving.

"They're to protect your feet," I tried to coax him to act normal, but he just blinked at me like *I* was the idiot who put booties on a cat. Which, to be fair…I was.

"Come on. You'll thank me later when your paws aren't frozen from the cold ground." Opening the back door, I gestured with my hand for him to follow. Stifling a laugh, I watched as he lifted each bootie-clad paw higher than necessary until he made his way onto the back patio.

He followed me down the steps and toward the river where I nearly lost my breath from the beauty just outside my door. I closed my eyes and listened. There was both a roar to the moving water and little plopping sounds from splashes landing in the depths. A dedicated wind had branches groaning against the pressure and rustling leaves scraped against one another. It was a masterpiece written by the most talented creator, making my hands ache with the need to stroke my brush against canvas.

When I opened my eyes again, I looked forward to where the small dock reached out over the water. Planks were missing from the foundation, and I found myself envisioning what it might be like to watch Deacon work on rebuilding it.

Back home, my parents always hired a handyman to come and fix things around their house. My dad had never been the type for homemade projects. He preferred to spend his time playing sports or chasing after a new marathon record for himself. My mother was the same way. We always joked that I must have been mixed up with another baby at the hospital because I was so dissimilar to my parents in the big ways.

Creation was in my blood, and I was excited to be around someone else who had the ability to create something from scratch. Even if he was a grumpy asshole. Art wasn't just in the finery of paints or sculpture. It was in one's ability to make something new out of what already existed. To breathe life in an undiscovered way.

Squatting, I ran my hand over Casper's fur, giving his back a good scratch. He rolled over onto the frozen ground and with a few wiggles decided it was much too cold and sprung back onto his paws.

"See, I told you the booties would come in handy." Mist gathered in front of my mouth as I spoke. The light rays coming through the tree line across the river were starting to dwindle as the sun sunk lower into the horizon.

Meow!

I chuckled. "I think you're right. It's time to head back inside to warm up." I took one final look around the forest that surrounded my little cabin and felt my chest swell with gratitude. There was a time when I thought I'd never see another day in my life. Now, seven years after the fire, I was here. In the cutest little town with my furry best friend by my side and a wealth of inspiration before me.

Life is good.

Steam rose from the hot chocolate on the coffee table as I lit the starter log in the small fireplace. It didn't take long before the starter log got going and the rest of the logs caught.

Settling onto the loveseat, I lifted the side of my sweater and rubbed at the scar lining my ribcage. The cold was really starting to irritate it, especially around the edges. I made a mental note to call my doctor on Monday to ask him what ointments might be best for it during the cold. The air was much drier here compared to Charlotte and if I didn't get the itching under control, I was going to drive myself crazy.

Casper chirped at me from the ground. I patted my lap to invite him up and he immediately jumped. Making two circles, he finally settled in and started kneading the blanket I had draped over my legs.

I let my head fall to the back of the sofa and took a moment to look around the space. The inside of the cabin was chic—modern even. It almost seemed to have a woman's touch, especially given the fresh flowers that were decorating the coffee table and both nightstands from the first day I'd walked in.

Sarah had said she'd helped Deacon renovate the place, but did she help him freshen it up with these flowers too?

My mind strayed to thoughts of Deacon having another woman help him with this place. Someone he might also share a bed with. My stomach turned sour. Some visceral part of me hoped there wasn't a woman in his life. Not that there was any chance I'd have a shot with him given his reaction to seeing me here. Not that I was even sure I *wanted* a shot with him.

I typically preferred men who didn't slam doors in my face.

Still. I didn't want to think of him with someone else and the feeling kind of bothered me. I shouldn't care what he does in his spare time and who he does it with. His life was none of my business.

Somehow, my mind still wandered to what it felt like to be held in his arms. The strength that surrounded me when I awoke to those beautiful green eyes and the guttural sound of his voice as he called after me. Tethering me to life when I was on death's doorstep.

It might have been the adrenaline or the simple fact that the man had saved my life…but I swore something transcendent passed between us that day. Beyond what words could describe, but I felt it. A divine connection that I was sure wanted us to be near one another given that we both had ended up in Pebble Brook Falls.

Pop!

Crack!

I startled at the sound of the dry wood catching fire in a

new spot. Letting out a long sigh, I stroked Casper's back and said, "I'm being ridiculous, huh, boy? Thinking there's some grand plan at work that brought us here."

He tilted his head back and looked at me with narrowed eyes, like he didn't care what I was thinking about as long as I kept scratching his back.

"Yeah, I don't blame you. I wish I had someone to scratch my back too."

Deciding to keep my thoughts away from tall, dark and handsome, I turned my attention back to the barren walls of the cabin. A misty forest scene flooded my mind. I could see every part of it. The way the sun's rays at dawn shone through parts of the mist through the branches of the large pine trees.

More and more details played out in my mind as I imagined where I might start with the mural. Before I knew it, I was so lost in my own imagination I didn't notice the room was starting to look hazy and the air smelled like...

SMOKE!

"Oh no!" Turning toward the blazing hearth, I realized black plumes of smoke were billowing forward, not up through the chimney like they were supposed to.

Grabbing Casper from my lap, I hopped off the sofa and ran toward the fridge with my phone. Dialing Deacon's number as fast as my fingers would let me, I headed out the front door to stay away from the soot filled air.

"Hello?" His gruff voice came through the line.

Taking a calming breath, I tried not to sound too

panicked. "Deacon, I think there's something blocking the chimney because smoke is filling the entire cabin."

Immediately sounding more alert, he asked, "Are you still in the cabin?"

"No. I grabbed Casper and we're both sitting on the front porch."

There was rustling in the background like he might be putting on a coat or something. "I'll head over there right now. Don't go back inside for any reason, okay?" There was an edge to his voice that made my heart flutter. Suddenly, the grumpy man I met on his front porch was concerned about my well-being…?

"Okay, I won't," I responded, peeking my head toward the window to see the smoke was growing thicker by the second. "But hurry, please?"

There was a roar of an engine through the phone. "I'm on my way." Then, the phone line went dead.

Chapter 5

Deacon

Blood pumped wildly through my veins as my heartbeat pulsed in my ears. Charlie was alone and the cabin was filled with smoke.

An image of her buried beneath ceiling rubble clanged through my mind as I shifted gears and pressed down on the accelerator of my truck.

Before her arrival—before I knew it was *her* who would occupy my rental cabin—I'd double checked everything to make sure it was in working order. The fireplace had been cleaned out, along with the chimney. Somehow, I missed something and now I couldn't get the picture of Charlie being stuck in the cabin surrounded by smoke out of my mind.

Even worse, it was my fault.

Again.

"She's not inside. She told me she was outside on the

front porch," I told myself out loud as I maneuvered the shift stick into a higher gear. "She's safe. *She's safe.*"

No matter how many times I repeated the words to myself, my heart rate didn't slow until I finally arrived at the cabin and found her standing outside, a white ball of fluff curled up in her arms.

She waved at me with a smile on her face. Anger boiled my blood.

What the hell was she thinking? Something could have happened to her, and she was smiling at me like everything was just fine.

Gravel slid under my tires as I slammed on the brakes and threw the shifter into park. Slamming the driver door behind me, I nearly ran to her. "What're you doing?"

Her brows pinched with utter confusion. "What do you mean?"

I pointed at the cabin behind her. "You should be further away from this place, not just standing right outside the front door. There's a gas line in there for the stove. If the fire would have reached it, there could have been an explosion." My breaths were heavy with each word as I towered over her. But she didn't step away from me. Instead, she inched closer and placed a hand on my forearm.

My skin burned where I felt her palm over my jacket. "Deacon, there's no fire. I think something's blocking the chimney, so there's a lot of smoke. But the fire didn't spread from the hearth."

Nostrils flaring, I ground my teeth together. I was acting

like a crazed lunatic. Of course there wasn't a fire. She'd told me that on the phone. It was just a blockage in the chimney.

I took her in for a moment, assessing for any kind of injury. There might not have been a fire, but smoke inhalation could cause long term problems.

Blue eyes stared up at me under the rim of reddish-brown lashes. Freckles kissed the skin of her nose and cheeks, giving her the look of a woman who should be somewhere on a tropical beach. Not in the middle of the Georgia mountains during the dead of winter.

Her closeness was making my vision grow hazy. I wanted her by my side, in my arms, away from any kind of danger. But that would be crazy because I hardly knew the woman. Even though I'd spent nearly every day of my life since the apartment fire thinking about her, I knew it wasn't normal.

There was nothing natural about how Charlie would haunt my thoughts when I couldn't fall asleep at night. Or how badly I wanted to see what those rosy, pink lips tasted like. I was a fiend for the woman ever since that day and it was so fucked.

I *am fucked*.

Because that fire wasn't the only thing that shifted my dreams into nightmares. Years in the military had warped my perception of the world. Always looking for the looming threats. Always assessing. There was hardly a moment when my mind was quiet—without worry, without fear.

And Charlie Banks had the uncanny ability of bringing out the worst in me. Because for whatever fucked up reason, the thought of something terrible happening to her was the most haunting thought of all.

"Deacon?" Charlie's soft voice brought me back from the spiral that was threatening my sanity.

I clenched my jaw when I noticed her hand was still on my arm. "Let me go see what's going on." Her hand slipped away when I moved past her toward the front door.

Thick clouds of smoke wafted past me when I opened the door. I nearly choked on the smell as it threatened to pull me back to those memories again. Determined not to go there, I kept my mind settled on the task at hand.

Grabbing the fire extinguisher from under the kitchen sink, I put out the blazing fire in the hearth so I could get a better look as to what was blocking the smoke path.

Coughing sounded behind me, and I turned to find Charlie waving her hand back and forth while her other arm still held her cat.

Rising, I said, "You don't need to be in here while I do this."

Her free hand settled on her hip, drawing my eyes down the length of her body. I was so amped up before I didn't notice she was wearing tight-fitted Long Johns pajamas. The cream colored top draped over her figure, showing the swell of her breasts. I nearly cracked a tooth from clenching my jaw when my gaze trailed further down her waist to the curve of her hips.

Fucking hell.

I forced myself to look back to her heart shaped face. One red eyebrow was arched as she said, "Neither do you.

This place is filled with smoke and none of us need to be in here until it all clears out. Let's just open the windows and come back in a little while."

"Come back?" I questioned. "Where are we going to go in the meantime?"

Her delicate shoulders shrugged. "Back to your place for a bit?"

Damnit. Just the thought of having Charlie in my home had ungentlemanly thoughts running through my mind. What it might be like to have her in my bed. To feel her soft skin pressed against mine. To see those perfectly pink lips moaning my name as I…

Raking a hand through my hair, I silently chastised myself. *Keep your fucking head on straight.*

She was already consuming every part of me, and she was all the way across the room with unbreathable air between us. How the hell was I going to survive having her in my space?

But then she brought her hand to her mouth and started coughing and the decision was made.

"My house. Go get in the truck," I commanded.

"I can help with the w—"

"In the truck." I pointed out the open door behind her.

Without another word, she spun around and walked out the door. It was all I could do not to stare at her ass. Letting out a haggard sigh, I quickly opened all the windows in the cabin and opened the back door so the smoke could clear out faster.

Finally opening the driver's door of my truck, I was hit

with the scent of smoke and something like vanilla cut through. It was warm and sweet and wholly *her*.

I tried not to breathe in too deeply but fuck if it wasn't intoxicating. With a groan, I slid across the seat and turned the engine on.

Meow!

Right. We weren't alone.

"Is it going to freak out while I drive?"

Charlie's giggle sent a bolt of electricity down my spine that had me stiffening. "*It* is a *he*. And he has a name. Remember?" That same right eyebrow arched at me and the smirk playing on her lips had her cheeks rising.

She was so damn beautiful it was difficult to look away. When her smile faltered under the scrutiny of my gaze, I finally looked behind us and shifted the truck into reverse.

"Just make sure he doesn't leave your lap until we get to my place."

The drive back to my house felt like an eternity with her in the passenger seat of my truck. My palm ached from white knuckling the steering wheel the entire way. I was thankful to be out of the small space and for the biting cold that woke me from my stupor when I got out of the truck and went to her side to open the door.

"Thank you," she nearly whispered when she slid off the seat and her feet hit the gravel.

The cat—Casper—gave a weird squeaking sound as we walked up the front porch and I opened the door for them.

As she passed me, I got another whiff of the warm vanilla scent. Not able to help myself this time, I closed my eyes and breathed in deeply. When I opened them again, I took in the long curls of her red hair and how they cascaded down her back. The ends nearly reaching the curve of her ass.

Everything about her was perfect. I knew it the moment I saw her seven years ago when those crystalline blue eyes shone with gratitude at the sound of my voice when I burst through her bedroom door.

But I'd ruined that perfection. I wasn't fucking strong enough to save her and now she would be scarred for the rest of her life because of me.

Following her inside, I shut out the cold behind me. I watched as she knelt to let Casper out of her arms. He pounced across the floor then sniffed the air like he wasn't quite sure if the surroundings were up to his liking.

Then, Charlie turned around slowly and started walking further into the living room. Watching her in my home made my stomach flip. So many questions ran through my mind.

Did she like it? Had I already ruined any chance of getting to know her? Did she blame me for the marred skin on her ribcage?

I already knew the answer to the second question. There was no chance in hell I'd be good enough for her. I just needed to put that hope to rest and never think of it again.

I was so twisted up in my mind, I didn't even notice her cat starting to rub himself against my pant leg.

"Um, what do I do?" I asked, catching Charlie's attention from where she stood next to my large leather sofa.

That damn giggle she let out had my heart lurching into

my throat. How it was possible to be *affected* by another person was beyond me.

I was starting to fray around the edges the closer she moved toward me. Suddenly, the large open floorplan of my home had become stifling.

She bent down in front of me and picked up her cat. It was purring in her arms when she lifted him up.

"When he does that, it means he really likes you and wants your attention." She extended the white furball toward me. "You can pet him if you want. I promise he won't bite."

He's not the one I'm worried about, I wanted to say but kept my mouth clamped shut.

Reaching out, my palm covered the entirety of the cat's small head. I tried to be gentle as I ran my hand over his ears, but his head sank with each pat from the weight of my palm.

"He won't scratch anything, will he?" I straightened back to my full height.

Her smile was wide as she responded, "No. He's well trained." A soft chuckle moved past her lips. "You're really not an animal guy, are you?"

It took me a moment to focus on the words she said and not the ruby red color of her lips. It seemed they darkened when she wasn't outside freezing her ass off.

Clearing my throat, I blinked out of my stupor. "I'm a dog guy."

She looked around the living room like she was waiting for a dog to come prancing through.

"I don't have one right now. I've been enjoying the alone time since I moved to Pebble Brook Falls."

"Oh." She shifted on her feet uncomfortably. Silence settled over the both of us, her gaze shifted to the ground.

Then, out of nowhere, she darted toward the front door. "This was a stupid idea," she murmured, moving past me.

It took me a second to realize what I'd said to make her scramble out of my home. Letting my eyes flicker shut for a moment, I internally groaned to myself. *I am such an ass.*

Before she got too far past me, I reached out and grasped the crook of her elbow.

"Charlie, wait."

She paused; her back was still facing me as she slowly looked down where my hand was gripped around her arm. I could feel the heat of her underneath the thin layer of her Long Johns top. The comforting smell of vanilla overwhelmed my senses and when her blue eyes lifted to meet mine, my breathing hitched.

Striking. That's what Charlie Banks was. Not beautiful. Not gorgeous. Those words didn't encapsulate what she did to me every time I looked at her. Because when I did, it was like taking a blow to the heart. A bolt of lightning hitting me square in the chest, setting my entire body on edge.

I wanted to pull her into my chest and feel the curves of her supple body against me. To bury my face in the strands of her fiery red hair. To lose myself in the depths of her ocean blue eyes.

But I did none of those things because I didn't deserve to. So, I let my hand fall from her arm.

My throat was thick as I forced out the words, "I'm sorry. I didn't mean for it to sound like I didn't want you here. I…"

Raking a hand over my head, I tried to find what I wanted to say through all the muck of emotions that were clouding my mind.

Letting out a sigh, I felt my shoulders drop. "I don't always say the right things. And I'm finding that to be especially true when I'm around you. So, I'm sorry."

Her face softened and I swore she leaned forward, like she might take a step toward me.

But she remained standing where she was, only a few feet away from the front door. Something about the view of her being so close to leaving upset me. I couldn't figure out what I wanted. Having her near me was suffocating. I could hardly breathe, let alone think in her presence. But there was a clear absence in my chest when she wasn't around. It was like she repaired something inside of me that had been broken from all the shit I'd been through in my life.

So, I did the one thing I probably shouldn't have. "Will you please stay?"

Chapter 6

Charlie

A warm glow emanated from the windows of my tiny cabin as Deacon pulled up next to my car. We'd spent about an hour at his place, letting the smoke clear out and the hearth cool down before heading back. Most of the time was spent in silence. He'd made me a cup of peppermint tea and honey to sip on as we sat on his leather sofa and watched Casper explore the space.

It was awkward at first. I didn't know what to say or how to act. Growing up there had rarely been silence in our home, even though it was just my parents and me. Even when it was just Casper and I in our various homes, I was always talking to him, and he was always meowing or chirping back to me.

After a few minutes though, I started to enjoy just sitting with Deacon. There was something comforting about his presence. Or maybe it was the fact that I couldn't stop the tingling sensation in my arm from where he'd grasped it, preventing me from walking out his front door.

There had been such earnestness in his eyes. A pleading that struck me right to my core and I couldn't get the image out of my mind. He was such an enigma.

One second it felt like he couldn't get rid of me fast enough and the next he was urging me to stay.

I felt it in my heart. That something had happened the day of the fire. There was some piece I was missing. I wanted to ask him. To get to the bottom of why he was so hot and cold with me.

But the thought of scaring him off with the question stopped me. As badly as I wanted to know, I couldn't risk pushing him away. Not now that I felt myself wanting to get closer to him.

Cold air hit my face when he opened his truck door. I watched as he moved swiftly in front of the hood, coming around to my side. Casper stirred in my arms when Deacon opened my door.

"Thank you," I said, slipping out of the seat.

He gave me a curt nod in response.

Despite the air appearing clear when we walked into the cabin, the smell of smoke still clung to the space.

"It's not as strong as before, but it still smells smokey. I'm going to put my bedding in the laundry while you work on the fireplace."

"Okay."

Casper darted into the kitchen where his automatic feeder

was and started feasting while I stripped my bed bare and tossed everything into the washing machine.

Aware of every movement Deacon made, I watched him from the corner of my eye lay down in front of the hearth and scoot himself closer so he could get a good look at what had caused the mess.

I moved to the sofa and asked, "Do you need a flashlight?"

He was silent for a moment, a vein in his neck bulging with the effort of twisting and turning to see up the chimney. When my eyes trailed down the length of his body, I realized just how large he was. His thighs pressed firmly against the fabric of his jeans, and I wondered what it would feel like to have that kind of power beneath me as I straddled his lap. What it might feel like to be beneath him as he rocked his hips against me.

Was he a gentle lover? Or was he the kind of man who rode hard?

"Charlie, are you okay?" I heard him ask.

My gaze snapped to his face that was shadowed from the hearth. I realized then that my breaths had quickened. I was practically panting over the man, and he'd caught me gawking at him.

"Yup!" I squeaked. "Perfectly fine."

Rising from the sofa, I decided I needed to get some space before I made a total fool out of myself. I went into the kitchen and washed out Casper's water bowl before refilling it again.

"It looks like part of a bird's nest fell through the

chimney and got stuck about halfway down. I need to grab a tool from my truck. I'll be right back."

Not trusting myself to speak, I simply nodded and went back to filling up Casper's water container.

When the front door was shut and Deacon was out of earshot, I knelt beside Casper and said, "I think I'm in deep trouble with this one, buddy." He looked up at me before leaning hard against my kneecap. "Do you think he's one of the good ones?"

When he let out a loud purr, I wasn't sure if he was telling me yes or trying to ward me away, but I selfishly took it as confirmation that Deacon might have a prickly personality, but that his friend, Sarah, was right. Behind his hard exterior, he was a soft teddy bear on the inside.

Deacon came back through the door with what appeared to be a collapsible grab-stick. Not having a clue what it did, I stayed silent but made my way back to the small living space.

"Let me know if you need any help."

A small smile pulled at the corners of his lips before he laid on his back and started stretching the stick upward, latching the small pieces together the further up it went. Deacon's large hand grasped the edge of the hearth as he hoisted himself further into the space.

I swallowed when my mind wandered to what those hands might be capable of doing.

My thoughts were cut short when a scraping sound rustled in the chimney right before a giant pile of sticks and ash came tumbling down, covering Deacon's face in soot.

Eyes squeezed shut, he lurched forward and started coughing wildly.

I hurried to his side. "Oh my gosh! Are you okay?"

He coughed one more time before leaning himself against the hearth. When he looked at me, his bright green eyes seemed even more vivid against the charcoal soot that covered his entire face.

When he scowled, I couldn't help the laugh that bubbled out of me. When his frown deepened, I laughed harder.

"I'm sorry," I breathed between laughs. "You should see your face right now. It's completely covered in ash."

He raised his palm and before I could say no, he ran his hand over his face, smearing the soot even more. "You've only made it worse," I laughed again and when his eyes settled on me, I saw the frustration rising which only made my giggle fit worsen.

It was the most ridiculous sight I'd ever seen. The way his eyes gleamed pine green against the gray color of the ash made it look like he was a wild animal in the forest peering through the night. Raising his hands, he looked at them with annoyance then grunted in defeat before leaning his head back to rest on the stone hearth.

Eyes closed, he murmured, "Well, I think we've found the problem with the chimney."

I looked to the open fireplace where the bundle of sticks, a thread of twine and some moss laid disassembled. Then I turned back to Deacon. "Thank you for helping me with it." I bit my bottom lip to refrain from laughing again.

"Stay here, I'm going to get you a washcloth." Deacon

didn't move as I went to the bathroom and wetted a washcloth.

When I went back to his side, Casper had become curious of all the commotion and was gingerly exploring the open hearth and broken bird's nest. I lowered to the floor and Deacon reached for the washcloth. I pulled my hand back so he couldn't reach it. "Let me."

Something shifted in his gaze like he was hesitant to allow me to help. For a moment I thought he was going to protest, but then he shifted his large frame, so his back was more straight against the stone, giving me better access to his face and neck.

My thigh rested against his as I scooted closer. Swallowing the dryness in my throat, I reached forward with the wet cloth and wiped the ash from his forehead. Deacon sucked in a sharp breath, and I yanked my hand back.

"Are you okay?" I assessed his face for any injury of where the sticks might have struck him, but didn't see any signs.

Those beautiful eyes grew wide for a moment, darting back and forth between mine. So many unspoken words were written in his expression. Part of me wanted to coax him to tell me something…anything. Questions of my own clanged around in my mind, but my lips stayed shut.

Neither one of us looked away as the silence between us grew. The tension was nearly unbearable when I felt the warmth of Deacon's calloused hand wrap around mine as he brought my hand and the cloth I still held to his temple.

"Keep going." His gruff voice sent a cascade of goosebumps over my skin. My arm hung in midair while I looked at him. This giant man sprawled on my living room floor had come back into my life for a reason it seemed.

My mom had always taught me to believe in divine signs. That if I followed my heart, fate would place me right where I was meant to be. As I took in the sight of Deacon's handsome face with inky lashes fanning over his eyes, a chiseled jawline and dark brows I felt a line go taut between us. It was the same tether that I clung to all those years ago.

The one that kept me alive.

Maybe most would chalk it up to coincidence. It wasn't like North Carolina was far away from Georgia. The likelihood that we might end up in the same place was a fairly comprehensible thought.

But there was something more at play here. I could feel it as he shifted slightly when I finally settled the cloth on the side of his face and swiped downward, revealing more of his tan skin.

We couldn't keep existing like this. Acting as passing ships in the night. Noticing one another without truly saying hello.

It…bothered me.

"Are we going to talk about it?" I asked hesitantly.

His gaze flickered like he knew exactly what I was getting at. "What is there to talk about?"

I half-laughed. "Oh, I don't know. Just the fact that you saved my life seven years ago and when I showed up on your front porch you slammed the door in my face."

He grimaced and shifted his face away from me. Feeling

brave, I slid the cloth under his chin and gently directed him to look back at me. "You don't think it's crazy that we both ended up in this tiny town an entire state away from where we first met?"

His deep inhale told me he was growing wary of my questions. "What I think is crazy is that you are attributing us being in the same small town as some sign that means more than it does." Those green eyes darkened to a shade of glistening emerald. "I moved out here to be alone. To be away from…people. Just because we met once doesn't mean there is more to the picture. There *can't* be more to the picture."

I hated that tears sprung to the back of my eyes. Honestly, I wasn't sure why they were there. Deacon spoke the truth. We were just two people who happened to have met in a tragic way who wound up in the same town. It didn't mean that fate played any part of it. No matter how much my heart yearned for it to be true.

But the seed of doubt he planted in my mind wasn't as strong as the pull I had toward him.

"You say there can't be more to it, but if that were true then you wouldn't react to me the way you have been. Or are you a grumpy asshole with everyone?"

It wasn't like me to curse at someone. My parents had raised me to be a lady with manners. But Deacon Calhoun got under my skin, and I wanted answers to his vague statements.

His bushy brows rose toward his hairline and my chest lightened at the sight of his half soot covered face in shock.

"I'm not an asshole," he stated defensively.

I just blinked at him.

His shoulders deflated. "Fine. Maybe I'm not the nicest person you've come across. But like I said, I chose this place to be away from people for a reason."

"And the reason is?" I cocked my head to the side. He wasn't going to get off that easily.

His lips popped open. "I…" He closed his mouth, and his nostrils flared with frustration.

I sat next to him in silence, waiting for his walls to come down and show me some semblance of the man who rescued me. The one with kind eyes, a tender touch with the need to protect.

A shadow passed over his face as he shifted his gaze downward. "I just need you to trust that I'm not the guy you might think I am. So, whatever you're trying to do, you just need to stop. It won't end well for you."

My heart cracked from his words, the room around us tilting slightly as what he said sunk in. And it was all ridiculous. *I* was ridiculous for thinking he felt the same way I did—a blossoming curiosity to know him.

It was probably just a trauma reaction in thinking that the thread between us that had kept me alive was more than just a fleeting moment in time. His rejection stung, more than I cared to admit. But I wasn't going to let it ruin my experience here. I couldn't.

I sucked in a deep breath. "You're right. I think I let the loneliness of being away from my home get the best of me." The emptiness of my words clanged around my mind, but he wasn't giving an inch, so neither could I.

Letting the washcloth fall from my hand, I reached across us and offered a handshake. "Friends, then?"

His eyes lingered on my face for a moment before they dipped to my lips.

Okayyyy. Maybe I wasn't crazy in thinking there was something between us. His mixed signals were giving me whiplash. But he'd made himself clear. He didn't want me to push the subject, so I kept my thoughts to myself.

"Friends," he grumbled before taking my hand in his and shaking it.

Hours after he'd helped me clean up the hearth and replace the old logs with new ones, I found myself lying in bed unable to stop thinking about the feeling of his palm pressed against mine.

I started to realize that it didn't matter if Deacon returned my feelings. I was already in too deep and, just like he'd said, I knew this wasn't going to end well for me.

Chapter 7

Deacon

Sleep evaded me again. My brain had buzzed all night long with thoughts of my conversation with Charlie. She'd wanted to know more about why I was the way I was with her.

I had been so close to telling her the truth. The truth being that for years, I'd been riddled with guilt from the day I couldn't stop her from being severely injured. And how that experience was another fuck up in my long line of making shit decisions that negatively impacted other people.

I'd wanted to tell her. God, I wanted to tell her so badly.

But when the time came and her bright blue eyes shone with wondrous curiosity, I shut down. That old part of me— the one who'd built walls a mile high—won out. Brick by brick, they shot up leaving me looking like an asshole…once again.

Since moving to Pebble Brook Falls, I'd found a way to open up to my friends. Johnny had been in the military, so he knew the cost those years took from all of us enlisted. He understood what it meant to be forced to make fast decisions and have your comrades' lives in your hands. It took a while, but when it was just the two of us, I was able to talk about my past. Not much, but enough that I was able to let some of the steam out.

Sarah had taken a less gentle approach over the years and basically forced me to be friends with her. We had an unspoken agreement though. She knew when she was inching too close to my edge and backed off before I had to tell her to.

I had the two of them and it had been enough for me. Now that Charlie was in the picture, I had no idea how to feel or what to think. Part of me wanted to lean in. To stop being so damn closed off. But the second I thought the words might slip from my lips, I clamped up.

Last night was a colossal fuck up and I would have to pay the consequences of seeing Charlie's disappointment when I went to the cabin this afternoon to work on the dock.

I ran a hand over my face and rubbed the sleep from my eyes. Coffee. I desperately needed coffee.

Meandering through my living room toward the kitchen, my heart kicked into high gear when I heard a knock on my door.

Judging by the lack of sun coming through the windows, it was barely sunrise. I reached for the doorknob and turned it. As the door swung open, I was shocked to find Charlie standing on my front porch.

A rose color bloomed across her cheeks from the cold air,

making her freckles stand out even more. The ball at the tip of her nose was rosy too and I found myself wanting to pull her into my arms to ward off the frost that was biting her skin.

Instead, I stood there frozen.

I hadn't noticed she was carrying something until her arms extended and I looked down to see a woven basket filled with what looked to be chocolate muffins. Most of them had sunken middles and dilapidated tops.

"I brought you these as a thank you for taking care of the chimney last night. And…" Her cheeks hollowed out and her gaze shifted to the ground between us. When she looked back up at me, I hated that there was conflict dancing in her eyes. "For making you feel uncomfortable with all of my questions. I have a tendency to pry, and I know it's not always fair for the person on the receiving end of the questioning."

When I didn't take the basket of muffins, she set the basket down on the ground, then she shifted to the side like she was about to walk away.

I'd already made such a mess of things last night, the last thing I wanted to do was make her feel bad again.

"Wait," I called out to her before she started making her way down the steps. She turned around, sunset colored hair flitting in the winter breeze. God, she was so beautiful. Charlie didn't belong in this cold tundra. But somehow, she'd found her way here and every chance I got, I ruined things between us.

I reached for the basket of muffins, and she handed it

over to me. "You didn't have to go through all that trouble. I was happy to fix the chimney. It's part of my job description as the landlord anyway."

"Right." She smiled sheepishly like she'd forgotten that part of the rental agreement. "Well, thank you anyway."

I nodded.

Gesturing toward her car over her shoulder with her thumb, she said, "Well, I'm going to get back. I hope you enjoy the muffins."

"I'm sure I will." I cleared my throat. "Oh, and I'll be by the cabin later this afternoon to start working on the dock."

"Great!" Her voice hitched up a few octaves. "See you then." Long curls bounced up and down as she turned and headed down the stairs toward her car. I was thankful that this time she chose to wear loose sweatpants and a baggy sweatshirt. Though, it didn't make watching her walk away any easier.

When she was in her car, I shut the door and set the basket of muffins on the kitchen counter. Charlie's presence this morning was like a ray of sunshine beaming through the dark clouds that always seemed to follow me around.

I knew that anyone who was close to Charlie had a significant gift in their life. She clearly wanted to get to know me, and I was a fool who couldn't keep the past where it belonged.

There was a nagging sensation in the back of my mind telling me Charlie was right. This all happened for a reason and the more I resisted it, the harder it was going to be for me.

The only thing I wanted after the war and after the fire was to find peace. I'd paid my dues in life and now was the time for me to rest. The problem was that it had already been a week since Charlie moved into the cabin, and I hadn't gotten a wink of sleep.

Something needed to change.

I just wasn't sure what that something was.

Frustrated with myself, I snatched one of the chocolate muffins from the basket and bit into it. Dry chunks of batter mixed with undercooked parts melded together in my mouth, creating a doughy paste.

"Blugh," I groaned before flipping up the garbage bin lid and spitting the bite of muffin into the trash. Then I moved to the kitchen sink, dunking my lips under the running faucet to gather some water in my mouth. I swished it back and forth and spit it out to clear the rest of my mouth.

That was fucking terrible.

As I stood there alone in my kitchen with the bundle of Charlie's muffins sitting on the counter, I smiled to myself for the first time in a really long time. Warmth spread down my neck, to my chest. The sensation felt bizarre, yet comforting. Like seeing an old friend after years of time had changed him.

She'd gone out of her way to bake me a thank you gift and even though the muffins were fucking terrible, she'd *thought* of me. It was one of the nicest things anyone had ever done for me in a while.

It didn't take me very long to decide I enjoyed the feeling and if being around Charlie let me have more of it, then I could learn to live with the discomfort our shared memories brought.

Metal pounding against metal struck through the sound of the river rushing below me as I worked another nail into the new board running across the dock. When I finished the row of nails, I noticed the swish of a white tail out of the corner of my eye.

Peering to my left, I saw Casper trotting over the frozen ground while Charlie struggled with her hands full of what appeared to be paint supplies. Slipping the hammer back into my toolbelt, I rose from the middle of the dock and crossed the yard to the back patio of the cabin.

"Let me help you with that." I grabbed the large white canvas from under her right arm while she set up the wooden easel.

"Thanks," she said breathlessly from the effort of carrying too much. After she finished setting up the paints and brushes, she took the canvas from me and settled it onto the middle of the easel.

"I didn't know you were an artist." I took a step back as she brought the kitchen stool in front of the easel and sat on it. She reached for a paintbrush, and it was the first time I noticed how slender and delicate her hands and fingers were.

I looked down at my right hand that I sprawled out. Dirt was buried under my fingernails and scrapes from splinters in the wood I'd been cutting and hammering all afternoon darted in all directions over the top of my hand. I didn't have to look at my palm to know callouses from years of hard labor had formed beneath each digit.

"Yup," she responded. "I went to Savannah's College of Art and Design. My parents helped support me until my paintings started finding buyers." When she turned to settle her eyes on me, there was a brightness there I hadn't seen before. Like talking about her art made her beam from the inside out. "I'm one of the lucky ones. I landed some spots in a few amazing galleries and found buyers pretty immediately. Now, I do a combination of commission work and selling original pieces."

"Wow," I said with genuine surprise. "I've never met an artist before."

Her brows pinched together. "Sure you have. Your friend Sarah does incredible work with her pastries. The chocolate croissant I had was art in food form."

I snorted. "You have a point with that. Her pastries are pretty incredible."

"Speaking of, did you have one of the chocolate muffins I made you yet?"

My stomach gurgled as I thought back to the chocolate paste I had to spit into the garbage earlier this morning. But there wasn't a chance in hell I was going to tell Charlie that her efforts were wasted. I'd eat every single one of them if it meant putting a smile on her face.

"I did. It was pretty good. Thank you again for making them for me."

A long strand of her hair fell forward against her cheek. My fingers ached to reach out and tuck it behind her ear, to draw my fingertips along the edge of her smooth jaw until my thumb stopped on her bottom lip.

The blue depths of her eyes shuttered for a moment, like she could see right past the walls I'd built between us, straight to the desire that roared through my body. I had a tight leash on it, but when I was this close to her my grip loosened.

She cleared her throat and looked down at the paintbrush in her hand. "I'm glad you liked them."

With the moment between us severed, I took a step back. I knew I was doing everything wrong. It wasn't fair for me to tell Charlie that I didn't want anything to do with her one day and then turn around and gawk at her like she was one of the seven wonders of the world the next.

I knew this…and still I couldn't stop acting like a fool when she was around—because the connection she'd spoken of last night was one I'd felt the day of the fire too. Maybe it was real, and I was avoiding any sense of emotions that tied me back to that time in my life. Or maybe I had some fucked up savior complex that ignited when I saw a beautiful woman in need of my rescue.

But there was a nudge deep in my core that told me I wouldn't be feeling this way about anyone else. It was *her* who had haunted my thoughts for years on end. The image of her suffering from my mistake was branded into my mind and if I wanted any chance of things being normal between us, I was going to have to figure it out.

I shoved my fists into my jeans pockets. "Okay, well I'm going to leave you to it and get back to working on the dock."

A question passed over her face as her lips parted for a moment. Then, the moment was gone. Instead of urging her to say what was on her mind, I retreated down the steps to the dock where I was safely away from saying something stupid that I would surely regret.

We both worked until the sun faded behind the trees across the river. My arm was sore by the time I gathered the scrap pieces of wood into a bucket to haul away in my truck. The dock was finished in record time. I chalked up the accomplishment to the frustration I felt towards myself and as I looked at the heavy hammer marks surrounding each nail in the boards, I realized just how much heaviness I'd been carrying in my mind.

Finally looking up, I saw Charlie was packing her painting materials up. The easel and canvas were already gone, probably moved inside already. My throat cinched as I tried to come up with something to say to her. Anything that would retract what I'd spewed from my mouth last night.

Because the truth was that I'd lied. There was no part of me that wanted to stay away from Charlie. Every bone in my body ached with the need to be closer to her and it made me wonder if that was why I'd been so miserable the last seven years. I'd run away from the only person my heart ever yearned to be near.

That was the thing about haunting memories though. They created barriers that stopped us from getting to what we needed most.

And when it came to haunting memories…I had more than most.

Chapter 8

Charlie

A week had passed since Deacon completed the dock repairs and I was finally starting to settle into my new home.

I'd gone into town nearly every day to sit with Sarah and Stephanie at the bakery. At first, the venture into town had been strictly for the chocolate croissants. Then, I started to enjoy how easy it was to converse with the girls. They were both so sweet and made me feel like I wasn't alone in my new town.

It was my every intention to make another trip to town this morning, but when I peered through the back door of the cabin while sipping on my morning coffee, I was greeted with a glistening blanket of snow. Snow had become rare in Charlotte, so I didn't have much practice driving in it. Despite my newly developed cravings for chocolate crois-sants, I didn't want to risk driving when the snow was pretty thick.

"Are you ready, buddy?" I asked Casper while fastening the final bootie onto his back left paw.

He chirped at me in agreement, and I was thankful he was starting to get used to his new footwear. This time, he only stood awkwardly for a few seconds before he bounded toward the front door with me.

I pulled down on the blush-colored beanie my mother got me this past Christmas. The fabric was soft over my ears, and I could feel the fluffy pom-pom move to the side when I slipped on my boots.

Casper nudged my leg with his face before I opened the door to the most beautiful winter wonderland I'd ever seen. A dusting of snow covered the top of the railing surrounding the front deck and the entire ground shimmered in the morning light. It looked like dozens of diamonds had been strewn about my front lawn, the view took my breath away.

I looked down at Casper who looked up at me and before he could get an idea of what I was about to do, I darted over the front porch and down the steps. Snow crunched under the heels of my boots while Casper's white fur blended into the scenery around us.

We ran around in circles, Casper chasing after me. The cold air burned my lungs, but I didn't care. The sky was moody above me, promising to send more snow that already had the surrounding pine tree branches weighed down.

Laughter fluttered past my lips as I fell to the ground and spread my arms and legs out wide, doing my best to make a snow angel in the little bit that covered the grass. Casper rolled his shoulder into it before plopping over completely, doing little wiggle worm movements so he could feel the coolness of the snow press into his fur.

I laid there for a while, giggling to myself as I watched Casper start to hop around in the snow, chasing after some imaginary bug that only he could see. Wet cold was starting to seep through my pants, but I didn't want to move. Not yet.

There was nothing that could take the lightness and pure joy away from me. I'd wanted this so badly. I thought my heart yearned for it before I even realized what *it* truly was.

Open space.

Freedom.

Silence.

Joy.

The divine experience that only being out in nature could bring.

In the short time of being in my new home, I'd already completed three canvases and listed them on my website for sale. One sold almost immediately, reminding me how fortunate I was to do my life's passion for a living.

Thankful for this life, I continued to lay in the snow. Watching endless gray clouds roll by, feeling my clothes grow wetter and colder by the minute. But that didn't matter because I was here, in the exact moment I'd wished and hoped for, for so long.

Speckles of white, green and brown paint covered my forearms. The mural was starting to come alive. After our morning in the snow, I brought Casper back inside so I could work on bringing some of the beautiful nature into our new home. The wall behind the loveseat had been transformed into a misty forest scene and as I stood back and assessed the work I'd put in for the last six hours, I felt impressed with myself.

My craft had transformed from the years I'd spent in college, and I was just now starting to find my voice as an artist. I wanted to create things that spoke to me through quiet whispers or loud yells.

And the nature surrounding the tiny cabin told me that there was such peace and mystery in the woods. What trials had the giant trees endured from the time they were a sapling until their roots grew deep into the earth? How much time had passed for the rushing water of the river to hone the pebbles lying beneath its surface?

There were so many questions that would go unanswered, and it was beautiful. The humbling experience of never knowing something. It kept me grounded and curious.

Satisfied with today's work, I gathered my brushes and went to the sink to start cleaning them. Lifting the faucet handle with my wrist, an angry gurgling sound rumbled beneath the sink.

"Oh no," I said under my breath as the rattling sound grew louder right before water spewed from the cabinets below the sink. Kneeling, I threw open the cabinet doors and saw that one of the pipes had burst and was quickly filling up the space. Water leaked onto the wood floors and started spilling further into the kitchen.

"Oh my gosh!" I yelled, having no idea what to do to stop the water from jutting out of the pipe. I smacked the faucet knob back into the off position, but that didn't stop the water from coming out of the broken pipe.

Hands dripping wet, I grabbed my cell off the counter and dialed Deacon's number. It rang five times before going to his voicemail.

"Shit, shit, shit!"

I called another three times, but he still didn't answer. "Come on, Casper!" I screeched as I took my car keys from the hook by the door and headed for Deacon's house.

I should have put on a coat, I thought to myself as I walked up Deacon's front porch steps. Snow had started falling again and my teeth were chattering as I shivered from the wetness that clung to the fabric of my long-sleeve shirt.

His truck was here which meant he had to be home. Two raps of my knuckles on the door and I heard footsteps sounding behind it.

Deep frown lines marred the sides of Deacon's lips as he took me in.

"Ttthere's a bbburst pipe in ttthe cabin," I said, unable to control the chattering of my teeth.

"Come inside." He ushered me through the front door quickly. Casper and I stood in his entry way while Deacon walked into his living room. He came back with a thick blanket and draped it over my shoulders.

My body relaxed a little as he rubbed my arms up and down, giving life back to my frozen limbs.

"What were you thinking going out in this weather without a coat, Charlie?" he chastised. But through the sternness in his voice, I heard the note of concern shine through.

I stole a deep breath, and my teeth finally stopped clattering together. "I tried calling you, but you didn't answer. The water is still running. I couldn't get the sink to turn off, so I rushed over here."

He blinked at me like my answer wasn't good enough for why I'd put myself in the position of getting hypothermia.

"You should probably go check on it," I urged, gesturing at the door behind me. "The water is still rushing into the cabin."

"I don't care about the fucking cabin, Charlie." He took a step toward me and grasped a wet lock of my hair in his hand. "The only thing that matters is you not getting sick from being out in the cold, soaking wet."

There was such a seriousness to his tone, like the idea of me being ill was beyond his ability to handle. My heart clenched at his display of worry. *This* was the same Deacon who had saved my life. The version of the man who made my heart flutter and had my mind whirling to find some way to get closer to him.

His voice was gentler as he let the strand of my hair fall over the blanket wrapped around my shoulders. "Take Casper and go sit by the fire, I'll be back soon."

"Okay." My voice was hoarse from the adrenaline of getting to his house as fast as I could.

Casper and I walked into his living room. Still feeling the wet cold from my clothes, I sat right next to the fire as Casper curled up on the ledge of the stone hearth.

Looking over the large leather sofa, I watched Deacon as he slipped on his coat and gathered his keys. When he got to the front door, he paused, his large shoulders tensed. Then he looked over at me and I swore there was a whisper of a smile on his lips before he turned back around and headed out into the night.

My eyelids had started drooping from fatigue by the time Deacon came back. As soon as I heard the door open, his presence jolted me awake. My clothes were still wet, but the warmth of the fire had kept the cold at bay. I gathered the blanket he'd given me around my shoulders again and rose.

He shrugged off his coat and set his keys and a bundle of something on the counter. Water soaked his pants legs from the knee down.

I swallowed. "How bad was it?"

His eyes were bright as he turned to me and said, "I was able to shut off the main line and used my wet vac to get the water off the hardwood. But the damage was pretty severe to the pipe, so I'll need to get a plumber in there to fix it. Apparently, my handiwork with the new sink didn't hold out very well."

My fingers combed through the still damp strands of my hair. "Gosh, Deacon. I'm so sorry. I feel like I've made a mess of the place and it's only been a week and a half."

Dark brows merged together, and he shook his head. "This wasn't your fault, Charlie. There was nothing you could have done to prevent the bird's nest in the chimney or the pipe from bursting."

He was right. But I was starting to feel like a major imposition to his once peaceful life. He'd said it himself. He moved out here to be alone and here I was in his space once again.

"I know." I threaded my fingers together and rubbed my thumbs over one another. "I just wish there was more I could do to take the burden off you." I half-laughed. "I'm sure this wasn't what you were thinking of when you decided to renovate the cabin and turn it into a rental property."

His right hand flexed at his side. "No, it wasn't what I had in mind."

My stomach sank as I held his fierce gaze. There was so much hidden behind the pine green of those eyes. The questions were buzzing on my tongue, but they couldn't find their way past my lips.

Suddenly feeling anxious, I unwrapped the blanket from my body and folded it neatly into a square before setting it back on the couch.

"I'll get out of your hair. Come on, Casper." I patted the side of my leg, and the sound made his eyes go wide. He did a quick stretch before hopping off the stone ledge and making his way to my side.

Keeping my eyes cast downward, I headed toward the front door. I knew if I looked at Deacon, some part of me would try to find a way to stay. But I'd clearly become an unwelcome burden, and it was time for me to go.

Focusing on my boots by the door, I walked past him. Or, I tried to until his arm reached out and his large hand circled my wrist.

"Where are you going?" he asked gruffly.

My chest heaved up and down as my breaths quickened. A tingling sensation pricked where the palm of his hand closed over my wrist. It was hard to deny that every time we grew near, my body came alive.

"It's late," I whispered, peering up at him. His lips pulled back into a tight line when I continued, "I'm going to a hotel to get some sleep."

"No." He stepped into my space. He didn't let my wrist go.

"Deacon," I said softly. "I've already become a nuisance. The last thing I want to do is bring that annoyance into your home."

Frustration flashed across his face. His nostrils flared and a muscle feathered along his square jaw. Then, he shifted toward the kitchen counter and swiped the bundle of fabric I'd seen earlier off it.

"I wasn't sure what to grab, so I just brought you some pajamas. The rest of your things are in my truck." My chin lowered as I noticed the clothes in his hand. *My* clothes. It was the sage green set I'd gotten for Christmas. The material was soft and lined with dainty cream-colored lace.

I looked back up at Deacon. Long thick lashes cast shadows over his tanned cheeks. Being this close to him, I noticed the veins that ran down both sides of his neck and just how broad his shoulders were. Under the layer of his flannel and T-shirt, I could see the muscles honed over years of doing hard labor. Everything about him was rough and yet…he was so damn handsome; it took my breath away.

"You want me to stay? With you?"

His Adam's Apple bobbed up and down as he swallowed. "It's too dangerous to drive on these roads. This was our first snowfall of the season, so they haven't salted the roads yet."

It was so hard to reconcile how he was acting right now with the guy who slammed his front door in my face. He was ice and fire, and I never knew which version I was going to get.

Something about that made my blood hum.

"Okay," I whispered, taking my pajamas from him. "I'll stay."

Chapter 9

Charlie

I tugged on the soft pajama shorts Deacon brought me from the cabin. He kept his home pretty warm, so I wasn't worried about being cold tonight.

I *was* worried about walking out of the bathroom half dressed.

From the moment he'd asked me to stay, it felt like something shifted between us. I knew nothing about this man, other than he used to be a firefighter in Charlotte and that he wasn't a big fan of people. But some part of me knew there was so much more to him than that and I craved to sit by his side and listen to the deep tone of his voice tell me about the unseen parts of him. But that was likely a wish that would never come true.

"This will just have to do," I murmured to myself in the mirror before I left Deacon's bathroom and nearly walked smack into a very muscular chest.

"Oh!" I squeaked as I found myself staring at sun

bronzed skin and tight pectoral muscles with a small dusting of black hair between them. Biting my lower lip, I let my gaze trail downward to Deacon's abdomen and that's when I noticed the burn scar that covered most of his right rib cage. The skin was tinged with angry shades of red and pink, probably from the heat of the shower he'd just gotten out of.

An image flashed in my mind of both of us on the ground, covered in burning rubble. His face was twisted in agony from the fire that burned his skin, but that didn't stop him from reaching out to me. Telling me to stay with him. Telling me to keep my eyes on him.

Just like that day, I couldn't tear my gaze away from him and the scar that would bind us together forever.

My hand instinctively drifted to my side where I knew there was a scar, much like his. But I balled my palm into a fist and dropped it to my hip.

"Sorry," he huffed, and my eyes shot upward to see him rake a hand over his short dark hair. "I thought you were going to be in there longer. I just came in here to grab some clothes." He lifted his right hand that held a pair of briefs and black sweatpants.

"Right. Of course. It's your room. I can just leave," I stammered, fighting the desire to take in the body before me that was the definition of a beautifully rugged man.

"No." His hand shot out, landing on the bathroom door frame. I was caged in, the smell of cedarwood and fresh soap hanging in the air between us.

"You happen to like that word a lot, don't you?" I

laughed, trying to distract myself from how good he smelled.

He didn't say anything. So, I just stared at him. Finding myself lost in what I realized weren't purely green eyes. There was a large fleck of golden brown in his right eye and swirls of pale blue melded into the green. I noticed as they flicked down to my lips. My breath caught in my throat as his head tilted to the side and he seemed to move closer to me.

Dizziness swarmed my senses, the background of his bedroom fading away as he grew closer still.

Kiss me. Please, kiss me, I silently urged him.

Heat licked up my spine as my entire body grew still under his spell. There was nothing I wanted more in that moment than for his lips to touch mine. To feel his warmth pressed against me as I explored the planes of his hard body with my hands.

Just as I thought he might have heard my hidden desires, his hand dropped from the frame, and he walked away–never looking back.

When he disappeared through the doorway of his room, I released the breath I'd been holding and spread my palm over my décolletage as the room stopped spinning and started coming back into focus.

It took me a few minutes to recover from whatever had just happened between us in his bedroom before I walked out and found him sitting on the couch with Casper curled into a tight ball by his feet. A glass of amber liquid was clutched between his fingers as he stared into the flames dancing in the hearth.

From where I stood in the hallway, I imagined what it would be like to paint him. I ran the pads of my fingertips together to ward off the need to grasp one of my brushes he'd packed away in his truck for me. I'd never been one to paint people. I could never get the proportions right and it had always frustrated me. I much preferred the wild landscapes of nature that called to be exposed. But there was a wildness in Deacon too.

Raw.

Unbridled.

Secretive.

Which is why I found myself drawing closer to him. Step after step, my feet carried me into the living room. I didn't think I could stop moving toward him, even if I wanted to.

The reflection of the flames flickered in his eyes when he looked at me. His large body took up most of the section of the couch and that's when it struck me.

Where am I going to sleep?

Deacon must have read my mind because he swirled the whiskey in his glass and then said, "I'll sleep out here on the couch. You can have my bed."

I glanced over my shoulder down the hallway. There were four doors, three of which I hadn't been through, but I guessed they were bedrooms.

"I can sleep in one of the guest bedrooms," I offered.

His gaze was piercing. "The only bed in this house is in my room."

I smiled. "You don't get many visitors then?"

He downed the rest of the liquor from his glass and stood. "Nope."

His strides were long as he walked toward me. "Let me just grab a blanket from my room and it's all yours."

Before he could pass me, I reached out for his arm and found my fingers curled into the side of his bicep. He stopped walking and I looked at where I'd grabbed him. His muscle dwarfed my small hand.

Heat curled in my stomach. "I can take the couch," I said with a quiet laugh. "You barely fit on it as it is. It'll be much more comfortable for me."

His chin lowered and that heat in my core turned into molten lead. "And what kind of man would I be having a woman sleep on the couch when there's a perfectly good bed for her to rest in?"

Not a very gentlemanly one by Southern standards.

"Sleep with me then." The words were out of my mouth before I realized what I'd said.

The green in his eyes darkened. The muscle beneath my palm went rigid as I felt my eyes grow wide with embarrassment. There was no doubt my cheeks were a flaming red. Unable to hold his gaze any longer, I shook my head and stared at the wood panels of the floor.

"I meant that we can share the bed," I gritted through my teeth. "I really don't want you to be uncomfortable tonight."

Rough fingers gripped the edge of my chin. I sucked in a breath as he tilted my head back so I was forced to look at him. "Is that really what you want?"

All thoughts emptied from my mind with the exception of *him*. His words, the curt tone of his voice, the coarse feeling of his touch against my skin. There was a slight tilt of his lips, like he was battling between the man he showed me and the man he truly was.

An enigma.

That's what Deacon Calhoun was.

And every single part of me wanted to discover the pieces that made him whole.

One resounding word came barreling through my otherwise empty mind. "Yes."

Telling Deacon I wanted to sleep next to him in his bed and actually sleeping next to Deacon in his bed were two wildly different things. When we were in the hallway, there had been safety despite the touch he held as he'd grasped my chin between his fingers.

Now, there were mere inches between our bodies, and we were both wearing very little clothing. My arms were ramrod straight at my sides above the covers. His room hadn't been nearly as hot when I'd taken a shower and changed into my pajamas earlier. Something had changed when I climbed into his king-sized bed and felt the mattress dip to my left when he joined me.

I brought the back of my hand to my forehead to see if I

was sweating, but my skin was dry as a bone.

Unable to stay still for long, I peered through the darkness at each one of my fingers to analyze my cuticles. Having been brought up as a lady, each finger was perfectly manicured, despite them often being covered in paint. Before long, I found myself staring at the ceiling tricking my mind into thinking the skip trowel texture was shaped into different animals.

Even that didn't work in keeping my attention for long as Deacon lay beside me. I'd tried avoiding looking at him for as long as I could, but curiosity won as I slowly shifted onto my left side, acting like I was just trying to get comfortable.

When my head settled back on the pillow, I stilled. Deacon was staring straight at me.

"You fidget a lot," he commented as I watched the way his lips moved with each word. They were the only soft things about him and my mind wandered to places it shouldn't have.

When I didn't respond, he asked, "Are you uncomfortable?"

I thought about it for a moment and realized the mattress was the perfect combination between soft and firm. The sheets were cool to the touch, but the weight of the comforter warded off the cold that no doubt seeped in from the window next to me.

"No," I finally said. Then, I realized he might not have been talking about the mattress at all. I slid my hands between my knees and brought them toward my chest.

"I can go onto the couch," he offered quietly.

My hand jutted out to stop him from going anywhere, but halfway to his forearm I stopped myself and slid my hand back between my thighs. "Please stay."

He didn't move to leave. We laid there together; our gazes fixed on one another until I finally felt brave enough to do what I'd wanted to from the moment I saw him.

"Are we ever going to talk about it?"

His eyes lingered on me for a few more moments before his neck turned and I found him staring at the ceiling. It was difficult to tell in the darkness, but it seemed like his jaw was clenched, his body more still than it had been before I asked the question.

A long exhale moved past his lips when he turned toward me again. "I've seen a lot of fucked up things in my life, Charlie. Some things that are so horrible, I can't find the words to describe them. But going back to that place where I found you..." His voice cracked and my heart thundered in my chest. "I'd rather live through all the other horrors I've had to face than go back there again."

Tears sprung to my eyes at his candor. It was the first real thing he'd said to me since I arrived. Not words that were trying to mask the hidden truth.

What he'd just told me…

The parts I remembered about that day were nightmarish. But that was a small fraction of what he'd probably endured that day. I'd been one of the lucky ones. There were many people who hadn't made it out in time.

I was thankful for the blanket as it hid the shiver cascading down my body as I took in the man before me.

The sheer size of him dwarfed his side of the bed, but the pain in his eyes told me that he was fragile under that tough exterior. Something about that day had shaken him to his core. And if this man, who'd apparently seen unspeakable things in life, couldn't talk about what happened that day, then I had to respect that.

After the fire, my parents had me see a psychologist to make sure I had support following the trauma. She'd told me that my resilience was beautiful, but that not everyone was gifted with the same ability to simply…move forward. There was no known reason for my strength. I wasn't special. But some part of me was able to find joy in life again without much effort after the fire.

Others, I knew, weren't as fortunate.

Seeing Deacon like this made me thankful for whatever part of my brain made me capable of walking away unscathed.

"Okay," I whispered. Even though I didn't get the answers I was looking for, the answer he gave me helped me understand him a little more.

And knowing just that small piece of him was enough to calm the torment of my need to know him.

A pacifying quiet settled between us, and I found myself drifting off to sleep under the steadiness of his gaze.

That night I dreamt of swirling snowflakes and strong arms that held me close.

Chapter 10

Deacon

Soft light swam behind my closed eyelids. I opened them and stretched my arms out wide to find the other half of my bed empty. Blinking away the sleep, I looked over to my right and my heart skipped a beat. Charlie wasn't there.

I shot forward as dread took hold of me and my mind tortured me with thoughts of something bad happening to her.

But then I heard the clattering of dishes through the open door of my bedroom and realized she must be in the kitchen making herself something for breakfast.

Falling back onto the pillow, I scraped a hand over my face.

Last night…

Cannot happen again.

Charlie got too close with her probing, and I had let my guard down. What the hell was I thinking letting myself sleep in the same bed as her?

Keeping my distance had always been the plan. Distance was my salvation when it came to Charlie Banks and last night I'd brought the woman into my bed. I'd created my own personal hell by letting her stay with me. I should have just driven her into town last night and put her in a hotel.

But no.

My dumbass invited her to sleep in my house and when I thought staying on the couch would be a good compromise, I crumbled as soon as she batted her lashes at me and those delectable lips shifted into a smile.

I blamed the damn night shorts she wore. The way the pale green brought out the blue in her eyes and made every one of her freckles stand out had me salivating to run my tongue over every inch of her petite body.

My cock jumped to attention, straining against the sweat-pants I wore.

Fucking great.

Having her stay for longer than a day wasn't going to work for me. I needed to get down to the cabin and find a way to fix that pipe. I made a mental note to call a plumber right after breakfast.

Pushing my shoulders further into the mattress, I closed my eyes and tried to think about anything I could to get my morning wood under control.

Hitting my finger with a hammer like I almost did the other day working on the dock.

Being shot at during the war in Afghanistan.

The knife fight I found myself in at a bar in Texas when I was stationed there.

Thankfully, it didn't take long for my hard-on to soften. I was fucking starving and whatever Charlie was making in the kitchen smelled amazing. I just hoped it was better than those muffins.

As soon as I opened my eyes, a flying ball of white fluff hurtled toward my face and before I could get my hands out from under the sheet, my mouth and nose filled with fur.

"Agh!" I groaned, twisting to the side and finally freeing my arms so I could pull the furball off my face.

I lifted Casper into the air and glared into his bright yellow eyes. The little fucker was purring so loud, he could rival a generator motor.

My eyes narrowed on him. "You get off on that shit, don't you?"

Meow.

He tilted his head slightly then licked his chops like I was his next meal.

"Don't even think about it. You're going to end up right back in that cabin later today. Mark my words."

The furry little rascal just stared at me like I was an idiot. I set him down on the floor before rearranging my sweatpants and heading into the kitchen. Sweet and savory notes filled the air along with the sound of some modern country artist whose name I didn't know. Charlie's back was to me as she flipped what appeared to be a severely misshapen pancake.

Her long red hair was set in disheveled waves that swung from side to side as she moved her hips to the music.

Fucking hell, I silently cursed as my gaze raked down her

back to where her night shorts must have ridden up without her knowing. The bottom curve of her ass cheeks played peek-a-boo under the frilly lace of her shorts hem. My cock stirred in my pants. Before she had a chance to turn around, I snuck my hand down the front of my briefs and tucked my cock into the waistband hoping it would help conceal just how badly my body called to hers.

Seeing her like this in my kitchen made my stomach do flips. Charlie Banks was all sunshine and rainbows. Given our interaction last night in bed, I expected to find her at least somewhat moody this morning. It wasn't beyond me to know I wasn't the easiest person to get along with. But she seemed to take me in stride.

It made me wonder what else she might take in stride.

The waistband of my pants stretched with my flexing dick. Having Charlie dancing in my kitchen—half naked—was not part of the plan. If I was going to survive this, I needed to go back to plan A and put as much distance between us as possible.

I watched as she flipped the final pancake and layered it onto the stack she had next to the stovetop. The delicate fingers that grasped my arm last night gripped the edge of the plate with ease. She was a painter, I reminded myself. She used her hands every single day and had considerable strength, no doubt.

When she noticed my presence as she whirled around with the plate, a beautiful smile spread her lips wide.

"Good morning, sleepy head. I made breakfast." She raised the plate of pancakes in the air before setting it down in the middle of the island next to another plate covered with a paper towel.

"Good morning," I responded cautiously, not used to having someone in my space, let alone cooking my meals.

"I hope you don't mind." Her smile faltered for a moment, and I realized she must have seen the discontent on my face. "I wanted to do something nice for you after letting me crash here last night."

This one is always doing nice things for others. But who does nice things for her?

Charlie's skin was practically glowing in the morning light coming in through the angled shades. Sunshine didn't cover it. Charlie was damn near ethereal and the way I wanted her was downright sinful.

"I appreciate it. Thank you."

I rounded the island and grabbed two plates and forks for us. The sweet scent of vanilla wafted toward me as she slid onto the stool next to mine.

"Your cat attacked me this morning," I said bluntly, remembering how the little rascal had pounced on my face, nearly giving me a heart attack.

She whirled on me. "Attacked you? What do you mean?"

The fluffball's ears must have been burning because I felt his body rub against my leg just then. He looked up at me with feigned innocence reflecting in his giant eyes. I glowered at him.

"He jumped right on my face while I was still lying in bed."

The giggle that came from Charlie's mouth made the

hairs on the back of my neck stand on end. It was so melodic and pretty sounding.

"That wasn't an attack. More like a gesture of affection. He wanted your attention, so he…made sure you were paying attention."

When I noticed the smirk on her face, I growled. She was too cute for her own good and it was starting to get under my skin.

Done with her games, I set the dishes and utensils in front of our seats and reached for the paper towel that was covering another plate full of bacon. Charlie sat in silence as I filled our plates with the breakfast she'd made and I tried not to look at her because I knew if I did, I'd lose control, just like I'd done last night.

And I needed to be in control.

Pouring syrup over the stack of three pancakes on my plate, I silently hoped they would be better than the muffins that were buried somewhere deep in my trashcan.

I took a bite and had to choke it down. I looked at the stack on my plate where I'd cut out a triangle to see that pockets of flour had spilled onto the plate. The mixture hadn't been combined all the way, so there were spots of dry flour.

I finally looked over at Charlie. She was mowing down on the pancakes like nobody's business.

"Do you like them?" she asked around a mouthful of food and something about it made her look so damn cute.

How the girl didn't end up with food poisoning or at the

very least, an upset stomach, was beyond me. I stole a glimpse at the large stack on my plate.

I'm going to have to eat this whole damn thing.

"Yeah, they're great. Thanks again for making breakfast."

The delicate column of her throat worked as she swallowed her bite down. "I was happy to."

Of course you were, I wanted to say. She was happy to do *anything* I was coming to realize. Whatever man claimed this woman as his wife was going to be damn lucky.

She was too good.

Too beautiful.

And it pissed me the fuck off.

The image of her making breakfast for another man while he came up behind her and kissed her neck. How her lips would call out his name as he worshiped her body. The long nights they would spend together.

I gripped my fork with a vengeance, the metal biting into my palm.

"Everything okay?"

My vision cleared from the personal hell I'd made for myself, and her face came into view. Despite the look of concern, her blue eyes sparkled. They were so bright with all her attention on me.

Just like they'd been when I found her huddled under a towel in the corner of her bedroom. Her eyes had been the first thing I'd noticed that day. They struck me to my core because even in the midst of the flames surrounding her, there had been hope reflecting in those crystalline blue depths.

"Yeah, I…um…" I cleared my throat as I tried to make sense of the thoughts warring in my mind.

Her auburn brows pinched together even more as she assessed me with concern.

"I was just thinking about how I need to fix that broken pipe so we can get you back to the cabin. It's probably going to be an all-day project."

The lines of her forehead smoothed as she leaned back a little. "Oh," was all she said.

I felt like a deflated balloon seeing the disappointment wash over her. *Did that mean she wanted to stay with me longer?*

"I just figured you'd want your own space again."

Her lips pulled back, but I could tell the grin she wore was forced. "You're right. It will be nice to have my own space again. There are some projects I need to finish anyways."

I nodded, suddenly feeling an urgency to take back everything I'd just said. The retraction was stuck in my throat though and I didn't know how to get the words out.

So, I did the only thing a man in my position could do. I stuffed my mouth with half-mixed pancakes and shut the fuck up.

"Are you sure you don't need me to come with you to help?" Charlie asked as we stood by the front door, and I laced up my boots.

"No. I'm going to call the plumber on the way and take care of some of the water damage to the wood while I wait. You're better off staying here." I gestured to her paint supplies that I'd brought in from my truck last night. "The house is yours. Light a fire. Get some work done. Whatever you need, just use it."

"Thanks for everything, Deacon." A rosy tint graced her freckled cheeks as she nodded, and I found myself wanting to find everything in the world that would make her cheeks glow like that.

But that wasn't my job. She wasn't mine to hold or kiss or do anything with. And I had to let that be okay.

My hand gripped the door handle and as I pulled the door open, bright white light shone in, assaulting my eyes. I raised my arm to shield my vision and heard Charlie gasp from beside me.

Blinking a few times, everything cleared, and I realized it wasn't the morning sun that did that. It was the several feet of pure white snow built around my porch.

"What the fuck?"

I stepped onto the wooden deck and looked around. Glimmering snow went on for as far as I could see. Charlie's car roof was barely visible, and the tires of my lifted truck were buried completely.

Out of the corner of my eye, I saw Charlie step onto the

front porch with me. Craning my neck, I looked down at her. There was an awed smile on her lips as she took in the sight.

"Has it ever snowed this much here before?"

I gazed back out onto my property, completely flabbergasted. "Never."

"What do we do?" she asked quietly.

The Blue Ridge Mountains in Georgia had been known to get snowstorms. Last winter had produced a couple that gave us some solid inches, but nothing to this degree. It had to be a record-breaking snowfall.

Tightness struck my chest as realization dawned on me. There was no way out of this.

My plan to get the tiny cabin back into living condition so Charlie could leave my house by tonight was a no-go. We were stuck here.

I was stuck here.

With the one person I had tried like hell to avoid.

Chapter 11

Charlie

"How did we get here, buddy?" I curled my fingertips over Casper's scalp. His ears twitched and he purred in appreciation.

An entire day had gone by since Deacon and I realized we were snowed in together. We both handled the situation by busying ourselves and avoiding one another as much as possible.

The first night I'd stayed with him, I saw a glimpse of the man my body desired. He was all dark and broody with long lashes over hooded eyes that told me the desperation I felt for him was mutual.

He'd been gruff and while he didn't tell me he wanted to share a bed; I could see the need in his eyes to be close to me. But then he shut down the moment I started asking questions.

It seemed there was a firm boundary in place and I was starting to think that maybe he just hadn't had sex in a long time and now that he had a pretty girl in his space, the temptation was too bothersome. Whatever connection we might have was likely just physical for him and I had to come to terms with that at some point.

Did I want the physical connection too? Would that be enough for me if things started to heat up between us? If I let myself give in to the small part of himself he might be willing to offer, would I be okay with it after the deed was done?

I'd been with men before. I'd even had a few serious relationships in my past. None of which turned into anything more, obviously. And none of which were with men who made me feel topsy-turvy like Deacon did. But that didn't mean it would be a good idea for me to give in to the temptation because I had a feeling that if I did, *I* would be the one who ended up with a broken heart.

But damn was that temptation pulling at me today.

Grasping the two mugs of hot chocolate I'd made, I peeked at him through the blinds of the window by the front door. His broad shoulders worked hard as he dove the edge of the snow shovel into the mountain of snow in front of his porch. I bit my lip as I watched him work, each movement of his strong body making heat pool at my center. Before long, I was practically sweating in my jeans and long-sleeve shirt.

I'd never really been around a man like him before. One who worked with his hands in such a proficient way. I couldn't help my mind from trailing off to thoughts of how he might use those hands on me.

My bottom lip suffered as my bite deepened. I was in big

trouble with this one, and maybe I should have just stayed inside and minded my own business. Instead, I followed that invisible string that had first appeared when he'd called out to me in my darkest hour and walked outside.

Cold air bit at my skin like a thousand needles pricking me at once. Casper meowed by my side as we walked through the windy swirls of fresh snow that started coming down.

Deacon looked over his shoulder at us and I was once again stricken with the handsomeness that was carved into every plane of his being. From his black hair that was starting to grow unruly at the nape of his neck to the strong structure of his jaw that always seemed to give away what he was thinking by how tightly he ground his teeth. The green of his eyes seemed shadowed today, darkened by the looming threat of the storm. And those plush lips that I thought way too much about had been drawn into a firm line.

I wondered, then, what it might feel like to see him smile. Full and wide. Like he had no care in the world or no trace of some horrific memory from past times pulling on his attention.

As he stalked toward me his lips turned downward into a deep frown.

Today wouldn't be the day I saw that smile, I realized.

Extending my right arm, I offered him a mug of hot chocolate. "I thought this might warm you up some. You've been out here working all morning."

His gaze set on me for a moment before dipping to the

steaming mug. When he didn't take it immediately, I lifted it a fraction and joked, "I promise I didn't poison it or anything."

Deacon's thick brows rose as he looked back at me. "You sure about that?"

Was that a joke? Did Deacon Calhoun just try to say something funny?

My lips pulled back and despite the frigid air, I felt heat bloom in my cheeks. "You'll have to taste it to find out."

He huffed a breath through his nose then wrapped his bare hands around the mug. His fingertips grazed against mine. The warmth of them shocked me and I sucked in a breath. In this weather…how could he still be hot to the touch?

I slid my hand off the mug and tucked it into my jeans pocket as I tried to ward off the butterflies in my stomach.

Yup.

I was in deep with this one and touching *any* part of Deacon was only going to lead to my own demise.

No matter how hard I tried to look away, I found myself gawking at his lips as they moved over the edge of the mug, and he took a long sip of the hot chocolate.

"What do you think?" I managed to ask when he lowered the mug.

The light caught his eyes, revealing those brown and blue flecks that danced amongst the green like old leaves falling from a tree against a gorgeous fall sky.

"I don't think it's poisoned, so that's definitely a plus."

I shoved him in the chest, playfully. He didn't laugh, but I caught a hint of a smirk and that was good enough for me.

"It's really good, actually. Thank you."

"Good." I nodded with conviction. If there was one thing I knew how to make, it was a decadent mug of hot cocoa.

We both sipped from our drinks for a few moments, taking in the snowmageddon that had us trapped together.

"I don't think I've ever seen anything like this before. It kind of messes with my mind if I stare at it for too long." I glanced up at him and found there was a pained look on his face.

I knew better than to ask him if he was okay, so I stayed silent, even though I couldn't tear my eyes away from him.

"I've only seen snow this high once. When I served in Afghanistan, our deployment ran through the middle of winter. Those mountains get colder than anything I've ever experienced before."

Afghanistan. The war. Another piece of his puzzle slid into place for me. If he'd been deployed while in the military, there was a high likelihood that he'd seen unimaginable things. Just like he'd said. Horrors that no human should have to face.

For some reason it hadn't clicked in my mind until now, the types of inhuman experiences he'd likely encountered over there.

Because I'd lived a sheltered, posh life since I was born, the idea of going to war, living in the mountains while risking my life was beyond my comprehension. I couldn't understand how that might shape someone. What fears and nightmares one might have to endure for a lifetime afterward.

The isolation out here. The desire to be alone in the wilderness… I'd only been here a short time, but the beauty that surrounded us had already captured my heart and calmed my mind in a way I didn't know was possible. I understood now why it was so precious to him. To his well-being.

Seeing me was probably a constant reminder of the life he had tried to leave behind. I was the person he'd saved from the fire. I knew I likely wasn't the only one he'd saved over his career, but I'd come here. Invaded his space. Asked him too many questions.

I'd probed and prodded. Disrespected everything he'd been through.

Guilt clawed at me with such strength all the air left my lungs.

Never in my life had I done something so selfish. Been so blind to my own intrinsic desires that I ignored what someone else was trying to tell me but couldn't.

My throat felt thick with the words *I'm sorry* and just as my lips parted to say them, a loud screech came from my left.

I whirled around to see what had made the sound. "Oh my God!" I yelled, my hands coming up shakily to cover my mouth. "Casper!"

"Shit!" Deacon cursed under his breath as he moved to my side.

While I was lost in thought, Casper must have snuck off.

He was in one of the pine trees clinging to the branch for dear life while a large hawk circled the tree.

I took in the mountains of snow between me and him and felt my heart begin to thud against my chest. Panic rose and tears sprung to my eyes.

"Deacon, what do I do?"

He was staring at Casper in the tree as the hawk continued to circle around. The way his eyes darted back and forth between the tree and the snow told me he was assessing the situation.

But as I shifted and saw the hawk's circle growing smaller, I knew there wasn't time to waste.

"I'm going to try—"

"Take this," Deacon interrupted me, thrusting the snow shovel into my hands. I grabbed it and watched helplessly as Deacon started wading through the several feet of snow towards the pine tree.

His large shoulders tilted from side to side as he climbed into the snow pile, stomping his boots along the way to create a sturdier path.

"Hold on, Casper!" I yelled across the way. If anything happened to him...*no*. I couldn't think like that. He was going to be safe. Deacon was going to get him and bring him back to me.

He had to.

The hawk took notice of Deacon slowly moving toward them and swooped toward the branch where Casper's claws were grasped onto the trunk.

"No, no, no!" I cried. I closed my eyes for a moment, not

able to bear witness to my little buddy getting hurt. Casper had been with me for so long and the thought of him suffering or worse yet…existing in this world without him had my stomach turning sour with such ferocity, I thought I was going to be sick.

When I opened my eyes again, I saw that Deacon was almost to the tree. His movements had become large and powerful as he swung his body against the thick snow with each step forward.

The hawk swooped down again, not caring that Deacon was so close. My heart lurched into my throat at the hawks near miss. Casper let out a strained cry that had my knees trembling.

"Please, Deacon," I whispered into the winter wind. "Please."

Every second that ticked by felt like a lifetime until I saw Deacon press his hands against the trunk of the tree.

He made it. Hope soared through my body, raising goosebumps along my skin that had nothing to do with the cold.

The coat he wore lifted up as his arms raised toward the branch. He was tall, but the branch Casper clung to sat a few feet above him.

"Jump, Casper! Come on, boy!" I moved toward the trail in the snow Deacon's body had made and patted the top of my thighs. Casper's attention shifted to me as he let out another strained meow.

He must have been terrified because I never heard him make that sound before.

I wiped the tears from my eyes and tried to smile, so he wouldn't think I was stressed. He'd always been so in tune with me. Following me around, being my comfort on the hard days and my celebration buddy on the best ones.

"Come on, rascal," I heard Deacon say as he wiggled his fingers to draw Casper's attention to him.

A flash of brown and white darted through the air just above Deacon as the hawk tried another assault. I gasped as its claws jutted outward toward Casper at the same time Deacon yelled, "Jump!"

Casper's shaking body flew through the air and just missed the hawk's talons before he landed in Deacon's sturdy arms.

"Got him!" Deacon called back to me.

"Yes!" I jumped up and down, no longer worried about the mess of waterworks on my face. My little guy was safe and that was all that mattered.

The hawk let out a long shriek before flying off to find some other prey no doubt.

Unable to wait for him to be in my arms, I sprang through the snow path.

"You're going to catch a cold," Deacon grumbled as he turned around and saw me bounding toward him and Casper. "Get back on the porch."

"I'm not going anywhere until I know he's okay."

"He's okay," Deacon said, but I ignored him as I closed the distance between us.

Deacon's forearms were wrapped tightly around Casper, little puffs of his white fur poked out in all directions, and he was still shaking. Reaching out my arms, Deacon gave him to me and ushered us back toward the porch.

"You're a stubborn woman, you know that?" His right brow arched upward as he looked down at me with what seemed like amusement, but I couldn't be sure. He was still so hot and cold with me; I never knew when he was jesting and when he was being totally serious.

I snorted. "I'm only stubborn when it comes to the things I love."

It was true. I'd always been a go with the flow kind of girl for most of my life with the exception of becoming an artist despite the odds stacked against me. And making the move to Pebble Brook Falls the moment I saw the listing of Deacon's quaint little cabin.

My parents had been devastated when I first told them I was moving, but when I explained needing a change of pace, they understood.

While I'd recovered fairly well from the trauma of the fire, I hadn't gotten away completely unscathed. The city life didn't call to me anymore. There wasn't anything wrong with it per say, I had just started to feel…overwhelmed.

After we'd gotten inside, I turned to Deacon and realized all his clothes were soaked from being in the snow for so many hours and then treading through it to save Casper. He'd jumped into action so quickly while I stood there frozen. I wondered if that had been due to his military training or was something innate that he'd been born with.

"Thank you for saving him." I rocked Casper back and forth, holding him close to my chest. He'd stopped shivering, but I could tell he was still pretty shaken up. "I...I can't believe I froze like that," I said, shaking my head in disbelief of myself.

When a tendril of my hair fell forward into my face, Deacon's eyes shifted to it. I tried to shake my head in a way that would get it out of my face, but it kept falling forward. His hand reached up, the strands of my hair falling through his fingers as he slid them downward.

I sucked in a breath, air whistling into my mouth as I watched him thread my hair through his fingers again until he finally tucked the piece behind my ear. When his thumb traced the cuff of my ear, I let my eyes flutter close.

His touch was gentle. The complete opposite of what most probably thought of just by looking at the sheer size of him—and at the rough calluses on his hands.

My gentle giant, I thought.

But when I opened my eyes and saw him retreat inward, I remembered that Deacon wasn't mine. No matter how badly I was starting to want him to be.

His words came out thick, like he'd just woken up from a long nap or something. "You're not the only one who's frozen during a difficult moment, Charlie. Fear does strange things to people." The distant look in his eyes told me he wasn't standing in the foyer of his house anymore. That his mind had taken him to faraway places.

"Well, I'm glad you were there," I offered, trying to pull him back to the present.

His eyes flashed, then he looked down at Casper and scratched behind his ears. "Me too. We wouldn't have wanted this little rascal to turn into hawk bait." Deacon's head tilted back and forth like he was contemplating what he'd just said. "Well, not today anyway. We'll have to see if he tries to jump on my face again tomorrow morning."

Holding Casper closer to my chest, I twisted away from Deacon and whispered, "Don't listen to him, buddy. He's just being a big meanie."

"A big meanie, huh?" Deacon's chuckle was raspy and warm and so damn sweet, it had my chest fluttering.

"Yeah." I beamed at him. "A big meanie."

"Well, this big meanie is off to take a long hot shower. I'll cook us some chili when I get out."

Cook us some chili. It was such a simple statement, but what I felt behind the words was monumental. It made me feel like I was part of Deacon's life in a way that I was starting to crave. That maybe there could be a spot for me here, which I knew sounded crazy. But that didn't matter to me. I'd already done wild things in my life, like picking up everything and moving to a small mountain town where the only person I kind of knew was a broody man who couldn't decide if he liked me or hated me.

As Deacon made his way across the living room and down the hall, I clutched Casper close to me and silently hoped that tomorrow would be more of the same.

Chapter 12

Deacon

Sweat clung to my skin in a thick sheen as I awoke to a dip in the side of the bed. Peeling my eyes open, I saw Charlie's bright face.

"What time is it?" My tongue felt thick and my throat hoarse as I tried to scoot up, but immediately thought better of it as my muscles strained.

"It's eight thirty," Charlie responded, her rosy lips tightened as she placed the back of her hand against my forehead. "You're burning up, Deacon. Where do you keep your medicine?"

"Burning up?" I tried to sit up again and saw the room start to spin, a sharp dagger-like pain shot through my skull, and I winced, squeezing my eyes shut.

"You're sick and you definitely have a fever. Just stay here and tell me where your medicine cabinet is, and I'll get it for you."

Even the quiet sound of her soothing voice sent rods of pain through my skull. *Sick. There is no way I can be sick.*

But as I assessed my body, I found that every muscle ached like I'd just done a ruck run with an eighty-pound backpack on. Every time I moved, there was a cold sensation that hit my skin from the sweat that soaked the sheets. And my damn head…it hurt. Badly.

"Fuck," I groaned, slowly opening my eyes to prevent another shard of pain from attacking my head again.

"Shhh," Charlie cooed. "Give me a minute, I'm going to go look for some medicine and new bed sheets."

When she rose from the bed, I reached feebly for her wrist and caught her just in time. I smacked my lips together, trying to get my mouth's muscles working properly again. Long red hair slid over Charlie's shoulder as her head tilted to the side and for the first time, I noticed there were different shades of red in it. Strawberry blonde highlights shimmered throughout the auburn and fire red shades. It reminded me of a blood orange sunset—wild and untamed but held such striking beauty that I couldn't look away, no matter how hard I tried.

"I don't have medicine," I croaked.

Long lashes fluttered as she blinked at me. "You don't have *any* medicine?"

I shook my head. "I never get sick, so I don't keep that stuff in my house."

"Okay." Her blue eyes darted around while she thought through the problem. "Do you at least have a thermometer?"

I tried to think, but the ache in my head was throbbing so

badly I could hear my heartbeat in my ears. "Under my bathroom sink maybe."

Warm hands wrapped around my right hand that was still holding onto her wrist. I stared at where our hands joined, seeing how easily hers fit in mine. Where I was rough and hard, she was all smooth and soft. The feeling of her skin pressed against mine was…I couldn't explain it. Comforting. Thrilling. It made me want to feel more and I hated that because I wasn't supposed to be this way. Not when I was the complete opposite of the kind of man she needed.

Unable to stand it any longer, I forced my hand back to my side and rolled my head to the right, so she wasn't in my direct line of vision anymore. She stood there for a few agonizing seconds before I watched her from my periphery disappear into the bathroom.

Frustrated as hell, I lifted my head and slammed it back into the pillow. Which was a huge mistake as searing pain roared in my skull.

"Agh." I squeezed my eyes shut again and silently chastised my stupid ass for doing that.

I was quickly discovering that I did many stupid things while Charlie was around. Thinking straight was nearly impossible in her presence. Part of me was annoyed by it. For so long, I had lived my life alone and I liked it that way. I didn't have to answer to anyone or take another person into consideration when I made decisions.

I thought I was going to live the rest of my life like that, and I was fine with it. Content even.

But Charlie Banks was quickly ruining my plans and even worse…I liked it.

She appeared through the bathroom doorway with a wide smile painting her lips. Her arm rose into the air and between her fingers she clutched a thermometer. "Found it!" She waved it through the air.

Her enthusiasm did something funny to my stomach, making it feel like a swarm of bees was flying around inside. I tried to stomp out the feeling, but as she grew closer with her little pajama set showing off the curves of her body, I found the bees attacking my stomach even more.

Leaning over me, she slipped the thermometer out of its plastic case and told me to open up.

"I can do it myself," I fussed, trying to reach for the thermometer, but she yanked it back.

"I'm only going to say this once, Deacon, so listen up." A stern look replaced her normally happy one as she pointed her finger at me. "You are sick as a dog and thankfully, you have someone here to take care of you. Being stubborn will only exhaust your body and keep you sick for longer, so I expect your full cooperation." With that, she lifted her right brow and popped her hip out.

"You're such a brat," I glowered at her.

"And you're a grumpy asshole," she snickered before gesturing for me to open my mouth.

So, she has some sass in her after all. Sunshine with some heat.

Rolling my eyes, I opened my mouth, and she slid the

thermometer in. We glared at one another until the beep went off and she took the thermometer from me.

The feistiness she carried just a moment ago vanished as she looked down at me with concern. "It's one hundred three, Deacon. That's pretty high for an adult."

"Yeah, I know." My body started to shake, and I tried to hide it beneath the covers, so she didn't worry but I was too late. Her eyes went wide as she took in my shivering body.

"I'm fine." I tried offering her a smile, but she only scowled at me.

"You are definitely *not* fine. But I know of something that could help."

I tried not to fall over as Charlie tucked the final edge of the clean fitted sheet onto my bed. She rounded the bed and hopped onto my side before spreading her legs a little.

Patting the mattress between her thighs, she gestured for me to come over. "Come on. Lay down here."

"No." I shook my head, which was a mistake as the room started to spin again. All the pressure from my sinuses was wreaking havoc on my stability.

"You said you wouldn't be stubborn."

"*You* said I couldn't be stubborn. I didn't agree to anything."

She rolled her eyes and pursed her lips and it was the cutest damn thing I'd ever seen in my life. Making Charlie frustrated was very quickly becoming a top five favorite pastime of mine.

"Will you get over here, already? I promise it will make you feel better." Pleading shone in her eyes. With a look like that, I couldn't deny her any longer.

Sliding her left leg off the bed to give me better access, I laid down on my back between her thighs.

"Scoot up a little bit."

"I don't want to hurt you."

"Hurt me?" she asked with a laugh.

"I weigh about three times as much as you, Charlie."

Even though I couldn't see her face, I knew she'd just rolled her eyes at me again. "I'll be fine. Scoot up."

Begrudgingly, I did as she said until my head was resting on her stomach and her thighs were snug against me. My breathing shifted and my heart rate sped up being this close to her. Feeling so much of her skin pressed against mine.

I hated that I wasn't in my best state. That my skin still had a sheen of sweat over it. But she didn't seem to care as she brought her legs even closer against my side.

"Comfortable?"

"Yes." I closed my eyes and noticed every point where our bodies melded together. My throat grew even more dry from the contact. She was so damn close and the faint smell of vanilla was soothing. I relaxed a little more and noticed how her firm thigh muscles provided a little more support around me.

"Good," she quipped. "I'm going to place the ice pack on your forehead now to try and get this fever down."

"Okay," I nodded slightly and braced myself for the cold.

Her touch was gentle as she brought the ice pack to my forehead, but I sucked in a sharp breath at just how damn cold it was and accidentally grabbed her shins from the jolting sensation.

"I know, it must feel freezing. I'm sorry." Once the pack settled onto my forehead, I felt her lean forward a little. "This should help distract you."

My eyes sprang open at the comment wondering what kind of distraction she had up her sleeve. Then, I felt her fingertips glide along my scalp with just the right amount of pressure to ease the pain.

"Ahhh," I breathed out, feeling my head grow heavier in her lap as my neck relaxed.

"Feels amazing, huh?"

"Oh yeah," I noted, drawing out the words. Chills spread out over my back and chest from her touch. "Where did you learn this?"

She was quiet for a moment as her fingers continued down the base of my skull where the pain was greatest.

"I'll make you a deal. A question for a question."

It was a dangerous game letting this woman inside of my head. Maybe it was the sickness or some delusional part of me that thought I had a chance in hell of being a normal guy for a moment. One who didn't have a fucked up past that kept me up at night. One who avoided any sense of closeness to others.

But I'd found that Charlie was good at getting close to people. She was too hard to look away from. And the pull I felt toward her... The strength I normally had to fight it was diminished from whatever sickness plagued my body right now.

"Okay." Her fingers stilled on me for a second like my agreement was striking. Which, I guessed it was given how I'd acted toward her for most of the time she'd been here.

I heard a quick breath move past her lips as her fingers started moving over my head again. "When I was little and would get sick, my mom would always let me crawl into her lap and she'd give me scalp massages to help with the headaches." Her laughter fluttered over me like a gentle breeze in springtime. It was…nice. "When it was just me in my apartment, I ordered a scalp massager for when I was sick. It was nice and helped with the headache, but there's nothing like the comforting touch of someone else trying to make you feel better."

Her world seemed like a fairytale, and I wondered if she'd ever experienced the pain of the world before the apartment fire. Maybe she just had a way of letting things go that I'd failed to master.

I stayed quiet, thinking about what she'd said and bracing myself for the question she was about to ask. I didn't like people prying into my life, which was why I'd found great friends in Pebble Brook Falls. Somehow, we all had a bit of darkness to us. Things we wanted to keep hidden away from the light. And we all agreed not to poke around when things were too sensitive.

Charlie wasn't like that. It seemed like she stared into the void, beckoning it to fight her, knowing all along that she was going to be the victorious one. She was brave, I realized.

"Did you build the tiny cabin yourself?" A wave of relief washed over me at her perfectly benign question.

I closed my eyes and let my body sink a little deeper into the mattress. "Not entirely. The structure was there when I bought the property, but I remodeled it this past year to use as a rental. My friends helped some too."

"Was Sarah the one to bring in the flowers?"

Opening my eyes, I looked up at her. "I believe it's my turn to ask the next question." Her eyes lit up as she bit the corner of her bottom lip.

"I guess I did agree to that." She winked at me and the simple gesture had my blood roaring in my ears. I shifted my gaze to the ceiling.

"Do you like it here?" The words were out before my muddled mind could stop them. I blamed it on the fever and not the growing curiosity I had for her.

There was no hesitation with her answer. "It's exactly what I hoped it would be. Wide open spaces brimming with nature's life and wonders. The decision to move away from the city was something I sat with for a long time before pulling the trigger." She let loose a breathy sigh as she combed her fingernails over my scalp, sending a ray of goosebumps down my arms. "I don't think I'll ever be able to go back."

"I know what you mean."

"Did you grow up in a city?"

The cold pack on my forehead slid a little bit as I nodded.

Charlie moved it back into place before she rubbed my temples in slow circles. "Charlotte, actually."

"Oh really? I mean, obviously I knew you lived there at some point, but I didn't know you were *from* Charlotte."

"Yup. My folks are still there, and they love it. It just never made sense for me. I always felt claustrophobic with all the people and big buildings. I didn't understand the allure of being on top of everyone else, especially when you're surrounded by strangers who hardly take the time for a good morning greeting."

"Yeah, that part was difficult for me too. I had plenty of friends, but after the fire…I don't know. They just seemed to kind of disperse and move on with their lives while I was stuck in the hospital for weeks." The sad notes in her voice made me angry. Her ray of sunshine was clouded by rain, and I hated it. I found myself wanting to find every single one of those people who made her feel alone during that time and punish them.

The anger had my head throbbing, but I didn't care. I hated that Charlie had ever felt that way. And I hated myself for not checking on her in the hospital.

My fire chief had told me she was in the same hospital as me when he and the rest of the guys came to visit me. I'd asked about her then but couldn't find the courage to seek her out. I thought she would have hated me and seeing her in a hospital bed because of my doing…it had been too much.

I wanted to tell her that I made a mistake back then. That I should have visited her if only to make sure she was recovering well.

I wanted her to know that I saw her. Every freckle on her beautiful face. The subtle way her nose wrinkled when she laughed at something. How the crystalline blue of her eyes reminded me of Bahamian waters—so stunning they didn't seem to belong in this world.

I wanted to tell her everything…

Instead, I just sat in silence as I watched her, those eyes that had haunted my dreams and many waking moments well with tears.

Chapter 13

Charlie

I worked hard to focus on the positive things in my life. The fire taught me how precious life was and I didn't want to waste a single moment of the time I'd been given.

But there were moments when I let myself feel the sorrow from the losses that came with that day. Seeing my friends disappear one-by-one had been heartbreaking as I sat in that hospital bed trying to be brave for my parents. Their worlds were rocked when they saw on the news that my building had gone up in flames.

The morning after, when I had woken up and saw their faces for the first time, I knew I needed to keep it together for them. I was their only child, their entire world.

But I wished that I had a safe place to land where I could have fallen apart. A friend…a partner…*anyone* who could have carried the burden for me for a little while.

Tears pricked the corners of my eyes, but I blinked them away. I wasn't back in that place anymore. I'd gotten out and my new home was shaping up to be my biggest adventure yet.

"No one should have to go through something like that alone, Charlie. All those people who you thought were your friends and didn't show up when you needed them most don't understand what they were missing out on. Because you're wonderful, Charlie. And they should have fucking been there."

He wasn't looking at me, but I could see the stern conviction in his eyes as he stared up at the ceiling. A muscle feathered along his jawline like he was trying to work his frustration down.

"You say that, but you also slammed your door in my face." I wasn't sure what came over me, but it felt good to say the one thing I'd been wanting to say since I arrived in Pebble Brook Falls. Deacon's welcome had been anything but warm and while he was starting to show me a different side of him, I was raised to demand respect. I had let him get away with giving me whiplash for too long already.

Drops of cold water slid onto my leg from the cold pack as it slid off Deacon's forehead when he rose to a sitting position.

"What're you doing? You need to be laying down," I barked at him.

When he turned around so he was facing me, I could see the struggle it took for him to sit up. He was so sick and despite the question I asked him and the growing frustration from our confusing interactions, I hated seeing him so vulnerable.

I moved to grab his hands and urge him to lay back down, but he quickly grasped my wrists with speed I didn't think he was capable of by the looks of him. His grip loosened a little as he slid his hands downward, and his thumbs were rubbing circles on the inside of my palms.

The feeling sent tiny sparks up my forearms and all I wanted to do was close my eyes and bask in how it felt to have part of me held by him.

"You should really lay back down," I whispered, not able to find the full volume of my voice from the bewitching circles he scribed into my palms.

His voice was oddly clear and steady as he said, "I need to look you in your eyes when I say this."

Oh.

Wavering back a little, I was perplexed by his words and the sudden willingness to answer my question. Or at least I hoped he was going to answer it.

The strength seemed to leave him a little as he wobbled slightly to the right. Perspiration formed over his brows and upper lip and as sick as he looked, he was still the most beautiful man I'd ever seen.

His nostrils flared as he took a steadying breath in and settled his gaze on me. I worried my bottom lip, wondering what he was going to say to me.

"I made a lot of mistakes the day of that fire. For one, I wasn't even supposed to be there. I was off duty when I was walking by the building and saw what was happening. Going in without any gear put my fellow firefighters at risk worrying about my safety. But I wouldn't change that decision for anything because you wouldn't be here if I hadn't gone in."

Chills skated along my skin because he was right. If Deacon hadn't come into my apartment when he did, I would have died probably a minute or two later. I shook the image out of my mind. I didn't want to think about those moments sitting terrified in the corner of my bedroom yelling as loudly as I could for someone to find me before it was too late.

"When I first heard your screams, I thought it was just the roar of the fire. I was on my way back down to aid with the survivors on the ground, but something kept telling me to keep going. When I saw you, I…" His throat worked as he swallowed and his grip on my hands tightened. "I'd never seen someone so beautiful before. Even through all the fear on your face, I saw hope shining in your blue eyes."

I sat completely still, not fully trusting my ears. Was I hearing things correctly? Deacon thought I was beautiful from the first moment he saw me, in my most vulnerable state, clinging to life as I had tried shrinking my body under the cover of the small wet towel.

I couldn't believe it.

But I also knew in my heart it was true. Because it had been his face I'd focused on when the edges of my vision started to fade. His voice, urging me to stay with him had kept me tethered to *life*.

Something had happened between us that day. At first, I thought maybe it was just the trauma of what we'd both gone through together. Especially, when our first greeting since the fire hadn't been the most comforting.

Everything was shifting now. The puzzle pieces sliding into place. And I still couldn't move, could hardly think with Deacon's hands on me.

There was an earnestness in his voice as he continued. "I've been in many dangerous situations over the course of my careers. Moments that I will never have the heart to speak about." His eyes cast downward, and I could feel the weight of those memories hanging in the air between us. I rubbed my thumbs across the edge of his palms, needing to do something to help me feel more grounded.

"Many of those moments, I could see when hope would leave the people around me. It looked as though a flash of realization swarmed them and suddenly fear took over. A thousand times, I've seen that happen, but not with you. Not even when you were minutes away from the most painful death there is."

I stopped breathing when his hand moved to cup the side of my face. Every part of me was bare to him. Deacon had seen something in me that I hadn't even seen in myself.

"You were the most magnificent thing I'd ever witnessed in my entire life, Charlie. And it scared the hell out of me." His voice shook and I knew it wasn't because of the sickness. Then his hand fell from my face, and I hated the cold that was left in its absence.

"That's why you slammed the door in my face. You were shocked to see me." My voice was barely above a whisper and the words felt thick on my tongue like I hadn't spoken in a long time.

The green of his eyes flickered as he nodded. "Shocked is an understatement."

I looked down where our hands were still joined. His were so large compared to mine and it made me remember how he'd held me that day, rushing us through the threatening flames. How, even now, I could feel the heat licking along my skin. My scar ached at the memory of its creation. But I didn't move to touch it. Not now.

"What about now?" Heart racing, I gazed up at him through my lashes.

His chest expanded on a deep inhale.

"Now, I don't want to let you out of my sight for a single second. And I don't plan to."

My heart soared and a wild giddiness took hold in my chest.

"You don't plan to?"

His fingers gripped my chin as he came in close. "Not a fucking chance."

We spent the next two days in bed together as I forced him to relax instead of trying to finish projects he had around the house. Casper was perfectly content snoozing on the foot of the bed while I monitored Deacon's fever and gave him scalp massages for his headache.

By the time supper rolled around last night, his fever had

broken. Tonight he was feeling almost like his usual self again and he was able to move into the kitchen with me while I worked on making soup. Minestrone to be exact.

"I can handle this, you know." I waved the wooden spoon in his direction. "You should be laying on the couch and getting some more rest."

"I've been resting all day, smalls. You're lucky I didn't try to bust out of that room hours ago. I thought I was going to lose my mind."

I snorted. "I might be small, but I can still take you in this condition. So, sit your ass down and rest."

A wide smile spread across his face, making my heart stutter a beat. It was the first time I'd seen him smile so brazenly. It was the most amazing thing I'd ever seen, and I found myself wanting to make him smile like that more.

"Yes, ma'am," he responded before he shot me a wink and slid onto the stool.

Turning back around to the pan of ground beef, I grinned to myself. I liked this version of Deacon.

Light.

Fun.

Devilishly handsome.

Too suave for his own good.

I liked it and I probably shouldn't knowing that I was already in way over my head with him. When he was around, I was putty on the floor. There was just something about the man that made me melt.

After what he'd told me earlier, I couldn't help but fall even harder. Right now, we were stuck in this house together as more snow continued to pile high outside. But I knew there would come a time when the snow melted and the reality of what he'd divulged to me would hit.

I just hoped he would still feel the same by then. That this thing between us was worth exploring.

"So, do you have a job you're missing out on right now?"

"You want to talk to me about work?" His voice was raspy from the cold. I could barely hide what the sound of it did to me as my cheeks stained red with heat.

"Mmhmm," I responded, staring into the pan of meat afraid that if I turned to look at him, my cheeks would give me away. *I want to know everything about you*, I wanted to say but kept my lips clamped shut.

"I, uh, decided to retire early."

I whirled around, shocked. "Retire early? Aren't you in your thirties?"

He shrugged nonchalantly. "I got lucky in the stock market. Really lucky, actually."

"Lucky in the stock market," I deadpanned.

"Yup." He nodded slowly. "While I was in the military, I put most of my earnings in savings and when I started working for the Charlotte Fire Department, I met a guy who was fucking brilliant in the stock market. He taught me some tips and after a while I started doing my own research. Got lucky with some biotech companies and was able to buy a good chunk of land out here when I decided to make the move."

I was in awe of him. At first glance, Deacon was a rugged mountain man who was obviously good with his hands, but I never would have guessed he would be the kind of man who made enough money in financial pursuits to retire in his thirties.

I quickly realized that was a terrible bias I held against men who looked like him and I made a mental note to eradicate that prejudice from my mind.

"How much land do you have out here?"

He leaned his large forearms onto the counter. "Fifty-two acres that run along the east side of the river."

I felt my eyebrows raise. "Fifty-two? Wow. That's a lot of land."

"I like my privacy."

"Casper and I have kind of ruined it for you." I laughed, but Deacon's eyes turned dark.

"You haven't ruined anything, Charlie."

His gaze bore into mine. Enraptured, I couldn't look away. The world seemed to still as he was the only thing I could focus on, just like the first day we met. Everything else drifted away while all the words emptied from my mind. We stayed like that—locked on one another like two magnets that couldn't be pulled apart.

Then the smell of smoke tingled my nose, and the connection was lost as I shifted back to the stove top.

"Oh no!" I gasped as I took in the charred meat. "Damnit!" Moving quickly to prevent the rest of the meat from burning, I reached over the pan and turned the burner off, but when I pulled my hand back, I bumped into the handle of the pan, jostling it over the stovetop.

"Ah! Ow!" I hissed, retracting my arm to my chest. "Shit!"

Before I could turn around, Deacon was by my side. "What happened?"

I raised my wrist and twisted it to the side so he could see where the edge of the pan burnt me. With a gentle touch, he took my wrist between his hands and inspected it.

I closed my eyes and gritted my teeth at the stinging sensation that permeated the area. "I burned myself on the pan."

His tone was tender as he cradled my wrist in his palm. "It doesn't look too bad, but let's get it under some cool water."

"Okay," I whimpered as he led me to the sink. Water rushed from the faucet when he turned the knob. I bit my lower lip as he tested the coolness of the water before sliding my wrist under it.

"Better?" he asked.

I peered up at him. There was still a paleness to his skin from how sick he'd been, but the color was starting to come back already. I could stare at him all day, I realized. Despite the pain in my wrist, I felt an urge to run my fingers through his hair like I'd done all morning to make him feel better. But this time, I wanted to do it for myself. I wanted to explore every part of his body. The parts that were honed from years of hard labor. The parts I hadn't seen yet. I wanted to spend the rest of my days getting lost in those green eyes, noticing all the changes within them from every kind of light that shone.

And most of all, I wanted to feel him pressed against me with nothing between us.

"I'd be better if you kissed me right now." The words I meant to keep in had slipped out, but I didn't care.

Deacon's breathing hitched and his gaze fluttered to my lips. When his head tilted downward slightly, butterflies flew freely in my stomach.

God, I needed him to kiss me. Please, kiss me, I silently coaxed him.

His head dipped further and I closed my eyes. But then I felt the gentle scrape of his closely shaven beard against the edge of my ear as he said, "Not yet, beautiful."

Chapter 14

Charlie

Not yet, beautiful.

Deacon's words swam through my mind for the past hour. I didn't know how to act throughout dinner and now that we were sitting on his sofa together watching the fire roar in the hearth with a cup of hot chocolate between my hands…well, I still didn't know how to act.

Did he mean that he fully intended on kissing me eventually? Or was he just trying to ward me off so I wouldn't bring it up again?

After another ten minutes of reeling through all the possible scenarios of what he meant, I decided to shut that part of myself off. If Deacon didn't want to kiss me, that was fine.

I was fine.

Everything was fine.

I sighed before taking a sip of my hot cocoa and tried to focus on the sweet warmth as it traveled down my throat.

Casper laid between us, and I was thankful for the barrier so that I wouldn't make a fool of myself again. Just being close to Deacon was proving to muddy my mind in ways I wasn't sure I would ever recover from.

But I could handle it. I'd become good at packing things away in a pretty little box so they didn't bother me anymore. Really, it was something I'd done my entire life without trying. Perspective was everything. You could either be grumpy that it's pouring down on you or you could dance in the rain. And I loved to dance.

So, I shrugged off the remnants of my sour attitude and gazed into the flickering flames.

After a few minutes, the leather sofa creaked, and I could feel Deacon's eyes on me. I slid my gaze to him and raised my eyebrows.

"What's going on in that pretty head of yours?" Another compliment that I tossed to the side. If Deacon wanted me, he was going to have to actually show me after all the shenanigans he'd been pulling.

But there was no reason for me to give him the silent treatment. We were stuck here together as wind whistled through the trees outside, bringing even more snow with it.

"I was just thinking about my papa and how much he loved having bonfires." I rubbed at my scar. The skin around it was getting more irritated by the day, but Deacon didn't grab my ointment from under the bathroom sink when he brought some of my things over from the tiny cabin.

"Oh yeah?" Deacon's smile wasn't as bright as the one from earlier, but he almost seemed more at ease with the gesture. Like something inside of him had cracked open and the barrier to his happiness had crumbled, giving him free reign to enjoy it again.

I decided that I loved every version of his smile right then.

Swallowing, I looked away. I was so far in over my head and the sensation of drowning was taking hold of me and I wasn't sure if Deacon would be my life raft or the one who pulled me under.

"Every fall he would have a big party at his house to celebrate the new season and after we'd barbeque for most of the day, we'd end it with a giant bonfire in his backyard. People from all over the neighborhood would come by to see it and gather around as the new season crept in."

A lightness took hold of my chest as I thought back to those times. "After a few glasses of merlot, he'd sneak over to me and pull me in for a side hug. Then he'd point to the fire and ask me if I could see the layers in the flames like he could.

"When I was younger, I thought he was just buzzed and crazy so I would laugh it off like he was just teasing me. But when I grew older, I took a moment to actually look and noticed there are, in fact, layers to the flames. The tip of the flame always burned a vivid yellow that would cascade downward into a sunset orange and even further still into shades of blue until finally ending with the hidden heat of the clear flame.

"I'll never forget the night I told him when I finally saw them. His face lit up like a shooting star and that was when he told me that people were much like those flames. We had the parts of ourselves that everyone could see. The parts that we chose to show to the outside world. The parts we only showed to those closest to us." My voice grew distant as I thought back to that pivotal moment in my life when something I'd tossed to the side had become so strikingly clear to me and the dawning realization that it had been in front of me all along. I just chose not to look at it. But when I finally did, it was pure magic.

I was thankful I saw what my papa did before he passed away and that he could share that life lesson with me.

"And what about the last layer of the flame? The clear part?" Deacon asked.

Calm curiosity danced in his eyes when I finally looked at him again. "That's the hidden part that we don't even show ourselves." My lips pulled back in a gentle smile. "But if we're lucky, someone will be able to uncover it for us."

Deacon's face fell and for a moment I could see the devastation he'd witnessed throughout his life written in the shadows that flickered across his face.

"Or at least that's what my papa said," I offered, trying to break the tension, but it didn't work.

Deacon stilled and I swore he saw those very hidden parts of *me* with those green eyes that I'd thought about more times than I liked to admit to myself since the first time I saw them.

"How do you do it?"

I rubbed at my scar again, suddenly feeling agitated. "Do what?" I asked defensively.

"See life through such rose-colored glasses and not have anything affect you."

His words felt like a slap in the face and my neck recoiled as I pulled back and gaped at him.

"Not have things affect me? You don't know anything about me."

He leaned forward and his eyes narrowed on me. Challenging me. "You're happy all the time. You make the best of things and don't bat an eye at trials that come your way. I know men who have fought in wars who, if they went through what you did the day of that fire, wouldn't be able to even be around an active hearth, let alone tell a nice story about bonfires. So"—his voice was stern as he moved closer to me—"how do you do it?"

"I…" Heat rolled over me in waves at his command and I hated how much I liked it when he told me what to do. When he demanded things from me. He was so bossy and gruff, and I wanted more of it because it pulled at something in me. Some hidden desire that hadn't shown itself until *he* came along.

"I live for the people who lost their lives." The words came out on a hushed breath. "It feels wrong to let the time I was given go to waste when their time was cut short."

His head cocked to the side. He was studying me like I was some abstract painting that he was trying to find meaning in. Part of me shied away under his scrutiny, but another part—perhaps the louder one—liked that he was observing me. I wanted his eyes on me. I wanted him to see me.

"Does that satisfy you?" I asked and then rubbed at my scar again. The itch was starting to drive me insane.

For a moment I thought he might have been frozen in place, then his gaze flicked down to where my palm rubbed against my ribs.

"It's bothering you a lot tonight."

My hand stilled.

"It's fine." I tossed my hair over my shoulder and tried to look away but found my eyes settling back on him again.

"It's the dry air," he said before rising from the couch and disappearing down the hall.

"Where are you going?" I leaned forward and called after him.

No response.

Casper's head popped up and he blinked slowly at me. He was probably wondering why I was causing such a fuss and disrupting his beauty sleep.

"Don't blame me. He's the one who's being a total weirdo right now." Disinterested in my antics, he settled his chin back on the blanket and closed his eyes right as Deacon reappeared with a small container in his hand.

"What's that?" I pointed at the container.

"Come to the edge of the couch." He gestured with his hands before kneeling in front of me.

I sat still for a moment contemplating whether or not I wanted to listen to him. He was being so damn bossy and right now, I didn't want him to get away with it. Mostly because I liked the idea of defying him. Testing his limits to see what he might do. What he might command me to do next.

Calm patience reflected in his gaze as he waited for me to move, and I had a feeling he was used to waiting out others given his military background.

Rolling my eyes and huffing in frustration, I moved to the edge of the couch.

"Lift your sweater," he ordered, nodding toward me.

"No."

"Yes," he growled.

"I can do it myself," I said sternly, zipping my lips into a tight line.

Something like irritation flashed across his face. "You've taken care of me all day. Let me do this for you." There was an earnestness in his voice that illuminated the connection between us once more. My mind whirled from his back and forth. One minute, he's rejecting me and the next he wants me to expose the most vulnerable part of myself to him like it's nothing.

Without another word, I lifted my knit sweater and watched his face turn to stone as he noted the large scar that ran from just below the cup of my bra down the side of my right rib cage. Most of the time, it was hidden from the world —myself included. Now, it was front and center for the man who gave me butterflies and infuriated me all at once.

Deacon's Adam's Apple bobbed as he swallowed, still staring at my marred skin. I wondered what he was thinking about. If it brought him back to that moment the way it did for me every time I saw it in the mirror. When the darkness finally took me, and his stunning green eyes were the last thing I thought I would see before my death.

I watched as he shifted in front of me and unscrewed the lid to the glass jar he held. His fingers dipped into the white salve. I held my breath as he smoothed the substance around his fingers.

"So it doesn't feel cold," he said, leveling his gaze on me. Even kneeling, he was taller than me sitting on the couch, and I wondered how many other people saw him like this. If he'd knelt in front of any other woman before.

The thought of him being with *anyone* else sent a jolt of jealousy through me. I shook the unwanted images from my mind.

When his fingers finally slid over my ribs with the balm, I felt a surge of relief. Not just from the itchiness of my dry skin, but from his touch that I'd come to crave. He concentrated intently, his brows furrowing slightly as he ran the salve down the swoop of my side and over the edge of my hip bone.

As my heart raced, I silently hoped he couldn't tell how affected I was by his touch. I was still trying to figure him out and while I knew I was vulnerable; I didn't want him to see just *how* vulnerable I was.

Then, his hand moved upward, and his fingers grazed the edge of my bra. I sucked in a sharp breath as heat pooled in my center and the apex of my thighs began to throb with need. He was close. So, so close.

Those pine green eyes looked at me and I could see the need that reflected back at me as his fingers stilled just below my right breast. He licked his lips and the room around me started to tilt when his palm splayed against my ribs. With the slightest pressure, he dug his fingertips beneath the underwire of my bra.

Breaths heavy, I felt my body give in to the battle that my mind had been trying to win. With my eyes fluttering closed, I leaned my forehead onto his lips.

"You keep dragging me around. Giving me whiplash. One second, you're rejecting me and the next, you're looking at me like I'm the most treasured painting in the entire world." Trying my best to break through the haze of lust, I leaned back and let the absence of his lips on my forehead sober me.

"I want to just let myself be with you, Deacon. But you keep making it so hard to know what you're thinking." I covered the hand he had over my skin with my own and continued. "When you touch me," I whispered. "I don't ever want it to stop."

Still as stone, Deacon just watched me as I tilted my face toward his and rubbed the tip of my nose under his chin and along his jawline. "I felt it then too. When I was in your arms the day of the fire and you were carrying me down the hall. I could have died right then and some part of me would have been okay with it because you felt like home. But I also knew that you wouldn't let my life end there. I knew with my entire soul that you would have done anything to get me out of that building. And you did."

His nostrils flared as he inhaled deeply and clamped his

eyes shut, shaking his head. "You can't say those things to me."

"Why? Why won't you just let me in?" My heart ached as I pleaded with him. Taking his head between my hands, he burrowed the side of his face into my grasp.

When he opened his eyes again, my chest was crushed under the weight of the fear that danced in his irises. "Because *you* are light in its purest form, and I am nothing but the darkness that will drive that light away. And I can't seem to stop wanting you, no matter how hard I try. I am no good, Charlie and I've already ruined a part of you once." He glanced at my bare skin where the scar was still exposed, his hand still splayed over top of it.

Everything clicked into place. Why he didn't visit me in the hospital. The slamming of his front door in my face. The hot and cold attention I'd received from him since I arrived.

This beautiful, incredible man who saved my life was broken. So terribly broken and that fragility woke something deep inside of me. A need to protect. To shield him from himself.

"Deacon," I whispered his name. "This"—Covering his hand with my own again, I pressed his palm further against my scar—"was not your fault."

A wave of torment shuddered across his face. His voice cracked as he spoke, "I stopped. In the middle of that hallway, Charlie, I stopped running. If I just would have kept going, the ceiling wouldn't have collapsed on us, and you wouldn't have—"

"Shhh," I pressed my finger to his lips. Looking down at

me, he stopped talking, but I could still see the regret of that moment written in the shadows of his face.

I needed it to go away. His pain. His regret. His self-loathing. I needed him to see what I saw in him. So, I pressed my lips to his cheek. Then the other.

When I pulled back, his long black lashes lifted and his chest rose as he inhaled deeply.

"It wasn't your fault, Deacon." I shook my head back and forth, then leaned forward again until our foreheads touched. "It wasn't your fault."

Our breaths intertwined and with every rise and fall of his chest, mine rose and fell too.

Then, I kissed him.

Chapter 15

Deacon

Heaven.

That's what it felt like to kiss Charlie.

My entire body seized up when she first pressed her lips to mine because I'd thought of this moment for so long. Dreamt of it in my wildest dreams, thinking it would never come true.

But as her little moan hummed against me, I couldn't contain myself anymore. I wanted her. *Needed* her. Like I needed the fucking air I breathed.

I slid my palm down the length of her side and gripped her bottom with my hands to pull her down onto my lap. Our lips parted and she let out a bubble of laughter that had my heart skipping beats.

Long strands of her sunset red hair fell over her shoulders. The crystalline blue of her eyes seemed to soften as I moved my hands upward to the sides of her face.

"I want to make you laugh every fucking day of my life,

Sunshine." Nuzzling my nose against hers, I felt her cheeks ball as she smiled. "It's the best sound I've ever heard."

Soft lips pressed against the center of my forehead as my fingers dug into her plush hips. "As long as I get to see you smile every day of mine." There was a huskiness to her voice I hadn't heard before. It was sultry and luscious and *fuck*... everything about her was carved to perfection by God himself.

Burying my hands in her hair, I kissed her again. This time, she opened up for me fully. Swiping my tongue against hers, I groaned at her warmth and sweet taste. There was nothing in this world that mattered more than this. It felt like falling as my stomach tightened and my heart beat faster. But the feel of her...it kept me grounded too. Kissing her was like coming home after spending years at war. It was the only place I wanted to be.

Her arms draped over my shoulders and when she started running her fingertips lightly over the base of my neck, goosebumps exploded down my arms. Everything with her felt like I was seeing the world again for the first time. It didn't matter who came before her because no one had made me feel the way she did.

Tangled together, she started rolling her hips forward in slow tantalizing motions that had my cock stirring.

When I gripped her ass and lifted my hips to give her the friction I knew she wanted, she bit my lower lip and dove her tongue deeper into my mouth.

"Fuck, yes," I murmured against her lips, and I felt her smile against me.

"There's too much clothing between us," she said, breaking the kiss. She frantically reached between us for the hem of my sweater, but I grabbed the sides of her arms before she could continue.

Letting out a little whimper, she stuck out her bottom lip at me and pouted. I laughed because it was the cutest damn thing I'd ever seen.

"What?" The word was a plea. "Why are we stopping?"

With a deep inhale, I breathed in her sweet vanilla scent and moved my palms back to the sides of her face. Her skin was flush, making the dusting of freckles over her nose and cheeks stand out even more.

"I just want to look at you for a moment." Her lashes fanned out over her cheeks as she leaned into my left palm. "I don't want to miss a thing."

The air between us was heady as we just looked at one another. Our breaths slowed as each moment passed by. I tried to memorize every detail of her beauty so if I ever lost the chance of keeping her in my arms, I'd at least have this. A memory I could hold onto forever.

The gentle slope of her pert nose was cute as a button. I drew my thumb along the edge of her jaw, bringing me to her rosy lips with a sharp cupid's bow on top. There was a small chicken pox scar right below her left temple where she probably scratched herself as a kid. Firelight caught the strands of her hair, turning them copper and a deep red depending on the shadows that bounced around the room.

"Stunning," I whispered as I grasped her wrists and

looked at her dainty hands. "I want to see what you've created with these hands. I want to watch you paint."

On a whispered breath she said, "Tomorrow. Tonight, I want to do…other things."

Looking into those sky blue eyes, I brought her left wrist to my lips and kissed the edge of her palm. She watched me with hooded eyes as I made my way down her forearm, kissing every bit of her soft skin.

"Other things," I echoed, coming back to plant another kiss on her wrist. "What might those other things be?"

"Must I say them out loud?" She stirred in my lap, and it took every bit of self-control not to grind my hard length against her.

"I'd like it very much if you did." Leveling my gaze on her, I swore the air vibrated between us with the tension we both felt.

As she leaned forward, her breasts rubbing slightly against my chest, she whispered in my ear, "I want you to kiss me between my legs. And once you've had your fill, I want you to slide your cock into me, so deep that I feel every single inch inside of me. But not too fast." She nipped the bottom of my earlobe with her teeth, and I groaned, no longer able to control myself as I ground my hips against her warmth that I could feel even through our clothes. "Because I want this to last all night long."

When Charlie pulled back there was a look on her face I hadn't seen before. Sultry eyes looked back at me. She was a woman who clearly knew her body well. Knew exactly what she wanted from a man, and I was damn near begging to give it to her.

"This is what you want?" I slid my hand up her thigh then between her legs where I knew she was soaking wet and ready from the moisture that had gathered against the fabric of her leggings.

"Yes," she breathed, head tilting back so far, the ends of her hair swished against the fabric of my jeans.

I rubbed her clit in slow circles as her grip on my shoulders tightened. Watching her writhe beneath me was like seeing one of the seven wonders of the world. It was so fucking beautiful, so alluring. My cock strained against my jeans, but I ignored it. This moment was about her.

With flushed cheeks and hooded eyes, she looked back at me. She bit her bottom lip as she started moving her hips against my fingers. With my other hand, I threaded my fingers through her hair and brought her lips to mine. We were a wild mess of tongues and teeth, the heat between us growing nearly unbearable as we quickened our pace. She ground against the palm of my hand as I continued to massage my fingers over her little nub.

"I want you to lick me, Deacon. I want to feel your tongue over my clit." Her breaths were hot against my lips as she spoke.

"My woman wants me to kiss and suck on her clit," I moaned as she ran the edge of her teeth against my jaw. "Let me fucking give it to her."

She paused for a moment and took my face between her

hands. A shy look passed over her face as she sucked on the bottom right corner of her lip. "Say it again."

My words repeated in my mind and then I knew exactly what she wanted. I could see it clear as day written on her face. "My woman," I repeated, nuzzling my nose against her neck.

She hugged me in such a sweet and tender way, it jarred me for a second. Sweet and tender wasn't my typical experience of anything in life. But that's what Charlie was. Feisty like the burn of bourbon, but sweet like smooth honey and tender like a gentle spring wind. She was everything I never knew I wanted. Never knew I *needed*. Because I'd denied myself even though I'd felt that string connecting us from the moment I laid my eyes on her.

"Is it crazy that I knew I was yours back then? That all it took was one look and I had fallen for you?" Her words were like a balm to my weary soul.

"Not at all, Sunshine." I kissed the corner of her mouth. "You're just a lot better at listening to your heart than I am. Because I knew it then too. I just…" I tilted my head downward and stared at the hem of her lavender sweater. "I had a lot of things get in my way."

"We don't have to think about those things right now." She slid her hands beneath my shirt. I shivered from the touch of her knuckles grazing my skin as she lifted it above my head.

"We don't have to think at all." She pulled me in close and trailed her lips along the top of my shoulder. I closed my eyes, taking in every moment that passed between us because I knew that come morning, everything might be different.

Placing my hands beneath her arms, I lifted her onto the edge of the couch and knelt between her open thighs.

Shadows from the fireplace danced across her freckled face. The blue of her eyes seemed brighter from the lust-filled glassiness. I loved seeing her this way. Undone and fucking ready for me to claim her.

She was *mine*.

Lifting her hips, she gave me the green light to take the next step. I gripped the edge of her black leggings and pulled them down, taking my time as I ran the top of my fingers over her thighs and shins.

Tossing them to the side, she giggled as she settled her ass back on the couch. The only thing between me and her sweet pussy was a blush pink thong with little daisies embroidered on it. I slid my pointer finger under the side edge and lifted.

"I like these."

Her voice was husky as she said, "Noted," then wiggled her hips to the side, trying to edge my finger where she wanted it.

I leaned forward and slid my cheek against her left thigh. Squirming under my touch, she laughed again. "That tickles."

"Sensitive?" I asked right before I dug my fingers into her inner thigh, massaging the muscle. Goosebumps rose along her legs as she squeezed me between them from the intense reaction her body was having.

"Yes, but I like it."

"Noted," I huffed on a breath. "What about this?" I rubbed both of my thumbs along the inseam of her thighs, right next to her clit.

She pouted, sticking out her bottom lip. "Now, you're just teasing me."

I smiled cruelly knowing exactly what I was doing to her. Then, I lifted her thong to the side, revealing her pink sweetness. Charlie's chest rose as she inhaled deeply. Keeping my eyes on her, I blew cold air over her sex and her head rolled back against the couch, her hands opening and closing against the blanket beneath her.

"Eyes on me," I demanded, wanting her to watch me as I tasted her for the first time.

Those blue eyes slid to meet mine, nearly hidden beneath long thick lashes. When she locked her gaze onto me, I spread her legs wider and licked her in one long stroke.

"Ahhh," she moaned, her rosy lips forming into a perfect o. The exact expression I'd wanted to see on her ethereal face for days.

She was sweet and salty against my tongue, and I loved every fucking bit of it. Devouring her with my mouth, I sucked on her clit. Licking every bit of her until she was soaking wet, her hips started to roll against my mouth.

"Don't stop, Deacon. Please, don't stop." Her voice was breathy with need as I felt her legs quivering beneath my palms that kept them wide.

"Never," I whispered.

I went to work, worshipping every little sound from her

mouth as my cock grew so fucking hard, I thought it might bust through my jeans. With one hand on her, I unbuttoned and unzipped my pants for some relief.

"You taste so good, beautiful. So fucking good. So sweet." She smiled lazily as her hips circled, my lips and tongue claiming her again.

"I want you, Deacon. I *need* you." Her bottom lip quivered as she sucked in a sharp breath.

"I'm here, gorgeous. I'm here," I whispered against her sex as she threaded her fingers through my hair and pulled me back to her.

Nothing had ever tasted so good as her against my tongue and I couldn't get enough as I lapped up every bit of her. Suckling and pulling on her clit, I pressed my thumbs against the side of her entrance, giving her more pressure. More friction. More of what my woman needed.

"Close," she breathed. "Deacon, I'm close."

I hummed against her with pure male satisfaction. She was mine and her body answered to everything I was giving her. Like she was made for me.

Fuck. Yes.

Charlie panted as I swirled the tip of my index finger against her entrance. She bucked against me, trying to move herself onto my finger. I gave her exactly what she wanted as I slipped inside her tight, wet center.

"You're so wet, baby girl. So wet for me."

She nodded with a lust-filled smile curling the corners of her lips. "Only for you," she murmured before my lips sealed over her clit again and I drove her buck wild with my tongue and finger moving in tandem, inching her toward the edge.

"Yes! Don't stop!" she cried out, her eyes rolling into the back of her head as she gripped the blanket like it was the only thing keeping her tied to earth.

Working in long fluid strokes, I kept my tongue on her, loving every second of her sweetness in my mouth. I pulled my finger out of her and slowly added another one to give her the fullness I knew she craved.

"Oh my god!" Charlie lurched forward and gripped the back of my hair, riding my face like she fucking owned me. I nearly burst at the seams watching her come undone for me as her orgasm took hold, wracking through her entire body in quivering waves. Her legs shook as she fell back onto the couch and I came off her, retreating my fingers slowly from the tight grip her pussy had on me.

When she looked up at me with a satisfied grin on her face, I took my fingers that had wrung the orgasm from her and sucked her wetness from them.

"You taste divine, Sunshine."

Chapter 16

Charlie

I'd done it.

I'd crossed the line with Deacon and there was no going back now. A part of me belonged to him—had *always* belonged to him. Now, though, the fantasy of being with him had turned into a reality. It wasn't just in my head anymore. The chances of me getting hurt were higher.

I knew this. Yet, I couldn't get myself to care about that risk.

As I took in the sight of him licking me from his fingers, I knew I was a goner. Deacon hadn't only called to my soul in a way I could hardly describe, but he'd opened a door for me sexually as well.

I'd never wanted someone so badly. Never had my body reacted to someone like this. Even after the crashing waves of my orgasm and the trembling of my body that came after it, my thirst wasn't quenched.

I wanted *more*.

And I wasn't sure I'd ever get enough.

Deacon caught me as I surged forward and wrapped myself around him. His lips parted when I kissed him, fully. Giving me his tongue, I could taste the remnants of my pleasure on him, and it was so damn erotic I nearly came again.

Tingling sensations cascaded throughout my body as he hugged me close to him, deepening the kiss until I was lost in the touch of his tongue and lips crashing over mine. I moaned, as his fingers threaded through my hair and the rise of chest from a deep inhale brought him even closer to me.

Nothing had ever felt so good. For so long I'd been a ship in a sea of uncertainty. Finding joy in the unknown whenever something new came my way. As a curious soul, I'd always been looking for something–anything, to keep me grounded. My art always had me asking questions. Moving on to explore the next thing.

But this. *Him*. He was my safe harbor after being thrown about in a sea of storms. He made me want to stay for a long, long while. And I wanted to explore every part of him. Every part of *us*. What we could be together.

Breaths heavy, I parted from him, immediately feeling the cold air brush along my lips where his warmth was now absent. "I want to feel all of you, Deacon."

"You're sure?" he husked, eyes falling to my lips again.

I smiled. "I've never been more sure of anything in my entire life." Tomorrow might bring something different. Uncertainty and doubt, maybe. But tonight, I knew exactly what I wanted. *Him*. Consequences be damned.

He nodded once, a sudden clarity taking hold in his green

irises. Like how he knew that bringing our bodies together—fully—would be the start of something we wouldn't be able to simply walk away from. Especially since we were still snowed in and there was nowhere else for us to go. If things went sideways, we would be stuck here together for who knew how long.

I brushed the anxious thought to the side.

I didn't care. If this meant I got to have Deacon as wholly mine, even for only one night, I'd seize it. Because living meant I had the chance to experience moments like this. And there was a time when I thought my life had been over, when I'd looked into the void of death and fought like hell to come back. Whatever tomorrow brought, I'd deal with it. But right now? Right now, I was alive.

"Lay down," I urged. He abided by my request, settling his head against one of the pillows that had fallen to the floor while he'd gone down on me. For a moment, I took in his large body sprawled across his living room floor. The only sound between us was the crackling of the fireplace.

He looked so at ease like this. With one hand settled behind his head so he could still get a good look at me. It seemed like all the worries he carried had melted away the moment we broke the ice wall between us.

There were so many versions of the man before me.

Valliant savior.

Grumpy asshole.

Tender lover.

All of them made him who he was, and I decided at this

moment that I liked each and every one of them…even the grumpy asshole version.

"Now it's my turn," I mused, settling between his legs as he propped his head up further making sure he could still get a good look at me while I finished what he'd started and slid his jeans down his legs.

Muscular thighs and toned calves revealed just how hard he worked to hone such a sculpted body. He was beautiful. Perfect even.

The firelight caught the ridges of his scar. Gently, I moved my fingertips over it, feeling the peaks and valleys as I remembered what it had been like to reach out for him when we were buried beneath the rubble. He had been so close, but I couldn't get to him. I couldn't breathe or move.

Deacon grasped my hand and brought my wrist to his lips. "It's not the way I would have chosen to bind myself to you. Through agony and horror. But it does"–his hand moved to cup my cheek–"bind me to you, Charlie. And I'm glad it does."

Leaning down, I kissed him. "Me too."

Then, I moved lower, pressing my lips to his jaw and down his neck until I hovered just above the beginning of his scar. He stilled his hands on me as I looked at him right before I ran my lips along the entire right edge of it.

"Beautiful," I murmured over his skin. "Every part of you is so damn beautiful, Deacon."

Shadows danced in his eyes from the fire next to us. "Tell me you want this."

He lifted himself onto his elbows and snaked his hand

behind my neck. His eyes shuttered as he breathed in deeply. "Words could never describe how badly I want you."

Heat blossomed in my core as he settled back down, those green eyes trained on me like I was the only thing in the entire universe.

I swallowed, my nerves running high with excitement as I leaned forward again and ran my hand along his hard length through his boxers.

He sucked in a sharp breath. "Don't fucking play with me, beautiful. If you want my cock, fucking take it."

Deacon's words and heady gaze had the back of my neck heating up and my core tightening. I'd never been able to orgasm twice in one night, but I had a feeling that was about to change given the way my clit ached with need for release.

I pulled his boxers down and wet my lips as I took him between my hands and started pumping him up and down. "Ah, yeah, baby girl. Just like that," he moaned.

Hearing his praise made my chest swirl with giddiness. I liked pleasing him. But even more, I liked how his body reacted to my touch. How he couldn't stop looking at me even as he strained his neck to lean forward.

A bead of pre-cum dotted the tip of his dick. The salty taste hit my tongue as I licked him from hilt to head, the silky hardness of his cock lighting a fire inside of me. One that only *he* could put out.

His hand reached down and wrapped around the long strands of my hair until he had them twisted around his palm. The base of my skull tightened with the slight tension of pain as he gripped me hard.

Yes. Use me. Take whatever you want from me, I wanted to say but instead opened my lips and slid my mouth down his cock until he hit me in the back of my throat. Over and over, I slid my mouth down him, letting him fill me. His hips started to lift as he met me stroke for stroke, still gripping my hair in a tight grasp.

"That's it. Take all of my cock in that pretty mouth. Take every fucking bit of me."

My pussy was soaking wet, craving to be filled by him. I could tell he was close with how his balls tightened and his dick pulsed against my tongue. He wasn't going to last long, and I wasn't ready to quit yet. So, I pulled my mouth off him in a resounding pop of my lips.

"Fuck," he groaned. "Don't stop." His voice sounded pleading as his head dropped to the pillow beneath him.

Crawling over him, I straddled his hips, hovering my slick sex just above his erection. "You said your woman gets what she wants." I took his dick in my hand and stroked it up and down before centering his tip at my entrance. "I want to see what you can do with this cock. I want to see just how wild you can drive me."

A feral grin split his face. "Wild doesn't begin to cover what I'll make you feel." Then, he slammed into me, burying himself so deep inside of me I nearly saw stars.

I cried out his name as he did exactly what he'd promised. He gave me what I wanted with every delicious stroke. Feeling Deacon fill me so fully was beyond anything I'd ever felt before. A perfect fit. So perfect, I didn't want it to stop as he held onto my hips and slowly withdrew himself so I could feel every ridge of him against me.

There were no words for the high I was on as he pushed back into me, my entire body tingled and vibrated with the electric current that buzzed between us. At this moment, nothing else mattered. He was mine and there was nothing in this world I wanted more.

Rocking into me again and again, I leaned forward placing my hands on his chest, my right resting just above his scar. The one that matched my own. The moment that would connect us for the rest of our lives, no matter what happened after tonight.

I ground my clit against him, my breaths growing heavier as I took in his beautiful face. The green in his eyes was bright like the first leaf on a tree after a long winter. Flecks of yellow and blue glimmered in the firelight.

Strong arms wrapped around me as I fell onto his chest, the sensation of our joining bodies so overwhelming, I felt lightheaded. "Good. Why does everything with you feel so good?"

He responded with a kiss to the crook of my neck that sent chills down my arm.

"Lean back for me, Sunshine." Deacon's voice broke through my lusty haze. The stroke of his hands on my back felt amazing as I lifted myself from his chest and leaned backward where his thighs supported me.

"I want to see you ride me." That devilish grin he wore was doing wild things to my stomach. Another assault of butterflies swarmed me as I settled into his saddle, his cock flexing deep inside of me.

Then he started moving. His hips lifted, filling me with his delicious length as his thumb swirled over my sensitive nub. I bit my lip, hanging onto the top of his bent knees as he stroked me over and over again.

"Deacon," I whispered, settling my eyes on his. "You feel amazing. So, so amazing."

His eyes narrowed on me with intention. He was a man who wanted more than amazing. He wanted to drive me *wild*. And he did just that as he pumped into me harder, stroking that deep spot inside of me that rarely got the attention it deserved.

Heat blossomed low in my belly, like a rose blooming in the summer sun. Deacon could see it as I edged closer to my climax. He leaned forward, the movement brought us even closer. There was no rhythm to the madness that took hold of me as I bucked my clit against him when he took my breast into his mouth and sucked hard.

It was just the friction my body needed to send me soaring off the edge.

The air vibrated with my scream of his name, my pussy clenching around his length like a vice. I loved it. Feeling every bit of him inside of me was pure ecstasy as I rode out my climax, his tongue and lips making work of my sensitive nipples.

In a voice so husky, I barely recognized it was my own, I gripped the back of his neck and whispered into his ear, "I want you to come on me. I want you to claim me, Deacon. I want to be yours."

A flash of hungry desire flitted across his face as he lifted his head from my breasts and devoured my mouth in a searing kiss that I felt all the way to my toes. Almost painfully sensitive, my clit throbbed as he picked up the pace. Our foreheads together, his eyes trained on me. Every ounce of pleasure he'd pulled from me reflected in those green eyes.

He loved this.

And so did I.

"Yes," he murmured against my lips, digging his teeth into my bottom one. "Fuckkkkk."

I worked my pussy on his cock, feeling him grow bigger inside of me. He was close. So damn close. Reaching behind me, I cupped his balls and stroked them gently as I bounced on his dick. Our chests were slick with sweat. A guttural growl emanated between us as he gripped my hips and slammed into me, chasing after what was his to take.

"I'm there, baby girl. I'm going to fucking come." He nipped the bottom of my ear lobe as he pulled me in close, then lifted me off him just in time. Leaning back between his legs, I watched as he pumped himself two times before he covered my stomach with his orgasm.

"Fuck!" he bellowed, rubbing the ridge of his dick along my sex.

The edges of my lips pulled upward, obsessed with every second of his undoing.

When he finished, we sat there for a moment. The haze of what we'd just done slowly falling away.

"You're amazing." He took my face in his palms and kissed my cheek. When he pulled back, there was a lightness to his eyes.

Happiness. Joy. Elation.

It all reflected back to me, making my heart flutter. There wasn't regret. The biggest fear I had was being stuck in this house with a man who wished he could take back making me feel that good. But that fear was dust in the wind.

"What now?" I asked, a bubble of laughter moving past my lips. The same joy I saw in him was soaring through my chest.

I was so, so happy. I'd never felt this way after being with anyone else. There was something different about this time. Something I couldn't quite place through all the endorphins running through me.

"First"—he kissed the left corner of my mouth—"we get you cleaned up." My face warmed as he placed another kiss on the right corner of my mouth. So tender. So gentle for such a gruff man.

"Then we do it again?" I asked, eyebrows raised.

His chuckle felt like diving into warm water as it surrounded me.

"Like I said before, my woman gets what she wants."

Chapter 17

Charlie

After two more rounds, my thirst was fully sated and I was left with the comforting feeling of Deacon's arms wrapped around me as I snuggled into his chest on the couch.

Hours had passed since we'd crossed the line with one another. I didn't want to look back and it seemed like he didn't either. The fear I had earlier of what the aftermath might bring for us had essentially disappeared. There was no trace of that man left. The one who had been so disturbed to see me on his front porch. All that was left was a man who held me like he never wanted to let me go.

And I liked that.

I *really* liked that.

"When did you get Casper?" The bottom of his chin grazed the side of my head; the little stubble hairs of his beard got caught in my hair and he smoothed them back down.

Our bodies adjusted as I snuggled closer to him, setting

my cheek on his still bare chest. The heavy thump of his heartbeat was soothing to me.

"My parents got him for me the Christmas after the fire. I think they wanted me to have a companion after they saw me struggle with so many of my friends. I told them I was okay, but I don't think either one of them believed me."

"Were you okay?" Deacon's thumb moved up and down my bicep.

"I was. Like I told you before, it was a struggle at first to see just how shallow the relationships I had with my friends were. But I didn't allow myself to stay stuck in that mindset. I have wonderful parents who stayed by my side the entire time and there are a lot of people in this world who can't say their parents would do the same."

I peeked up at him. "If we're always looking at the things we don't have, we tend to miss the most beautiful parts of our lives."

Closing my eyes, I took a moment to let the current moment sink in. A moment I didn't realize just how badly I'd wanted until now.

"Wise words coming from someone so young."

I half-laughed. "You can give credit to my grandpa again for that one. He always had the best sayings. The kind of life lessons that stick with you, no matter how long ago he told them to you."

"Hmm," he hummed thoughtfully. "Was Casper as mischievous of a kitten as he is now?"

Casper rose his head from where he was laying down at

the other end of the sofa. He always had a sixth sense of knowing when someone was talking about his misbehaviors.

"A thousand times worse," I snickered. "He used to get into literally everything. One time, I was in the middle of a really big commission piece, and I left the room for two minutes to grab another cup of tea. When I came back, my paints were everywhere, and Casper's white coat had turned into a kaleidoscope of colors."

Deacon's chest rose and fell as he laughed. "Did he also have a habit of attacking your face in the mornings?"

"Yeah," I drew out the word. "I thought I broke him of that a few years ago, but you must have brought out the wild side in him." Looking up at Deacon I saw humor dancing in his irises. A stitch hit my heart. The sex with him had been amazing. He made me feel things I didn't know my body was even capable of. But none of that compared to how he looked at me right now. Like I had brought him peace in the midst of a terrible storm.

"Did you have any pets growing up?"

"We had some family dogs. Never any cats though."

"Oh yeah? Why's that?"

We both shifted our attention to Casper as he stretched, his entire body elongating until the front half of him almost fell off the couch.

"Too unpredictable."

I laughed at that. "For someone who's made a career out of unpredictable situations, I find it interesting that it would bother you so much."

"Maybe that's why. I've had my fill of it and now I need

some stability in my life." Deacon's lips met my temple. I shuttered from the feeling of his kiss and wrapped my arms around his waist, wanting to be closer to him in any way possible.

"He's not so bad though," he murmured against my hair. "Although, if he ends up darting outside in the snow again, I might just leave him out there until he figures it out for himself."

Sitting up quickly, I pushed on his shoulder. "You would never," I scolded.

Deacon's head tilted to the side as he raised his eyebrows. "Would I?"

Darting my gaze between his eyes, I couldn't tell if he was pulling my leg or not. Then, he smiled broadly and dug his fingers under my arms and into my sides, tickling me.

"Ah!" I squealed, shoving his arms away from me, but he kept the tickles coming.

"You honestly think I would leave *your* cat outside in the snow?" His laughter mixed with mine until he finally stopped, and I could catch my breath. "I'd chase that little rascal to the ends of this earth if it meant making you happy."

My breaths were heavy as I registered Deacon's words. "You would really do that for me?"

His hand dove underneath my hair, landing on the back of my neck where his strong fingers started working on me in a slow massage. "I'm beginning to realize that I'd do just about anything for you, Sunshine."

The dark shadows that had haunted Deacon's face from

the first moment I saw him on his front porch had seemed to lift, not even a small trace of them left behind. Whatever had changed between us. Whatever had given him the courage to leave that day behind us…I was thankful for it.

I booped his nose with my index finger. "Right back at you, Grumps."

His eyes widened. "Grumps?"

"Short for grumpy butthead."

He snorted and his nostrils flared. "Is that right?"

"Don't worry." I kissed his cheek. "Grumpy suits you."

"As long as it doesn't chase you away."

"I think you've already done all you could to chase me away. For some reason, I kept sticking around."

Deacon's gaze shifted to my lips as I ground my hips against him, feeling that heat from our earlier escapades rising again.

"And I'm really glad you did." His lips found mine as his hand moved up the back of my head, fingers twining through my hair. This kiss was unlike all the others that had been filled with scorching passion. This one was tender and sweet. Where he was normally hard, Deacon softened, moving his tongue against mine in long fluid motions that had my body melting against him.

Every part of me was singing with the sensation of butterfly wings fluttering over my skin. His kiss consumed me. Taking everything I was and making me anew. He was everywhere, touching every corner of my soul. Leaving a piece of himself behind to fill the parts of me I never knew were broken.

When we finally parted, it felt like another piece of our puzzle slid into place. The portrait of us was taking shape in such a beautiful way, it nearly brought tears to my eyes.

I could tell he felt it too. This one moment that was ours —had *always* been ours. Just waiting for us to be brave enough to reach out and take what we wanted.

Then, a loud slamming sound emanated from behind me. I jumped in his arms, and he held me close. "What was that?" I asked with a startled breath.

I watched his eyes as they looked up and past me. "I think it was the screen door slamming shut. Let me go check it out."

Intertwining my fingers with his, he rotated my hand until my wrist faced toward the ceiling. A line of sparks shot up my arm when he leaned down and kissed the inside of my wrist. My eyelids fluttered at the contact. Then, he was gone. Leaving me and Casper on the couch while he inspected the cause of the noise.

"Wait." I whisper-yelled. "I'm coming with you."

He stopped a few feet from the front door and turned around. "Why are you whispering?"

I shrugged and looked at him sheepishly. "I don't know. What if it's an axe murderer who is trying to break in to kill us and take our spot on the couch?"

Deacon's eyes narrowed on me. "If your first thought was that it's an axe murderer, then why are you coming with me to check it out?"

I rolled my shoulders back. "In case you need backup."

With a lopsided smirk, Deacon stalked toward me and

took my face in the palm of his hands. "Baby girl, I'm a trained special operations soldier who's been to war more times than I can count. I think I can take on *one* axe murderer and keep you safe."

"What if he's a really big one?" I giggled.

Deacon seemed to grow a few more inches as he rotated his own shoulders backward. "There are very few men I've come across in my life who are bigger than me. And if he is…well…we're both fucked."

I burst out laughing as Deacon kissed the tip of my nose and chuckled. "Come on." He grabbed my hand and led me toward the door. "Let's see what we're up against."

Deacon opened his front door and wisps of snowflakes whirled around us, settling onto the wood floors of his home before melting. Cold air blasted my face as we stepped onto the front porch, my socks doing nothing to protect my feet from the frigidness of the frozen wooden planks.

"Oh my gosh." I brought my hand to my mouth. "It's even higher than it was yesterday."

Deacon stepped further out, snowflakes dusting his black hair as he leaned on the porch railing and looked upward. "As soon as it stops, I'm going to need to get some of this snow off the roof."

"Are we at risk of having it cave in?"

Frost had already gathered on his eyebrows when he looked back down at me. "I checked all the trusses when I first moved in here. They're solid, but I don't want to take any chances."

I nodded, holding my hands to my mouth and blowing

hot air into them. Deacon moved toward the screen door that was open, lying flat against the large logs that made up the paneling of the house. He assessed the latch on the door and started fiddling with it.

"I think we've found our axe murderer." He looked up at me.

"Is it broken?"

"Yeah. The locking mechanism broke off, so the door has nothing to keep it secure anymore. I'm going to need to take it off the hinges and bring it inside or it'll keep us up all night."

The icy air had moved its way down to my bones by the time Deacon had gotten the door off the hinges. He'd told me to go inside and sit by the fire numerous times, but I loved watching him work and I didn't want him to have to be out in the cold by himself.

I had a feeling Deacon would have been fine with the door slamming off and on throughout the night. He'd probably had to learn how to sleep in loud places given his time in the military. I knew he was doing this for my benefit.

When he brought the door inside, I went into the kitchen and brought back some paper towels to wipe the floor clean from the wet snow.

"I could have taken care of that." Deacon's voice was low as he knelt beside me and took the soaked paper towel from my hand.

"This is my home too."

His hand stilled. I wanted to slam my foot straight into my mouth. This wasn't my home. This was Deacon's home.

That *I* had intruded with my cat. I needed to calm my jets and not say anything else that might have him running for the hills. "For the time being, I mean. Let me help."

I loosed an anxious breath when he nodded and brought me back another paper towel.

Keep it together, Charlie. One amazing night with a man does not mean he wants you to take ownership of his house.

His heavy footsteps creaked on the floorboards as he headed into the living room and settled onto the couch. After the floor was dry and I discarded the paper towels, I sat on the sofa next to him, but not touching him.

"Is that what it was like in Afghanistan? The snow piled up that high?" He was staring into the fire, and I realized he must have put a few more logs onto it while I was cleaning up because it was bigger than before.

My stomach twisted into knots as I noticed the shadows in his eyes had reappeared. The intimate bubble we'd shared before had popped and I was left with the one version of him that I couldn't break through.

Much to my surprise, he shifted and turned his attention to me. "Sometimes worse," he stated plainly, and I tried not to let him see how much his response affected me.

Talk to me. Give me that smile again. Please.

When he said nothing else, I settled into the quiet and tried not to let this change in his demeanor ruin the night we'd shared. He was allowed to have his feelings. It was okay that he shifted like this.

Or at least that's what I told myself, so I didn't break down.

I pulled Casper into my lap, needing something to keep me grounded. He purred loudly as I scratched between his ears and ran my hand down his back.

"I lost a lot of good friends over there," Deacon's husky voice broke through the silence like a bolt of lightning.

The green in his eyes darkened as they settled back on me. "It's difficult for me to think back to that time."

"I'm so sorry, Deacon. I shouldn't have brought it up."

There was a heavy pause between us. I felt like a jerk for pushing him. Just because I was able to manage the trials I'd faced in life with ease didn't mean everyone had the same experience as me. Some people didn't want to talk about what they'd been through. Some just wanted to forget.

"Don't do that," he whispered into the space between us, the planes of his face solid as stone.

"Do what?" The words were thick on my tongue.

"Regret asking questions you want to know the answers to."

I looked down at the floor. "It's none of my business. Sometimes I just need to keep my mouth shut."

The rough pad of his thumb slid under my chin as he gently shifted my face toward him again. My breath hitched as I took in his devastatingly beautiful face. The sharp edges of his jaw and pronounced cheekbones. His thick lashes that made him look boyish up close, curbing the edges of his gruff nature. And those lips. God how I already loved those lips and everything they were capable of making me feel.

"Don't stop being curious just because it's hard. God..." His head dropped low for a moment before he lifted his chin and shook his head at the ceiling. When his gaze landed on me again, he said, "I wish I possessed your ease with being open. I wish I could lay all my cards on the table and not have the aftermath impact me the way it does. I want to try… I *am* trying with you, Charlie. Just…give me some time. I've never done this before. Not with anyone."

Heat stung my eyes. I blinked to stop the tears from forming. "Take as much time as you need. I'll be right here when you're ready."

He smiled his brilliant smile that I knew he kept hidden most of the time. Then he pulled me into his lap and wrapped his arms around me.

The only sound was the beat of his heart against my cheek and the crackling logs in the hearth. The sounds I fell asleep to. A gentle lullaby that I wanted to hear again and again.

Chapter 18

Deacon

Bright white light landed on my living room floor from the window Charlie sat in front of. Her easel took up most of the corner with the large canvas settled on top of it. Her paints sat to her right as she combined colors onto her palette.

The long auburn strands of her hair were tied up high on the top of her head. Tendrils of curls draped loosely down her back and behind her ears. I paused behind the couch, taking in the view of her working. She was so small compared to the giant painting in front of her.

It amazed me how she was able to make the image of the tiny cabin's backyard come to life. The way she moved the brush across the painting, taking care with the high and low-lights of the trees and water, made the image come to life as if I were standing right there. The crunchy winter grass beneath my feet and the smell of crisp fresh air in my lungs.

Last night had changed a part of me that I wasn't prepared for. I was falling for her. This woman who had barreled into my life, unannounced and without abandon. A part of me had known there was something between us. The day of the fire, and my inability to make things right with her after, were a testament to that truth. A string of some sort had tied us together. Binding our souls…if that was even a thing.

God. I sounded like a fucking puppy dog who'd been at the shelter for too long and just wanted a home of his own. If my guys were still here, they'd be giving me shit for how tightly I was wrapped around her dainty little finger.

Charlie Banks was doing strange things to me. I watched her delicate neck bend as she tilted her head to the side to get a different perspective on her painting, and I felt it. That incessant pull to be near her. To hear her sweet laughter and to feel her supple body pressed against me with nothing between us. I wanted to sink into her. To stare at those beautiful depthless eyes forever.

And it fucking terrified me.

But I couldn't let the fear in. If I did, I'd fuck this all to hell and end up chasing her away. And all I wanted was for her to stay right here with me.

"Mmm, something smells amazing!" she called out, not knowing I was only a few paces behind her. Frozen. Like a fucking coward.

I'd managed to keep myself in check since last night but allowing myself to be vulnerable wasn't something I was used to and my grip on this new experience was starting to slip.

Before I had a chance to get my shit together, Charlie

spun around on the wooden work stool I'd brought in for her from the garage.

"Good morning, handsome!" Her cheery voice was like a knife to the heart.

Don't fuck this up, Deacon. Don't you dare fuck this up.

She hopped off the stool and bounded toward me, Casper followed in her footsteps, prancing beside her. The smile she gave me was brilliant, like the first rays of sunshine casting through a cloud after endless rain. Warm and striking. It took the breath from my lungs.

"Is this one for me?" Completely unaware of my stupor, she nodded toward the plate in my hand.

"Yes," I finally managed to say. The single word response seemed to break me from the shackles I'd put around my own mind. "I thought you might be hungry after all the work you've been doing."

Despite our time together last night, she'd gotten up with the sun and set up her art corner in my living room before I'd made it out of bed. Seeing all her things there, like her art supplies belonged in my home, had awoken some insurmountable fear in me. This feeling that I had to protect her at all costs. And everywhere I looked there was a looming threat, waiting to take her away from me.

"That's so sweet of you." She took the plate from me and slid her other arm around my waist. "I really appreciate you doing that. I was going to make *you* breakfast before you woke up, but I got so carried away with my work."

I pulled her close against me, not wanting to let her go. There was no resistance as she settled her cheek against my bare rib cage. Right against the scar that mirrored hers. A constant reminder of my failure. Despite her telling me the injury wasn't my fault, I knew better. I'd taken seconds of precious time letting my emotions take over when I should have focused on getting her to safety.

Something snagged at my heartstrings with brute force as she kissed my forearm that was wrapped around her.

I was starting to lose it. The control I exerted over every part of my life. The one thing that had kept me from cracking under all the pressure I'd been through in my life.

I needed to step away. If I didn't rein things in…I squeezed my eyes shut as my heart rate skyrocketed and my breaths quickened.

"Are you okay?" Charlie tilted her head back to look up at me. Placing a hand over my heart, I stilled, wondering if she could feel what was happening inside my body.

"I'm fine. I was just…wanting to take a closer look at your painting." I couldn't look at her. Because if I did, everything would come crumbling down and I needed to regain control.

She paused for a moment, and I knew she was questioning whether or not I was telling the truth. Thankfully, she didn't push it. Instead, she let go of her hold on me and walked back toward the painting.

It took me a moment, but with a deep breath in, I let my shoulders drop and tried to empty the worries from my mind and followed her to her easel.

Setting the plate of food down on the small side table, she turned to me. "What do you see?"

"In the painting?" I asked.

"Yeah. What do you see?" The blue in her eyes shone with delight that had my chest cracking in two; widening further so that there was room for these new feelings. Feelings I hadn't let myself experience for a very long time.

It was startling and exciting and fucking terrifying.

I couldn't let myself lose focus. I couldn't let myself slip back to that place of fear. So, I looked at her painting and tried to focus.

At first glance, I saw exactly what it was. An image of my tiny cabin's backyard. It was beautiful and appeared effortless. All the colors blended together just like they did in nature.

The longer I stared at it, though, the more I started to see beyond the initial image. I saw the depiction of the forest and river through Charlie's eyes. The way *she* wanted it to be seen. Where the river was normally tumultuous and violent with its rapids over the rocks, she'd painted it as serene. Tranquil likeness of the trees were highlighted with a light layer of fog. Not eerie and unnerving. But soothing and inviting. It was…peaceful.

"I see you," I whispered, throat thick with emotion as I turned back to her. "All I see is you."

Like a blossoming flower, she unveiled herself to me at that moment. The way her entire face lit up had my chest nearly bursting. Not from fear…from something else. She was beautiful beyond anything I'd ever seen before.

She leapt into my arms. Her laughter and smile sent a

flurry of tangles into my stomach. I laughed with her too as I spun us around the living room.

When she was in my arms like this, I could let everything else fall away. The worries. The judgment I'd made toward myself. All of it had vanished with the sound of her joy.

It was dizzying–the back and forth.

As I settled her back down in front of the easel, she beamed at me. "Do you understand the kind of compliment you just gave me? It's literally an artist's dream to be recognized through their work." She rose to the tips of her toes and still had to stretch as she planted a kiss to my cheek. "And you just made my dream come true."

"Is that right?" I raised my eyebrows at her before snaking my hands behind her waste and dipping them into the back pockets of her jeans.

"Mmhmm." She nodded, biting her bottom lip. Fuck. My cock was already twitching seeing her bite that lip. "I feel like I should reward you for that." Then the little vixen winked at me.

I tilted my head at her and smiled. She had something up her sleeve as she twisted in my arms. Her ass pressed firmly against my dick as she turned her back to me and bent over, dipping her finger into the puddle of syrup on her plate of pancakes.

"Keep teasing me like that, woman, and I'll take you right here." I ground my molars together as I tried to contain myself.

When she whirled around, the right edge of her lips was tilted upward in a knowing smirk. Syrup rolled slowly down her index finger. "But what if that's exactly what I want you to do?"

A guttural sound ripped through my throat as she planted her sticky finger over my left nipple and painted me with the syrup. "Oops," she noted before sticking her finger in her mouth and sucking off the remaining sweetness. Her freckled cheeks hollowed as she sucked. My head fell back as I gripped her hips hard.

"Fuck me," I groaned, drawing out the words.

"My pleasure," she said delectably before placing her palms on my sides and licking the dripping syrup from my chest. My fingers dove deeper into her soft hips as she swirled her tongue around my nipple, licking every bit of me clean. She looked up at me, those blue eyes intense with mischief.

My own little sunshine. So sweet and innocent in one moment, only to blind me with her sexiness the next.

"Mmm," she hummed against me as she licked her way down my torso until she was on her knees in front of me.

I was panting like a fucking dog as she slid her small fingers under the waistband of my sweatpants. A wave of goosebumps rose along my stomach as she licked right above the edge of the waistband in one long go. Taking her hair and twisting it into my hand, I gripped hard, pulling her head back.

She arched a delicate brow at me. "Is my grumpy man on edge this morning? I thought three rounds with you last night would have worn you out." Charlie tested me in ways I'd never experienced before, but this was on a whole new level.

I fucking loved it.

I grasped her hair firmly and bent down until my lips grazed her ear. "You want to test my stamina, baby girl?" I snorted. "Be careful what you ask for."

Rising back to my full height, I held onto her hair with one hand and dove into my pants with the other. Releasing my cock over the edge of my pants, I watched the light in her eyes grow brighter with excitement.

"Keep your hands together behind your back." Her shoulders adjusted as she interlaced her fingers, her closed fist falling just above her ass. "That's my good fucking girl." I pumped my cock twice then let it fall before I gripped her chin in my hand. "You want to use this pretty little mouth to test me? You want to see what I can fucking do to you?"

She nodded on a whimper.

"Open." I pressed lightly on the corners of her lips until they opened wide for me. Her tongue was warm as I pressed the head of my cock against her.

"Yes," I hissed between clenched teeth. "I'm going to fuck the sass right out of that pretty little mouth."

Slowly, I guided her mouth onto my cock until she took me fully, wet heat surrounding every inch of me. She kept her eyes on me as I pulled out and let her tongue swirl over the tip. Like my dick was her favorite lollipop, she sucked on me hard, pulling me back to her even though her hands were still behind her back.

"Fuck yeah, baby girl. I love watching you take all of me."

"Mmmm," she murmured, the vibration in the back of her throat hit me in the best way.

Picking up the pace, I gathered the loose strands of her hair that had fallen and bunched them together again in my hand. She was so damn good at this. Licking the ridge of my length every time I pushed inside of her. My balls tightened. I was already getting closer. She felt so good. So fucking good.

Opening her mouth wider for me, she already knew what I wanted as I hit the back of her throat, gripping her hair hard with every thrust. "You take me so well," I grunted as tears started to stream down her face from the effort. Not tears of pain, but of pure fucking ecstasy as she sucked me off, loving every second of it.

Tumbling toward the edge, I didn't want to come this way. I wanted to be inside of her, stroking her pussy nice and deep.

With the most effort I'd put into anything in my life, I retreated. Charlie gasped for breaths with a delicious smile on her face. Releasing my hold on her hair, the tendrils fell forward over her shoulders, covering her breasts like some exotic mermaid.

Fear. Doubt. Worry. All the things I ran away from. All the things I wasn't good at.

But this. With her. The physical. I could do this all day long.

Extending my hand toward her, she looked at it, head cocked to the side. "Are you already done with me?"

I huffed a breath as she slipped her small hand into mine. "Not even close." I guided her toward the back of the couch and as she stepped in front of me, I planted my hand over her left breast. The edges of her scar seemed calmer than they had last night when she was itchy and irritated. The salve had worked, and I was thankful. I hated seeing her even the slightest bit uncomfortable.

Charlie tilted her head back, eyelashes fluttering as I moved my other hand to the small of her back, drawing her close. My cock pressed against her belly. I flexed it against her and her lips pulled back into a smile.

"I'm so wet for you, Deacon." The sultry sound of her voice acknowledging the want she had for me had my entire body tensing with the need to claim her. My head dipped low as my hand skirted up her chest and over her decolletage until my fingers wrapped around her exquisite neck.

She bit her lower lip.

"Do you know what that fucking does to me?" My grip tightened against her skin.

"I think I have an idea," she smirked.

"Why do you insist on testing me? Crossing all my boundaries and making me *fucking feel*? I didn't ask for this." I walked her backward until her ass hit the back of the couch.

"I didn't ask for you to come into my life and wreck me," I said against her lips before I trailed my tongue along the open seam. Her little gasp of air had my dick throbbing to be inside of her.

"You didn't ask," she replied. "You begged me, Deacon. I could see it in your eyes. You wanted me from the second you saw me all those years ago." She glared at me. My little sunshine fucking *glared* at me. Feisty didn't begin to cover what she possessed behind that sweet facade. She was nothing but bright blue flames. The kind that burned the brightest.

"Stop. Fighting. Us." Her words had my mind spinning.

No. I didn't want to go there. I didn't want to face all this yet. I just wanted to feel her and not think.

Whirling her around, I pushed her against the edge of the sofa until her front was flush with the leather. She moaned as I slipped my hand in front to find four buttons I hadn't noticed before. My fingers fumbled with frustration as I tried to unclasp them as quickly as possible.

Her breathy giggle lightened my chest.

"Why are there so many damn buttons?"

Cheeks flushed, she peeked at me over her shoulder. "To add a little more of a challenge."

I leaned over her back and nipped the bottom of her ear lobe. "Challenge accepted," I drawled before I clasped both sides of the front of her jeans and pulled hard. A loud rip had two of the buttons flying toward the floor, landing with subtle thuds against the hardwood.

"So impatient," Charlie giggled as I yanked her pants down and pulled them away from her feet.

"Mmm, I like these on you." I tugged on the frilly black lace of her thong.

"I thought you might."

The fact that she wore black panties just for me had my mouth watering. Charlie Banks was my fucking dream girl and here she was bent over the back of my couch with her perfect little peach in my face, ready for me to take her.

"Always plotting, I see."

"Only when it comes to getting you inside of me," her husky voice was like velvet over my skin.

Taking both her wrists in mine, I held them tight behind her back as I smoothed my palm over her ass cheek. "You're about to get all of me, baby girl."

With my other hand, I slid her thong to the side revealing her beautiful pink pussy. Rubbing my fingers over her clit, she strained against the hold I had on her wrists.

"Damn. You're fucking dripping wet for me."

She wiggled her ass, showing me how ready she was. Lining myself up at her entrance, I nudged her with the head of my cock.

"Is this what you want?"

"Yes," she crooned, eyelids already growing heavy as she looked at me over her shoulder.

With my free hand, I gripped her ass and slid into her slowly. She was so warm and tight, I had to control myself from pounding into her. We'd had our fun last night, but this time I wanted to take it slow. I wanted to feel every part of her.

Her head dipped as she cried out right when I made the final inch and buried myself completely inside of her.

"Ah, so fucking good," I groaned, nestling even deeper. With my feet, I pushed hers into a wider stance until she was completely open to me, then I slipped my hand between our thighs and rubbed her clit as I pulled out of her all the way.

When I sank back into her, her legs started to quiver. I loved making her feel like this. Loved seeing her wild side come out.

My fingers slipped over her wet clit as she started to back into me. "Deeper, Deacon. I need you deeper."

A loud smack of her ass hitting my pelvis resounded around us as I slammed into her. When she cried out, I knew I'd hit her spot. "Yes, don't stop. Please."

Matching her desperate rhythm, I pounded into her. Her pussy clenched around my cock, tightening so hard around me I could tell I was getting her right where I wanted her to be. Delirious from the pleasure I gave her.

Charlie challenged my manhood with her delectable sweetness. I'd always prided myself in being able to last, but when it came to fucking her…it was hard to keep my grip.

A wild frenzy took hold of me as I let go of her wrists and dug my fingers into her luscious hips. Our labored breaths synced together as I slammed my cock into her over and over again, so fucking hard the couch started to inch forward.

"Deacon, I'm coming. I'm coming!" she panted before letting out a wild scream that had my balls cinching upward.

"Fuck!" I pulled out of her and stroked my shaft twice

before my release sprayed over her pert ass. I caught her smiling at me as she wiggled her butt again.

Those blue eyes watched as I pumped my cock, the final bits of my release seeping over my hand.

She licked her lips, eyes dipping to my cock. "I can't wait to see what part of me you'll claim next."

I snorted. "You might need to give me a few minutes first."

"Oh?" She pouted, sticking her bottom lip out as I picked up my sweatpants and wiped her clean. "I thought you were supposed to show me what you're made of."

There she was again. My little sex vixen who liked to push me to the teetering edge of my limits.

Charlie turned around so she was facing me again. I stepped into her space, snaking my hand around the base of her neck then I ran my thumb along the edge of her bottom lip. The one she'd used to guilt me into fucking her only a second ago.

"I might need a moment, but there's no way I'm done with you yet, baby girl," I said before kneeling in front of her and claiming her sex with my mouth.

I spent the next hour ravishing her body until she could hardly keep her eyes open. All I could think to myself was that I'd never tire of this. Never tire of *her*.

Chapter 19

Charlie

Droplets of water dripped down my back as I wrapped the light blue towel around me. Deacon and I had gone at it all morning and despite the growing soreness between my legs, my body still craved to be touched by him. *Wanted* by him.

I bit my lip thinking back to how he bent me over his couch and fucked me so hard I thought we were going to break the furniture.

It was good for him. Physical touch. Before we'd started our escapades this morning, I saw him retreat inward. I noticed the faraway look in his eyes that told me he was slip-ping away. I understood that if there was a chance for this to be real…a chance for us to make it past the snow melting, that I would have to keep him with me and fight against the fear that I now knew took hold of him.

Emotion lodged in my throat as I looked at myself in the mirror. My skin was glowing even though it was the middle of winter and there was a brightness to my eyes I'd never seen before. Deacon had left his mark on me, and I was all the better for it.

He was becoming my safe haven. The one I wish I'd had back then, when I had to be strong for everyone else even though the only thing I wanted to do was break down. Deacon was the person I could be all versions of myself with and the thought of all that going away once the snow melted, and we were forced to face the reality of the connection we had was starting to scare me.

I didn't get scared often.

There was too much joy in this world to let fear control me. But the happiness I'd found with Deacon was a once in a lifetime kind of happiness. Deep in my bones, I knew it. Knew how rare it was.

I just hoped I was right about the tether that connected us and this wasn't some cruel trick of fate.

Sighing, I gave myself one last glance in the mirror before I went to his linen closet to grab him a towel since his last one was in the washer.

I opened the door, and my gaze trailed upward where a puzzle box sat on the top shelf. Securing my towel around me, I reached for the box and pulled it down and laughed. On the top of the box was an image of puppies playing in a field. There were too many to count. Most of them had their mouths wide open ready to chomp their neighbor or were getting ready to take a bite of grass.

My heart warmed at the picture and thinking of Deacon trying to match the pieces of their adorable little faces.

"Hey, Sunshine," Deacon called through the closed bathroom door. "Is it my turn yet?"

"Almost!" I said back, not quite ready to give up the space.

Sunshine… The nickname he'd chosen for me made my heart burst with glee. It was such a sweet name. Bright and lovely. So different from the *baby girl* he'd chosen for when we were intimate.

Two nicknames.

Two versions of our relationship.

What about the third version? The one where he ran away from us. From what we had together. There was a darkness in Deacon that had been created from the war he'd fought in and the awful things he'd witnessed as a firefighter. Those parts held onto him and I couldn't help but wonder if there was room for them between us. Or if those parts would eventually drag me down too.

I shook my head, trying to loosen the doubt. My heart tugged and I knew I was falling for Deacon. It was one thing to think about the possibilities between us and quite another to have them starting to play out. To see his brilliant smile at something I said. To feel the warmth of his embrace and the pure ecstasy that came from his touch.

Closing my eyes, I inhaled deeply. If I was going to ask him to be brave and to give us a fair chance, I needed to do the same thing.

Opening my eyes, I reached for the handle and opened the bathroom door to find Deacon laying on his bed, arms bent wide as he rested the back of his head in his hands.

With the puzzle box in tow, I climbed onto his bed and straddled him. He shifted his arms and settled his hands on my hips and smiled at me. I smiled back as I lifted the box in front of him.

"Puppies?" I asked with a smirk.

He took the box and assessed it. "I haven't looked at this in a long time."

"I knew you were a big softy behind all that grump, but I didn't take you as the puzzle making type."

The smile he wore dropped slightly, but it didn't go away completely as he said, "I did a lot of puzzles with my friends overseas. There's a lot of down time when you get deployed and one of my buddies would always bring a puzzle with us. They'd always be of something sickeningly adorable. I think it helped for us to look at something that didn't have to do with violence and death. Even if it was just an image printed onto puzzle pieces."

I swallowed, my stomach sinking at the thought of Deacon being exposed to so much horror.

"I brought this one on our last deployment, but we never got to make it. My friend was killed in action before I even had a chance to show it to him."

"Oh, Deacon." I reached for his hand, surprised when he didn't pull away from me. "I'm so sorry."

Glassy eyes looked up at me. It was the first time I'd seen past his wall with clarity. He was hurting and all I wanted to do was make it stop. But that wasn't for me to decide. Sometimes, we just had to live through the hurt.

"Why don't we make it now. In his honor." It was a bold

move. One I wasn't sure was even right in this situation. I'd never known someone who had lost friends in war. Maybe I was stepping out of line.

Deacon sniffed and cleared his throat. "Yeah. Yeah, let's do that."

"Really?" I tried not to sound too surprised, but excitement flared in my chest.

"Only if you make us some hot chocolate first." He patted the side of my hip and I slid off of him.

"Now that is something I can definitely do."

"Casper!" Deacon and I both scolded him at the same time as he blinked at us innocently before swatting another puzzle piece to the floor.

Deacon leaned out of his chair and picked up the piece. "See! Unpredictable."

I laughed. "I'm pretty sure knocking things off a table is a predictable cat move."

Deacon showed the puzzle piece to Casper and said, "This is not *yours* to play with you little rascal."

I nearly snorted into the mug of hot cocoa as Casper just swished his tail back and forth, scattering a few more pieces around the table. Several were nearly knocked off the edge again.

"Okay." Deacon lifted Casper into the air and placed him in his lap. "If you're going to misbehave, you go to cat jail."

I burst out laughing. "Cat jail?"

Deacon's bright eyes met mine. "Yes. He can't knock any more pieces off the table while he's in my lap."

Casper settled down until I could only see the tips of his ears poking up from the edge of the table. "I'm pretty sure you just gave him exactly what he's been wishing for all along."

Deacon just looked at me with his brows scrunched together.

"Your affection."

His brows rose as he looked back down at Casper who was now purring in his lap, eyes closing and opening lazily. "You sneaky little fucker," Deacon admonished him in a whisper.

"I can't believe you were outsmarted by such a tiny creature. Your brain has to weigh at least four times as much as his."

Deacon grunted as he glared at me.

The grump makes another striking appearance, I thought to myself but thought better of saying it out loud.

We finished spreading out the rest of the puzzle pieces, turning them all over so disjointed puppy parts were all over the table.

"Did you do puzzles growing up?" Deacon asked after we'd completed the left border.

"My parents and I used to do one every year at Christmas

time. It's one of my fondest memories with them. We'd stay up late and make copious amounts of hot chocolate until we all got stomach aches and couldn't drink anymore." Images of those times filled my mind, and I felt a wave of gratitude wash over me as I thought of how lucky I was to have such an amazing childhood.

"Eventually we turned it into a competition though. We all came up with words we'd use to say loudly every time we got a piece in. When someone else would say their word, it made you want to try harder," I laughed. "It also messes with your head if you haven't placed a piece in a while."

"Hm," Deacon huffed. "I kinda like the idea of that. What was your word?"

I beamed at him. "Boom."

"Boom?" he chuckled, and I blushed.

"*Yes*. Boom."

"Like an explosion."

"Listen, I thought I was a hot-shot kid and boom seemed like the appropriate word at the time."

"I like it." He nodded with a smirk.

Crossing my arms over my chest, I sat back in the chair. "Well, it's mine. You have to pick your own."

"A little protective over your boom?"

Deacon was teasing me. He was actually poking at me and not because he was grumpy and irritable. He was actually trying to joke around.

My heart fluttered as I leaned across the table and pecked his cheek.

"What was that for?" His grin was lopsided and adorable, making him look younger than he usually did.

"For being cute," I replied.

"Cute?" He sighed dramatically. "You're not allowed to tell any of my friends that you think I'm *cute*."

I stilled. It was the first time either one of us had made any mention of life beyond the snowstorm that kept us cooped up in his home. A flutter hit my chest as my heart skipped a beat.

"So, um…" I cleared my throat and tucked my hair behind my ears. "What's your word going to be?"

Those beautiful green eyes settled on me for a moment. Assessing. Questioning what had just happened between us. I wondered if he realized what he'd just said and the weight it carried for me. For us.

Then he blinked and the moment was gone as he mirrored me, sitting back in his chair and crossing his arms tighter over his chest, careful not to disturb Casper.

"Alert." Deacon's lips quivered like he was trying to hide a smile.

"Alert," I repeated, trying it out. "It's definitely not as good as boom, but it'll work for someone like you."

"Someone like me?" he chuckled.

"Yeah." I shrugged. "You know…someone with inferior puzzle making skills."

He leaned forward and rubbed his hands together. "Ohhh, you have no idea the monster you've just unleashed." Then he scanned the table, picked up a puzzle piece and slid it into place along the border we'd created together.

It fit perfectly.

"Alert!" he shouted loud enough for Casper to awaken and nearly scurry off his lap.

"You are *so* going down," I growled at him, and he laughed a full belly laugh.

For the next hour, we downed three cups each of hot cocoa and *alerted* and *boomed* until our eyes hurt.

Deacon finally settled back in his chair and rubbed his hands over his face. "I'm pretty sure I've won this round."

"You most certainly did not win. There were far more booms than there were alerts. Casper agrees." I nodded at where my furry little boy still laid in Deacon's lap.

"Oh, right. Like he would side with you when I've been the one giving him chin scratches all night."

"Whoa there, Grumps." I lifted my hands in mock defense. "I'm pretty sure he would side with the one who's fed him his entire life. Not with some man who *just now* decided he liked him."

"Care to test that theory?" Deacon's brows rose, the green of his irises shimmering with roguery.

"Stay, Casper," I said to him as I put him down in front of the mat by Deacon's door before walking back to my spot near the dining table.

Deacon glared at me playfully from where he stood behind the couch.

"Ready?" I asked him and he nodded.

"1, 2, 3!"

We both knelt to the floor and called for Casper to come to us. At first, Casper just sat there looking between us like we were both crazy, but then he stood up on all fours and started walking toward us.

"Come on you little rascal!" Deacon snapped his fingers like a fiend catching Casper's attention.

My jaw popped open as Casper started walking toward Deacon. *That little stinker!*

I did the only thing I could do and maybe it was messed up of me, but I used the T word. "Casper! Come here, boy. Don't you want a treat from your mama?"

Deacon rose on his knees and looked at me with shock. "You sneaky, sneaky woman."

I cackled then we both went back to work calling for Casper who was taking his sweet ass time looking between both of us while making slow steps forward. I kept offering him treats that I didn't actually have in my back pocket, and he finally started shifting in my direction.

Right when I thought I had him in my grasp and I would win, Deacon's voice went two octaves higher as he patted the ground and said, "I'll let you sleep on the bed tonight!"

Casper stopped mid-stride, his front right paw hanging in the air. Then he shifted his head toward Deacon like he suddenly understood the entire English language. Then the little stinker pranced to him without a care in the world. His tail swished back and forth with glee as I sat there empty handed, and *my* cat bounded into Deacon's arms.

"That's my boy!" Deacon bellowed, scooping Casper into his arms and standing tall.

Deflated, I rose to stand and walked over to them. Scratching behind his ears, I brought my face close to Casper's and hissed, "You little traitor. After all the years we've had together, and you betray me like this? Ugh." The little furball had the audacity to purr at me like he was perfectly content with his decision.

Deacon shifted to the side, so I no longer had access to Casper. "Hey, don't be mean to my little guy just because you're a sore loser."

Hands on my hips, I shot him a withering look. He gave me one back. There we both stood, in a glaring contest before we both broke within seconds and burst out laughing.

Tears streamed out of the corners of my eyes as I hunched over, clutching my stomach. Casper bounced in Deacon's arms as his laughter radiated around us.

When we both caught our breath and the giggle attack had subsided, Deacon looked at me. My mind flashed to the first time I saw his stunning green eyes through the hazy smoke of the fire. They had been my lifeline then. Such beauty in the midst of what I was certain were to be my last moments on earth. But now...seeing them so bright and joyful... My heart cinched with a feeling that I'd never felt before. One I wasn't quite ready to admit I was feeling.

When he reached out for my hand and brought my wrist to his lips, my entire body buzzed.

"Your laughter is the most beautiful sound I've ever heard, Charlie." He pressed another kiss to my palm. "Don't ever stop laughing."

Heat hit the back of my eyes. I had to bite my lower lip to keep it from trembling. "I promise I won't."

Chapter 20

Charlie

"Hey, mama!"

"Charlie! Oh, honey. It's so good to hear from you. Your father and I have been worried sick." My mother's voice cut out slightly from the poor reception that the snowstorm likely contributed to.

"I'm sorry I didn't call you earlier, the cell service has been terrible here. It's so good to hear your voice. Is Dad around?"

"Yes, let me grab him." There was rustling in the background and then I heard her call my dad's name. A few more seconds later and then, "Okay, honey. We're both here on speaker phone."

"Hi, Daddy!"

My father's low voice broke through. "Hi, sweetheart. How's the cabin holding up for you in that weather? Do you have enough food? Are you warm enough? How's Casper doing?"

I laughed at the rapid-fire questions. My father always worried about his little girl and even though he knew I was independent and could handle things on my own, he still liked to check up on me.

"Everything's fine. Although it was a little touch and go there for a second."

"What do you mean?" They both asked in unison. That was my parents. Always in sync with one another since before I could remember. I loved that about them. They were predictable and given everything that was transpiring between Deacon and I, I needed a little bit of predictability. Especially since the snowstorm had quieted and it looked like it was starting to melt some.

Bundling the blanket around my shoulders, I watched my warm breath fog in front of me as I took in the white land-scape on Deacon's front porch. I told my parents about the bird's nest in the chimney and how the entire cabin filled with smoke. That part frightened them given the fire from years ago, but I assured them everything was fine.

"When the storm started to come through, the pipes in the cabin froze over and busted. There was water every-where. I felt so bad for my landlord because everything was going wrong."

"Oh my gosh, honey. That sounds like quite a series of bad events. Did he manage to get the pipes fixed for you?"

I paused. Not quite sure how to tell them that I was staying with a man I barely knew who had also been the person to save my life…and that I was falling for him. Hard.

In the end, I knew I would tell them everything. We'd always been that way, and it felt wrong to start lying now even though I knew they would be concerned. Everything I'd done with Deacon…it wasn't like me to move so quickly with anyone. I was more of a slow burn kinda gal.

Clearing my throat, I peered up at the porch ceiling and braced myself. "Actually, he wasn't able to get them fixed before the snow came. I've been staying in his house for the time being."

Silence echoed loudly through the phone. I could see it now, my parents looking at one another with worry in their eyes as they tried not to be too overbearing with all the questions they wanted to ask.

"Are you safe, Charlie? Do you need us to come and get you?" my dad asked. I rolled my eyes and smiled.

"Yes, Dad. I'm perfectly safe. I, um, actually knew him from before I moved here."

"What do you mean?" my mother chimed in.

Biting my lip I sucked in a deep breath. Here we go. "My landlord is Deacon Calhoun. The guy who saved me from the apartment fire."

There was a gasp from my mother. They mumbled something to one another and my heart raced as I waited for their response.

It was my father who spoke first. "This certainly seems like divine intervention, sweetheart. I mean to have ended up in the same small town almost seven years after the fire… wow!!"

"Divine intervention or not, all I care about is if he's treating our daughter right."

My parents had always been deeply feeling, spiritual people. They saw signs in everything, and this situation was no different. I felt it too. The day of the fire, I knew there was something special between Deacon and me. Not that I told anyone that—including my parents. But my ending up here wasn't something they would simply chalk up to chance.

Part of me wanted to be wrong about my connection with Deacon because if I was honest with myself, it was a huge disappointment that he hadn't come to see me in the hospital or at least tried to contact me at some point. My information had been shared all over the news. It was well known who I was given the status of my parents and how well involved they were in the Charlotte community.

Back then, I had to hide how I felt about him. It was ridiculous thinking that you could feel a connection to someone after meeting them only for a few minutes. So, I attributed it to the adrenaline and tried to stomp out all thoughts of him from that day. But now…I understood without a shadow of a doubt that I had been right. There was something indescribable between Deacon and I. Something that had brought us together again.

"He's not my boyfriend, mama." Even though I really wanted him to be. Drops of water fell from the snow on the roof. It would all melt soon and we would have to figure out what we were doing. What everything that had happened between us meant.

"I don't care if he's your boyfriend. Right now, you're living together, and I just hope he's treating you right."

"Of course he is. You really think I would put up with a man not treating me well?"

They were both quiet and I sighed. "Okay, maybe I've made some mistakes with men in the past. But I've learned my value and if he wasn't treating me well then, I'd make sure he did."

"We just don't want to see you struggle, Charlie. You're too nice sometimes. I'd hate to see you let anyone else walk all over you again."

It was a part of myself that I was equally proud of and resentful toward. My parents were right. I *was* too nice sometimes and I'd had to learn the hard way that not everyone gave as much of themselves as I did. I just wanted to see the good in people. The idea that others would just take and not give in return seemed awful to me. I couldn't comprehend it.

The aftermath from the fire had opened my eyes though. And I hadn't exactly had the best string of relationships before that. I'd dated several guys who seemed great at the beginning, but wound up cheating on me or taking advantage of how much money my artwork brought in.

"I promise he's not like that and Casper loves him."

"Really?" my mother asked, shocked. "That cat barely stands us being around. The only person he likes is you."

"Yeah," I snorted. "Until he met Deacon. They're basically best friends now."

"That's wonderful. I'm glad you're having a good time despite the storm snowing you in."

"Thanks, Dad."

I filled them in on my latest art piece before hanging up the phone and slipping it into my jeans pocket. Extending my open palm under the awning of the porch, I caught a droplet of water, watching it splash across my skin. Tinier drops scattered, leaving a cool zap in their wake.

When the door opened behind me, I turned around to find Deacon standing with his hands in his pockets. My breath caught just from the sight of him. It had only been twenty minutes, and my heart already missed his presence.

"How're your parents holding up?" He strode toward me, took my hands in his and blew hot air against them to warm them up. I blushed from his touch remembering how he'd kept me up all night last night.

"They're doing okay. Worried about me."

"Did you tell them you were staying here?" His voice was gruff.

"I did."

And, his raised eyebrows seemed to ask.

I blew out a breath. There was no way I was going to tell him how my father thought our second meeting was divine intervention and that maybe we were meant to be. Deacon was already easily startled. I didn't need my families woo-wooness scaring him off.

"My mama said that she'd beat you up if you mistreated me."

He smiled widely. "She sounds like a badass."

"Tiny but fierce," I added.

"Just like her daughter." He brought his hand to the back of my hair and brought me closer, kissing my forehead.

"The snow is starting to melt."

Deacon pulled back and looked over the top of my head at his property sprawled out behind me. "Seems so."

"What will happen once it does, and we're no longer trapped here?"

"I'd hardly say my time with you has made me feel trapped." His gaze darted between my eyes like he was assessing if that was how I'd felt—trapped.

When I didn't answer he ran his fingers down the long locks of my hair, playing with the ends. "I'm not sure what will happen. This is new territory for me, Sunshine. I do know one thing for sure though." His fingers moved to the bottom of my chin as he gently tilted my head back, so I was looking at him fully. "I don't want this to end."

I was floating and his grasp on my chin was the only thing grounding me because he'd just said what I'd only hoped to hear him say. He didn't want things between us to end. He wanted to try.

It was all I could ask for and he was willing to give it to me.

"I don't want things to end either."

DEACON

"You're almost done with this one." It was more of a question than a statement. I rubbed my palms over Charlie's shoulders as she made tiny little strokes of white over the river water. The painting seemed done to me a few days ago. I thought it had been perfect then, but now that she was adding even finer details, it all seemed even more real. Like I could walk into the image and feel the mist from the river on my face.

"Just a few more things to fix, then yes." Tilting her head back, she looked up at me. The pale blue of her eyes matched some of the wisps of paint along the river scene. I ran my hand over her decolletage and up the delicate column of her throat as I brought my lips to hers.

"It's stunning," I whispered across her mouth. Then, I felt her smile against me and my heart skipped a beat. The things she could get me to do with that smile. The list was endless.

When she lifted her head to get back to work, I moved to her left and leaned against the windowsill to watch her paint.

"How did you get started with art?" I asked, watching the small muscles of her forearm flex and shift as she moved the brush along the canvas.

A giggle had the balls of her cheeks blooming light pink. "As my parents tell it, they caught me drawing on everything in the house. If there was some kind of marker or crayon available, I would find it and use it to make everything around me prettier."

Thinking back to her asking to paint murals in the tiny cabin, the story made a lot of sense. Her long locks of hair shimmied across her back when she turned her head to look at me.

"One time—I think I was about eight—my parents walked into my bedroom and every single wall was covered in flowers I'd drawn with some markers I'd snuck home from a friend's birthday party. Most parents would have been furious, but mine just put me into art classes and art summer camps. I think they knew from that point forward; it was my passion. They've always been really great at supporting my dreams."

"You're lucky in that way."

Her eyes softened. "I know." The wood of her paintbrush tinged against the glass mason jar filled with murky water as she swirled it around. "What about you? Have you ever been into anything creative?"

"I can show you."

Her brows popped up. "Really?"

Extending my hand for hers, I said, "Come on."

When she slipped her hand into mine, I gave it a tender squeeze. I loved holding her hand. Everything of hers was so tiny compared to me, but I knew she was strong. Charlie had the kind of quiet strength that only came with conviction in her truth and the confidence that she knew what she wanted from this life. There weren't many people in the world like her.

Heading for the garage, I stopped with my hand on the

doorknob. I'd never shown anyone my woodwork before. Not outside of my parents. It was the one thing I'd always kept for myself. But I wanted her to see it. Wanted to share every part of myself with her.

"Ready?"

Even though the hallway was dark, there was a bright-ness to her eyes. Excitement. It made my heart hammer against my ribcage.

"Yes!"

I opened the door, and we stepped into the garage-turned-woodshop. Sawdust littered the floor and after a few weeks of not being in here, a fine layer of dust covered most of my works in progress.

"Oh my gosh. Deacon!" Charlie moved through the space with her hand covering her mouth, eyes wide in awe. "This is incredible."

I watched as she stopped at the mid-sized grandfather clock I'd been working on before her arrival. Her fingertips moved over the etched birds above where the glass clock would display. "Those little guys took me forever to get right."

"I can imagine," she breathed. "They're so beautiful."

"Thank you."

As she wiped the wood dust from her fingertips, she looked back at me. "How long have you been doing this?"

Rubbing my chin with my hand, I thought back to the first time my dad bought me whittling tools for Christmas. "I was pretty young. Probably around the same age you started going to art classes. My father always gifted my mother and I wood pieces for Christmas. He'd make jewelry boxes for her and wooden toys for me. When I got a little older, we'd work together in his shop. I mostly started with whittling."

Reaching for the small frog on the shelf behind her, I handed the tiny trinket to her. She moved it over in her hands, assessing my work. I grasped the back of my neck, suddenly feeling nervous. "This was the first thing I ever made. The proportions are pretty awful, and his eyes are way too big, but I was proud of it back then."

"As you should have been. Deacon, you have an incredible gift."

She held my gaze for a moment before giving me the frog back and continuing to make her way around the larger pieces. Stopping at each one, I felt a sense of anxiety take hold wondering what she thought about them all. Her opinion mattered to me.

I cleared my throat. "When I got older, my dad showed me how to make furniture. That's when I became obsessed. Most of the wooden pieces in my house I made."

"The dining table?" she asked, voice excited.

"Yup."

"The headboard in your room?"

"Mmhmm."

"What about the rose side tables in the living room?"

"Those too."

"Have you ever sold your work?"

I laughed at her incessant questioning. It was so *her*. "It's not really something I'd ever thought about before. I've always just done it for myself."

She ran her teeth over her bottom lip as she thought about what I'd said. "I get that. But if you ever wanted to consider selling some of your work, let me know. I can help you with the business side of things." The words came out of her mouth in a rushed excitement. Her enthusiasm for my work hit me like a damn freight train. Aside from my parents, I'd never had anyone tell me my work was good because I'd hidden it away. Just like everything else.

Hearing a compliment from Charlie's lips made me stand a little taller.

"I'll consider that."

She shot me a wink that made my heart stutter before she went back to observing my work. "Whoa!" Charlie knelt in front of the half-finished bench I'd started last year and couldn't find the inspiration to finish.

"This is amazing." She brushed her hands over the back of the bench where half of it was carved with vines and bloomed orchids.

"Where were you planning on putting this one?" She beamed up at me with curious eyes.

"I was thinking about the front porch, but I don't know. I'm not sure." Halfway through working on the bench, I realized I'd made it too big for just myself. It was a piece that was meant for two people to share and since I didn't have anyone else in my life, it didn't make sense for me to finish it.

Until now.

"I know the perfect place." She rose to stand in front of me and dug her hands into the front pockets of my jeans.

Snaking my arm around her waist, I pulled her closer. "Is that right?"

"Mmhmm." The reddish orange curls of her hair dipped into her face as she nodded. "You should put it on your front porch so we can drink our hot chocolate on it together."

My stomach did a weird flip-flop at the thought of having her sit on this bench with me. The piece I'd unconsciously made for two people to share. Maybe some part of me always knew she'd come back into my life one day. A thread of hope that despite all my shortcomings, she might actually want to stay.

I brushed the hair from her face and placed a kiss on each one of her freckled cheeks. "I think I can do that."

Her body close to mine, she moved her hands from my front pockets to the back ones. I fucking loved it when she claimed my body with such ease. Like it was second nature for her.

"And if you're really nice, you might even let me paint it."

I inhaled deeply and tilted my head back and forth like I was thinking about it. Even though the thought of her touching one of my pieces with her gift was a fucking honor.

"I think we might be able to arrange a deal."

Her rosy lips spread wide, showing her bright white teeth. It stole the breath from my lungs.

"Good." She gave me a curt nod. "Because I think you and I could make something really special together."

Me too, Sunshine, was what I wanted to say and almost did. But the words got caught in my throat.

Charlie spun out of my arms and spent the next few hours asking me endless questions about my work and how I grew in the craft. I didn't stop smiling the entire time.

Chapter 21

Charlie

My fingers hurt from how much painting I'd done today. With Deacon's admission that he didn't want things between us to end, even once the snow melted and we had to go back to the real world, I'd been inspired to create more than I ever had before.

"Let me help you with that," Deacon offered, coming up behind me at the kitchen sink.

I was scrubbing the last bits of paint from my fingers when he took over. His large body engulfed mine from behind. I sank into him, loving how warm his body was. Any time he was near, the winter cold was warded off and I often found myself refusing to leave his side.

His rough hands moved over mine as I leaned my head into the crook of his shoulder and chest. Outside the kitchen window, the sun shone, and birds started coming back to life, landing in the trees surrounding his house. Soon I'd have to go back to the tiny cabin. Even though this was where I wanted to be. Barefoot and happy in Deacon's kitchen with his arms wrapped firmly around me.

"Almost there." His hot breath tickled the cuff of my ear as his fingers rubbed against mine where only a little bit of white, green and brown paint remained speckled over my skin.

"What're the plans for tonight, Grumps?"

"Hmmm," he hummed deeply. "I was thinking we could sip on some whiskey by the fire. What does my sunshine girl think about that?"

"Whiskey…I've never had it before."

I could feel the surprise on his face even though my back was to him. "Is that right? Well, you're in for a treat then."

"Doesn't it burn?"

His chest rumbled as he chuckled. "All good things burn a little bit. Whiskey's one of them."

"I guess I'll try it."

"You guess? I guarantee by the end of the night you'll love it." My toes curled at his innuendo, and I had a feeling he was right. Whatever Deacon wanted to introduce to me, I would end up loving. Because it was part of him—his enjoyment. And I loved seeing him happy.

"All done." Soft lips met my cheek before he reached for a tea towel and handed it to me to dry off my hands. "I'll meet you in the living room."

"Okay." Hanging the towel back on the oven door handle, I felt an unnerved feeling come over me. This space had become my home in just a week's time. Somehow it felt like I'd been here forever and that made me weary of what it might be like to leave once the snow melted and we got the tiny cabin situated.

Would I still be happy? I thought so given that the few days I'd been in the tiny cabin had been wonderful and refreshing. But *he* wouldn't be with me. We wouldn't share in the little moments of waking up next to one another, the passing glances between us when he paced around while I worked on my pieces or seeing how sweet he was with Casper.

I was both excited that he was willing to give us a chance and sorrowful that this season of being with him was going to end. Things were going to look different when all I wanted was more of the same.

Grabbing a blanket from the couch, I wrapped it around myself before settling in front of the fireplace. Casper's tail flicked back and forth as he slowly made his way over to me.

"I bet if I was Deacon, you'd be moving a lot faster." He just lazily blinked at me like he had no regrets for how much he adored the big grumpy man. "Not that I blame you," I said, picking him up and placing him in my lap. "I'm kind of obsessed with him too."

Orange and blue flames put on a show in the fireplace. It amazed me how something so beautiful could cause so much damage in such a short amount of time. I rubbed at my scar, making a mental note to rub some more of Deacon's salve on it before going to bed tonight. Whatever concoction was in that, I needed to figure it out because I'd never had the itching be relieved for so long after using it. Normally, I had to apply my petroleum-based lotion at least once a day, but his salve lasted for days at a time.

I heard more rustling in the kitchen before footsteps sounded toward Casper and me. I needed to pull myself out of this rut if I didn't want to ruin the rest of our night together. Worry wasn't normally something I battled with. Even when I first started going off on my own in life, without the support of my parents, I'd been nothing but excited. Completely invigorated by all the possibilities. Then, I'd felt the same again when I transitioned out of college and had no idea how I was going to support myself as a brand-new artist when the potential for failure was way higher than success.

I *always* saw the bright side of things.

There was just an unsettling feeling deep in my gut that I couldn't turn off and I didn't know why. All I'd wanted was to hear Deacon say that he was excited about a future with us. That what we shared wasn't going to end once the snow melted. That he was willing to *try* for us.

And he'd given me that.

So, why the hell am I still up in arms about this?

As Deacon rounded the couch with two glass tumblers in his hands, I shook the question from my mind. I was being ridiculous.

He gave me one of the glasses then sat down in front of me, cross-legged. His large thighs strained against the fabric of his jeans. My mouth watered as I thought back to riding him last night. How powerful I'd felt with his huge body beneath me, getting off on how he looked at me.

I stirred in my seat, feeling my clit ache with the need to be touched by him and tried my best to focus on the cool sensation in my palm from the iced whiskey drink he'd made me.

"This is Four Roses, one of my favorites." He brought the glass to his nose and sniffed lightly.

Following suit, I sniffed the amber liquid and caught floral, honey, and spice notes. It must have been expensive because there was no sting to my nose like there often was when I got a whiff of hard liquor.

"It smells nice."

He smiled. "Now, here's the trick. With a whiskey like this, you want to sip it. It's not like one of your fruity cock-tails where you can down it in one go."

I frowned at him. "How did you know I like fruity cocktails?"

He leaned toward me and kissed the edge of my mouth. Chills ran down my arms and when he pulled back, I found myself leaning forward, chasing after his touch. "Because I know my woman."

I blushed.

There it was again. *My woman.* If I was his, surely that meant—No. I needed to get *out* of my head and into the present moment. Guessing what was going to happen between us would only send me into another worry spiral and that wasn't me.

"Maybe I like spicy margaritas."

His green eyes flickered with amusement. "No way."

I snorted.

"But you *are* going to enjoy this." He nodded at the glass in my hand. "Take a small sip."

"So bossy," I teased.

"Do it," he commanded, his voice lowering an octave.

Like he was in control of my every movement, I lifted the glass to my lips and felt the rush of the cold liquid hit. Taking some into my mouth, I let it sit on my tongue for a moment before I swallowed. It was smooth and crisp, like biting into a freshly picked apple at the beginning of fall.

There was no awful burn down my throat, but it did bite a little. Just enough to get my attention.

"Wow," I breathed. "That is really good."

"That's my girl." Deacon winked at me before taking a long swig from the tumbler. Thick black lashes fanned out as he kept his eyes trained on me. I licked my lips, watching his Adam's apple bob up and down as he swallowed. When he pulled the glass away, my mouth watered from the sight of his full wet lips.

My mind wandered to how those lips felt against my sex and how he looked when I rode his face.

Blinking away the debaucherous thoughts, I took another sip of the whiskey. Already starting to feel a little buzz latching onto the edges of my mind, I said, "We should play a game."

"What're you thinking, Sunshine?"

I couldn't help the smile tugging on the corners of my lips. "How about two truths and a lie, but the stripper version."

"There's a stripper version of that game?" he chuckled.

"Mmhmm." I nodded slowly. "If you guess the lie incorrectly, you strip. If you guess the lie correctly, the other person strips."

Mouth open wide, he downed the rest of his whiskey, the thick column of his throat working. I was mesmerized by him. Every little movement he made was so damn sexy. There was no mistaking the wetness between my legs that seemed to grow more and more every time Deacon spoke or even moved a muscle. Looking down at the glass of whiskey in my hand, I silently cursed it for making me extra horny. I was already wild for the guy; I didn't need the help of alcohol to make that even worse.

"I'll go first," I offered. Deacon put the glass down and sat back on his hands, his large chest flexing against his T-shirt.

Focus, Charlie, I chastised myself. If I was going to win, I didn't need any distractions from him.

"Okay. I've ridden a mechanical bull. I've always wanted to be kissed in the rain. I won a baking competition in high school."

His eyes narrowed slightly like he was trying to read into my mind. I giggled, taking a sip of whiskey.

"I don't think you won a baking competition."

I almost choked on the amber liquid. "Ugh! How did you know?"

He looked down at the floor between us and smiled to himself. "The other two just seem more like you."

I groaned. "Well, that's really annoying."

"Annoying that I won, and you lost?" The right side of his mouth tilted upward in a roguish smirk.

"Yes!" I laughed.

"Well, go on then." He nodded toward me. I set the glass down on the stone hearth and rolled my eyes.

Slowly rising to my feet, Casper scattered off, finding a new spot to lay on the couch. I locked my eyes on Deacon and played with the hem of my sweater, giving him a little show with my hips swinging back and forth. He sat back, leaning on his hands again with a heady neediness shadowing his eyes. He wanted me. And I fucking loved that he wanted me.

Slowly lifting my sweater, I felt the graze of my own knuckles moving smoothly over my stomach. I pretended they were *his* hands taking his time as he undressed me. The air was thick with heat between us, but I still had goosebumps rise from my navel to my chest when I made the final exposure of my white lace bra as I brought the sweater over my head and let it fall into a heap on the floor beside me.

Deacon's gaze raked down my body. His tongue darted out between his lips as he took me in. With anyone else I still would have been self-conscious, covering my mid-section and scar with my arms. But for him I could be vulnerable. I could let myself be bare and know that he liked every imperfection. Deacon's lust for me was a balm to any insecurity I'd ever had.

In a voice that didn't seem wholly mine, I said, "Your turn."

He shook his head slowly. "Fuck the game." Then he patted his thigh. "Come here, Sunshine."

Biting my lower lip, I took a few steps until my feet were planted firmly on both sides of his thighs. Still wearing my pants, I could feel the heat of my needy sex as I stopped right in front of his face.

"Undress me," I commanded, sliding my hand over the top of his head, threading my fingers through his dark hair. A low growl emanated from his lips as he seized my pants' button and hastily took them off me.

"Always wearing the prettiest things." He flicked the edge of my sage green thong against my skin.

"Just for you," I said in a hushed voice.

When his head dove forward to lick me, I stopped him. Those green eyes pierced through me, desperate wanting reflecting in them. "I just want you, Deacon." Bending down, I brushed my lips against his. He shivered as we parted, and I watched as he lifted his hips from the floor and stripped himself bare.

Rough knuckles scraped against my skin as he rose to his knees and unclasped my bra before sliding my thong down my legs. When he sat back down and I settled into his lap, he took the blanket I'd been using from the floor and wrapped it around my shoulders.

Placing my arms over his shoulders, the blanket draped

around us, creating the perfect cocoon of warmth. His hands moved to cup the sides of my face, stilling me against him. I could feel the hard ridge of his cock against my wet sex. But I didn't want to rush this. And neither did he.

When his lips found mine, I melted against him, our chests touching and our breaths becoming one. Dizziness swirled my mind and tingles spread all over my body. It felt like kissing him for the very first time. It felt like he was mine all along and mine to keep forever.

Our tongues moved over one another. Slow, languid strokes that had my entire being whirling with electricity. He was the spark that lit my soul up with bright beautiful light and I never wanted to be without him. Deacon was showing me everything he was in this moment.

Sweet.

Tender.

Loving.

They were the parts he kept most hidden and yet, here they were. On full display. Just for me.

Large hands ran up and down my back as I opened for him, finding that need down deep in my core as I started to rock against him.

"I want you, Deacon. I need to feel you inside of me. Please." My lips quivered on a shaking breath that matched his. Where I felt my entire soul call to him, I knew he was there waiting to answer. I could see it in his eyes. The readiness to open up to me. To fully let me in.

He pulled back only until there was enough room for him to slip his hand between us and guide the tip of his length to my entrance. Deacon groaned in pleasure as I slowly swirled my hips, his cock thickening even more as I slid myself down his shaft.

"You feel so good," I moaned, collapsing forward as his arms snaked around my waist. It took a moment to adjust to the fullness of him. Grasping the base of my neck, he pulled down until he was buried so damn deep, I started to see stars.

"You're mine," he whispered against the cuff of my ear before he settled his face into the crook of my neck and started grazing his teeth and lips along every inch of my sensitive skin.

I leaned backward, feeling him tense inside of me. "Say that again." Emotion lodged in my throat.

Taking his fingers to my forehead, he swept a long tendril of my hair to the side before lining my bottom lip with the edge of his thumb. When his pine green irises flicked back to meet mine, he brought our foreheads together, lips only a breath apart. "You're mine, Charlie."

Closing my eyes tightly, I let his words sink in deep, all the way to the depths of my soul. Then I kissed him so hard our teeth nearly clinked together. He buried his hands into my hair as I rolled myself against him. The feel of his thick cock inside of me while I ground my clit against his pelvic bone had me spiraling.

To be this connected to him, to feel this close… Heat started burning the back of my eyes as our movements became one. Where I rolled forward, he met me with the exact friction I needed.

"You're so beautiful, baby girl. You take my breath away." His lips moved against the crook of my neck as he sent a trail of kisses down the side of my arm.

I don't want this to end. I don't want things to go back to the way they were. I don't want to ever be without you.

All the things I wanted to say to him died on the tip of my tongue. I felt too good in his embrace to let my fears take hold, even if they were making themselves known with great force.

I wanted this moment with him. Even if it was the very last one I ever got, it would be worth whatever pain came next.

I pressed a kiss to the side of his cheek and whispered, "Don't ever stop showing this part of yourself, Deacon. Please, don't ever stop." His kindness, gentleness and openness. It blew me away and I only hoped more people could see what laid behind the walls he'd built so thick.

He stopped moving for a moment and looked at me. *Really* looked at me. I held his gaze, and I could see he knew exactly what I meant. That he was safe with me. He'd taken a chance, opened himself up and I was here. In complete awe of the man he kept so securely hidden.

"You're amazing." I brushed my fingertips along the side of his face.

Like a damn bursting free, Deacon unleashed himself on me and I finally felt the full force of what it was like to be in his presence.

Capturing my lips with his, he kissed me so deeply, so profoundly, I knew I'd never be the same. It felt like he was saving my life all over again. I was bound to him. Breathless and aching we moved together, tangled in one another's embrace until there was no part of us that was separated. We'd become one and as we found the release our bodies needed; a single tear trekked down my face.

I'd given every single piece of myself to him and all I could do was hope he would want to keep them.

Chapter 22

Deacon

Hot liquid ran down my throat, warming my insides from the frigid cold that didn't seem to want to leave Pebble Brook Falls. Or maybe it was just Charlie's absence that drove my bones to feeling frozen. I'd become selfish, not wanting her to leave my side even though we'd been in the same house for a few weeks now.

Charlie Banks had become the candlelight in my darkness, warding off the shadows of my past with just a simple smile. Helping me find laughter again. God, I couldn't remember that last time I'd laughed this much. It had to have been years—before my time as a firefighter and maybe even before the war.

The way we connected last night had changed everything. This was no longer a quick fling that would end as soon as she was able to go back to the tiny cabin.

I wanted her.

I *needed* her.

And I'd never needed anything in my entire life. I'd always been a simple man, content with having very little. I preferred my alone time in the quiet, but ever since she burst into my life, I'd found everything *before her* dull and tiresome.

Charlie had brought me back to life and while I clung to the lightness in my chest, I was also terrified that something bad was going to happen. The fear ate away at me. It was like a gnat flying around, biting me every chance it got. It was too small to see how to get rid of it, but it was there. Sucking the joy out of the moments I shared with her.

Staring at the ground, I shook my head. I needed to figure my shit out because I saw the shift in her last night too. The look in her eyes had told me she was falling. That she was in this for the long haul.

And I wanted that too. Charlie saw through the razor-sharp barbed wire I kept around myself to the person I was before war and tragedy had tainted my existence. More than that, though, she helped me become that version of myself again.

I needed to be better for her.

I had to be.

Or I'd lose her. I knew it.

"Come on, boy!" she called to Casper who was taking a tentative step into the snow that was now only a few inches thick on the ground. Charlie was hesitant to let him outside after the hawk debacle, but I assured her that he was safe with me outside.

That didn't stop me from having a talk with him about

not venturing into any trees though. The little rascal was starting to grow on me. I liked having him around. I liked having both of them around.

A sinking feeling hit my stomach as I thought again about what it would be like without them here.

It would be quiet.

Too quiet.

Before, I had enjoyed the silence this house brought me. It kept my mind clear of things I didn't want it to stray to. Now, the thought of silence had goosebumps skittering along my spine.

I needed to convince her to stay. That as crazy as it was, I was falling in love with her and the last thing I wanted was to be parted from her.

My chest ached as those bright blue eyes met mine from across the yard. So vibrant. So full of life. God, I hoped I wouldn't suck it all from her. I hoped this wasn't a fluke and that the parts of me she'd uncovered last night would stay visible. That I would be brave enough to stay in her light and not retreat back into my darkness.

She deserved to see the best of me.

Those long dark red tendrils of her hair fluttered in the wind making her look even more angelic against the white winterscape. I'd always thought she belonged on a beach somewhere. A place in the sunshine that would darken her adorable little freckles and show the shine of her hair. Somewhere that matched the warmth of her smile.

But after these weeks with her, I'd come to realize that she was exactly where she was meant to be.

With me.

"There you go! Don't be scared, Casper!"

I smiled as Charlie patted her thighs, coaxing the little fluff ball to venture closer to her. When he finally made it all the way to Charlie, she scooped him up in a hug and spun around. Laughter—glorious, easy laughter—flitted through the air, lightening my chest and chasing away the remnants of my demons.

"You're such a brave boy!" she crooned. Bringing her face close to his, she nuzzled her nose against Casper's before looking back at me.

"What're you doing up there all alone?"

I smiled. "Just watching." *Watching every little thing you do because you're so damn perfect.*

With a hand on her hip, she pouted. "That doesn't sound like very much fun. Why don't you come out here with us, Grumps?"

Oh, with pleasure, Sunshine.

Anywhere Charlie Banks called me to, I would follow. If Johnny or any of my military buddies were here to see me, they'd say I was pussy whipped. While I wouldn't argue with them—I'd give my left nut to make sure I could claim Charlie's sweet pussy as my own for the rest of my life—there was more to this than just sex.

She *meant* something to me. And I wasn't sure the last time a woman—if any—had that kind of impact on me.

Setting my coffee mug on the railing of the porch, I trudged through the snow and stopped right in front of her. "Here I am, at your command."

She booped my nose with her pointer finger. "Now, isn't this much better than being up there missing out on all the fun?"

Looking around us, I inhaled a heavy breath of the cold air, feeling it line my lungs with a needle-like sting. "And what sort of fun do you have in mind?"

There was a mischievous glint in her eyes and her pert little freckled nose twitched before she smiled widely. "A little friendly competition of sorts."

"Why do I have a feeling I'm about to get ganged up on?" I rubbed my hand over Casper's face as he purred.

"Because I'm a champion snowball fighter. And you're about to lose."

My head tilted back as I laughed. "Is that right?"

"Mmhmm." She nodded, then bit her bottom lip.

"Didn't you say the same thing about puzzle making? That you had far superior skills."

She placed a hand on her hip and glowered at me. "And your point is?"

I tucked a loose strand of hair behind her ear. "My point, Sunshine, is that you lost at puzzle making. Horribly, I might add."

Her mouth popped open in shock before she swatted my arm. "Deacon Calhoun. I didn't make you out as a liar!"

I chuckled. "The only one lying about their skills, sweetheart, is you."

She gripped the lapels of my jacket and yanked me forward. Rising onto her tiptoes, she ran her teeth along the edge of my jaw before placing a kiss on my neck. "We'll agree to disagree on this. Only because I hate arguing with you."

I snorted before I grabbed her ass and gripped it hard. "Here I was thinking you got off on it."

She snickered then bit her bottom lip as she batted her eyelashes at me.

I stole a chaste kiss before running my thumb along the edge of her rosy lip. "Keep biting that lip and I'll strip you bare and fuck that sweet cunt of yours right here in the snow."

Her eyes widened a fraction at my expletive, but she didn't back down as she leaned forward and nipped at my ear lobe. "I'm not falling for it, Grumps. I'm about to beat your ass and then we'll see who ends up bare in the snow."

A feral sort of thrill ran through me at her challenge.

"It's on."

Leaving her stranded, I darted behind her and immediately started building a wall of snow. The ice bit into my skin as she squealed and darted away from me, finding a spot with Casper right in front of the porch.

She didn't have a chance to start building her barrier before I nailed her in the shoulder with a snowball. Little flakes splattered everywhere.

Unimpressed with our game, Casper bounded for cover by the front door.

"Hey!" she shouted across the yard. "We didn't say *go* yet!"

"Go!" I yelled back right before I threw another one her way then continued building up my little wall of ice.

Mist clouded around my mouth as I took in heavy breaths from the excitement. Something like joy flickered to life in my chest. I was having *fun*.

I couldn't remember the last time I'd felt this light. All I knew is that ever since she'd come around, the feeling had started becoming more familiar.

I liked it.

Just as I lifted my head to see what she was doing, snow pummeled into my face.

"Woohoo! You suck! I win!" Charlie's trill voice permeated the air.

Shaking my head back and forth, the snow fell from my face and I could see Charlie doing a little dance, wiggling her hips back and forth as she moved in a small circle.

With her back to me, I reeled my arm back and watched as the tightly packed ball of snow smacked her right in the ass. Startled, she gave a little hop and yipped.

Rising from the safety of my wall, I pointed at her and clutched my stomach as I laughed. "Who sucks now?!"

Whipping her hair around, she glared a hole into my face for a few moments. Then the second she darted beneath her wall again, I moved behind mine and started building a small artillery of snowballs.

When I came back up again, I realized she must have had the same idea as me because she started throwing snowball after snowball in my direction.

"You're going down!" she laughed between each word, continuing to hurtle more snowballs at me—most of them missing their mark.

I followed suit, both of us rising from our stations. When I ran out, I knelt down, taking her hits while I packed together the biggest snowball I could manage.

Finished with my masterpiece, I lifted the monstrosity into the air, readying my attack. Her eyes flashed, growing wider as she realized what I'd done.

"No way!" she laughed and yelled at the same time, holding her hands up in defense.

Reeling my arm back, I grunted as I threw the giant snowball as hard as I could. I watched as it soared through the air. Like a punch to the gut, my stomach sank as I realized my aim was off. The snowball moved quickly several feet above Charlie's head until it landed in a flurry of white onto the edge of the porch roof where there was still at least a foot of snow piled high.

Charlie craned her neck to look above her. Time slowed the moment I realized what I'd done. Two cracks formed along the edge of packed snow on the roof and it started to slide.

"Charlie!" I screamed just as the snow slipped from the roof. Charlie covered her head with her arms and ducked down just as the snow slammed into her back, forcing her to the ground.

My legs moved faster than ever before as I ran toward her submerged body. "No, no, no!" My heart lurched into my throat. I thought I was going to be sick, but I kept it down. Focusing solely on Charlie as I finally crossed the yard.

"Charlie!" I called to her through the snow as I slid to the ground and immediately started digging through.

Frozen to the bone, my hands ached as I clawed through the snow. Frigid wetness bit through my gloves from the effort, but I didn't fucking care. Flashes of that day sprang to my mind as I kept digging. Images of her beautiful face, those bright blue eyes both terrified of her looming death and hopeful that I'd be able to save her.

I've done it again. I've fucked up the only good thing in my life. Oh, God. Oh, God!

My mind reeled with self-loathing as my chest squeezed so tight I couldn't breathe.

"Charlie, please!" Something hot and wet started to roll down my face as my vision blurred. Tears. I hadn't cried in years. Not since I came home from war without three of my brothers. Not since I had to watch as their bodies were buried, and their loved ones suffered.

But Charlie... Charlie was my fucking soul. The only person who could bring me back to life after every fucked-up thing I'd seen in this world. She was *mine.*

And I'd screwed up again. I couldn't keep her safe. Just like I couldn't keep my brothers safe.

"Charlie!" I cried out just as my hands uncovered her black puffer jacket. Moving faster, I moved the snow from her sides until I could reach around her stomach. Gripping her sides, I pulled her from the snow, the momentum jolting us backwards with her landing on top of me.

Scurrying to see if she was okay, I sat up and pulled her entire body into my lap. "Charlie! Please answer me. Please tell me you're okay." Her eyes were closed as I held her face between my hands, a large red mark already marred the right side of her beautiful face.

She blinked and a guttural sound escaped from my throat.

"Deacon." Her voice was raspy as she settled those ice blue eyes on me. "Deacon, I'm okay."

Drops of water splashed onto her cheeks and I realized my tears had fallen, leaving little wet marks on her freckled skin. She wrapped her arms around me when I brought her close to my chest and hugged her. I took in a deep breath of her warm vanilla scent and thanked whatever divine powers were at work that she was okay.

"Is Casper alright?"

Shit.

Not ready to let her go, I let her pull back only slightly so I could look around for the little guy. Thankfully, I saw him right away, sitting on the top of the porch steps watching us closely.

"He's fine."

She sighed with relief.

"Do you want to try to stand?" I asked, wanting to test her body for any sign of injuries.

When she nodded, I rose and helped to steady her with my arms. She staggered a little bit and my heart raced, nearly beating right out of my chest.

"Does anything hurt?"

She blinked, then looked around her body for a few seconds, moving her arms and legs a little. "Just some soreness in my lower back, but nothing sharp."

My lips tightened. "Charlie, I am so sorry." My voice cracked on the last word. I cleared my throat, trying to ward off the thick emotions clogging it.

Her grip on my forearms tightened when she looked up at me. "Deacon, this wasn't your fault."

I looked off to the side because the angry red mark on her cheek was wrecking me. I knew it would bruise. That tomorrow morning, she'd wake up with a reminder of my stupidity and carelessness.

One day, she'd realize that I was no good. That the only thing she would get with me was a life filled with pain and regret. Then she'd leave. And I'd be left in the darkness once again.

So.

Many.

Thoughts.

Ran through my mind.

All of them dark. All of them *without* her.

"Deacon." She pressed her palm to the side of my face, forcing me to look at her. "I promise you, I'm fine. It was just a freak accident."

"That *I* caused." I pounded a fist on my chest and hurt flashed across her face.

"Don't do this to us." Her words were barely a whisper. "Please don't."

"You need to stay away from me, Charlie. You'll only get hurt."

Tears welled in her eyes, and I hated myself for causing them, but I knew it was true. She had to stay away from me.

What just happened was a sign. A reminder–the people I cared about always suffered. They always got hurt. It was better if I was alone.

So, I did the only thing I could think of to make sure she stayed safe.

I walked away from her.

Chapter 23

Charlie

I'm losing him.

The thought struck me like a bolt of lightning as I sat across from him at the dining table. A deep frown was etched into his face—a constant reminder of what happened yesterday.

When I woke up this morning, blue and black splotches had appeared on my right cheek where my face met the compacted snow as I took the hit to my back and fell. Dazed from the impact, I admitted, it had been unnerving when I woke up in Deacon's arms having to remember that seconds ago, I was buried under feet of snow.

He'd told me I'd probably lost consciousness for a few seconds, but that was almost all he'd said to me for the rest of the night. Aside from checking on my face and making sure I stayed awake for a long time in case I presented with any other symptoms of a concussion.

Deacon had changed in an instant. The light in his eyes

from when we were having the snowball fight had snuffed out completely. He looked even worse than the first day I arrived, surprising him on his front porch. At least back then, he was angry.

Now, all I got was heavy silence and solemn looks. His silence was heartbreaking.

I can fix this; I'd told myself this morning when I woke up in the bed we'd shared for two weeks now to find it empty for the first time. There was no good night kiss last night and he had stayed on his side of the bed, leaving me alone in the darkness.

When I couldn't stand it anymore, I told him I wanted to work on the puzzle hoping it would break the icy barrier between us and he'd finally talk to me.

It worked…sort of. He'd sat down across from me and stared at the scattered pieces. But at least he was here and not brooding in some other part of the house.

Acting as normal as possible, I slipped one of the pieces into place. "Boom," I attempted in an excited voice only for it to come out in a flat whisper.

Peering at him through my eyelashes, I caught him looking at me, but he immediately averted my gaze. I dipped my head lower, trying to get him to look at me.

Nothing.

I rubbed at my aching chest.

Frustration and hurt simmered in my veins. After all we'd shared together and after everything I'd *thought* we'd overcome from the past and he was choosing to let an *acci-*

dent get in the way of something really special. I wouldn't stand for it. Wouldn't allow him to take this away from us.

I hated what he was doing. A sense of betrayal struck me in the heart. It was just like those days I'd spent in the hospital. Not a single friend came to visit me. I was alone in the fight. Abandoned. Tossed to the side without care.

But *this*. With *him*. It was much worse.

Because I'd given Deacon my heart. He had it in the palm of his hand and he'd just decided to throw it away. Like I was *nothing*.

Tears blurred my vision, but I refused to wipe them away. If he looked at me, I wanted him to see what he was doing to me—to us. This was a choice. And he was choosing wrong.

Just when I opened my mouth to tell him everything I was thinking, Casper jumped onto the table. Puzzle pieces slid to the side, some of them falling to the floor as he trotted across the table and sat right in front of Deacon.

Meow.

Casper nudged Deacon's chin with his nose and gave him two licks on the cheek. He'd never given me a kiss before. Not once.

I held my breath as Deacon sat back in his chair, putting distance between him and Casper. Then he slipped his hands under Casper's belly and set him down on the floor.

A loud shriek permeated the air as I slid my chair back with force. I couldn't stay in here any longer and watch him bury his head in the sand—blinding himself to what he had right in front of him. The *love* he had in this house and how he was ruining it for himself.

I could feel his eyes on me as I trailed into the kitchen and made myself a cup of hot chocolate.

"Chocolate will never let you down, honey," my mother used to always say when I would come home with hurt feelings from school or when I got a poor grade on a test. She'd always break me off a piece of her dark chocolate bar and once the delicious bite melted onto my tongue, I knew she was right.

There would never be a day when chocolate disappointed me.

As I took a long sip from the steaming mug, I let it calm my nerves. The frustration started to dissipate, and I felt my mind clear. Taking a deep breath in, I let my shoulders drop and tried to let go of the anger. Anger was just fear in another form and if I didn't want Deacon to let fear win, I couldn't either.

Peeking around the corner, I saw Deacon was still in his seat at the table, staring blankly at the wall. He was so far into his own mind, I thought he might stay trapped there forever. Unable to see that he had a way out. He didn't have to live like this anymore.

Setting the mug of hot cocoa on the kitchen island, I knew I had to do something. Deacon had fought to save my life, risking himself in the process. There was no way I could just leave him to his own devices when he was down this bad. No matter how much it hurt to be on the receiving end of his rejection, I had to try and figure this out.

Taking another deep breath and letting it go, I rounded the kitchen wall and headed toward him. A muscle ticked along his jaw when I moved closer. I could tell there were a lot of things moving around in his mind. So many things he probably wanted to say but couldn't.

But we didn't have to talk. I could show him how much he meant to me.

Attempting to do just that, I stopped behind him and ran my hands over his shoulders and down his chest as I hugged him from behind. Placing a kiss to the cuff of his ear, I saw the goosebumps rise along his skin, but he still didn't move. He was a stone, lodged in his seat. Unmoving. Relentlessly stubborn.

So, I craned my neck until our lips were close. He glanced at me, and I saw the flash of pain in his eyes. Like just a simple look in my direction caused him such agony, he couldn't do it for too long.

It broke my heart. Splintering it into a million pieces.

Still, I wouldn't stop. He hadn't stopped trying to save me, even when his side was burned badly, and he could hardly walk. He'd found the strength to stand and carry me to safety.

Now, it was my turn to carry him.

Moving in, I tried to kiss the corner of his mouth, but he shifted his face away from me.

"Deacon," I pleaded, fighting against the coarseness in my throat. "Talk to me, please."

I knelt beside him and rested my hands on his thigh. When he didn't respond, I continued. "I can't begin to imagine what kind of battles you have to face every day given everything you've witnessed in your life. But what happened yesterday was *not* your fault. It was an accident. And I'm right here." My voice cracked on a sob, the emotions I tried to keep hidden under layers of frustration were breaking through.

"I'm right here," I whispered again. "Can't you at least look at me?"

Those beautiful green eyes finally shifted as his head turned and he looked right at me. "You're not safe with me, Charlie." His voice was low and rough from being silent for so long. "I think we've proven that time and again now."

I shook my head in confusion. "I'm the safest I've ever been with you, Deacon. I trust you with my life."

"And look where that got you yesterday," he snarled.

Shocked by his anger, I recoiled. He blinked and dread consumed his face. "I'm not good. I'm too fucked up."

"Don't say that!" I cried, gripping onto his forearm.

"It's true." Silver lined his eyes, and my heart broke a little more. "Everyone who gets close to me either dies or gets hurt. That's the way it's been for a long time. And there's no way in hell I'm going to let that happen to you. Not anymore."

"So, you just get to choose to end things between us because you're scared? What about what *I* want?" I slid my hands into his and gripped hard. "Deacon, I'm falling in love with you."

His eyes widened in surprise. It was the most reckless thing I'd ever let myself do—falling for him. But there was no helping it. He was the one I wanted.

The tenderness in his eyes stayed there for a few more

moments, then something shifted. He pulled his hands away from mine and his face turned to stone.

"Love doesn't fix things, Charlie. This world isn't some fairyland you've dreamt up in your mind. It's harsh and terrible shit happens every single day." His nostrils flared and I knew he was internally fighting against every word that came out of his mouth. I could see it in his eyes. The way he warred with himself. How his past tarnished his present and future. He was being vicious with me so *I* would be the one to walk away.

"I don't pretend to live in a fairyland world, Deacon. But I do know that we have something special. We've *always* had something special, but you've been too scared to let yourself have it for longer than two seconds. You're running away from a good thing!" The words were harsh. I knew it. I just needed him to see how ridiculous he was being. How fear wasn't going to give him the life he wanted.

But maybe that was it. He carried so much guilt from things that have happened in his past that he doesn't want to let himself be happy.

He looked at me. Silence rang around us as I watched my world unfurl in his eyes right before he said, "This"—he gestured his hands between us—"isn't going to work."

"You don't mean that." Tears spilled down my face as my throat closed tight. "You don't mean that!"

"I do." He cried with me. The green of his eyes was bright as a blade of grass from the gloss of his tears. "If you stay here, you'll get hurt and I can't have that." His hand moved to reach for my face, but he stopped himself. It fell to his lap with a light thud.

"Fight for me," I whispered. "Fight for us." I *needed* confirmation from him. I *needed* him to fight for us.

If he was willing, I'd stay with him through all of this. I'd battle his demons right beside him. But if he wouldn't fight *with* me…

The last shred of my heart scattered to the wind as Deacon rose from his seat and walked past me, leaving me sitting on the floor, hurting worse than the flames from that fire that nearly took my life.

Chapter 24

Charlie

Drops of my tears splashed onto the paper as I finished the note for Deacon. He was still in the garage, hammering away at something. The beats became an endless drone after almost an hour of him taking his emotions out on whatever piece he was working on.

He was out there, all alone, when he should have been in here with me trying to figure out how we could move forward from this.

Echoes of his words played out in my mind. He thought he was no good. That love wouldn't be enough to keep me safe. Through his eyes, the world was an unjust place that took and took and took from him, but I saw the complete opposite. Everyone suffered. He wasn't alone in the pain of being human. Bad things happened to good people all the time. But we had a choice to let the pain of our misfortunes swallow us whole or we could fight and see all the good that surrounded us. The *good* that held us steady through the storms.

I couldn't stand his hammering silence any longer. I needed to get out of this cabin. I needed to get some fresh air and a new perspective on how to get through to him.

Placing my empty hot chocolate mug over the edge of the note so it would stay, I knelt to the floor where Casper was sitting patiently, swishing his tail back and forth.

"I'm going to head into town for a little bit, buddy. I'll be back tonight to feed you dinner." He nudged my hand as I ran it over the top of his head and gave him scratches between his ears.

Despite what was happening between us, I knew Deacon would take care of him in my short absence. I just... My heart couldn't take the weight of the reminders of the joy this cabin held. Everything was a constant reminder of the affection I shared with Deacon and how he was choosing to let it be destroyed by fear.

Rising, I gathered my purse and keys after slipping my coat on. The snow had melted just enough for me to drive. I'd head into town. Maybe walk around for a little bit, then come back.

Back to where I belonged.

If Deacon would still have me.

The bruise on my cheek stung when the winter air hit it as I stepped onto the front porch. A hawk's cry rang loudly above me. Another reminder of how Deacon had risked himself for my happiness when he got Casper down from the tree.

The shards of my heart stuck me deep in my chest. Every part of my soul ached and wept.

It was one thing to make a choice that led to your own heartbreak. But it was quite another to have the choice made for you. My hands were tied and I was running out of options.

Stepping down the porch stairs, the edge of my right boot slipped out from underneath me.

I let out a startled yip as I caught myself with the railing. There was a stitch in my left knee from the quick bend, but otherwise I was alright. Closing my eyes for a moment, I took in a deep breath, feeling the air line my lungs with a subtle sting that broke through the onslaught of endless thoughts. I settled on that feeling, taking another breath in.

Leaving this place—if only for a little while—felt wrong. This cabin and these days with Deacon had etched themselves into my bones. Leaving marks that would be there for the rest of my life. This place was a part of me now and I, a part of it.

Opening my eyes, I knew what needed to be done. We both needed space. Clarity. And that was something I could give us. It was the one thing I was in control of.

Carefully, I bounded down the remaining steps and got into my car.

Turning the key over, the engine sputtered, then died. "Come on," I coaxed it, giving it another try to no avail. "Come on!" I said more sternly this time, turning the key for the third attempt. The engine roared to life, and I sat back in my seat feeling both remorse that the car worked and regret that I was about to leave this place that had so quickly become my home.

"I'll be back within a few hours," I said to myself, shaking my head at the ridiculousness of my emotions. This wasn't a forever goodbye…at least not yet. And maybe that was what made this so damn difficult. With Deacon being so out of sorts and unpredictable, I didn't know if this was the last time I would leave this place feeling a thread of hope that everything would be okay. I was only one half of this puzzle and maybe some time and space wouldn't be enough.

For a moment, the darkness of that future gripped me tightly. Sorrow and grief took hold in my chest and my throat burned with tightness. I hated these feelings. They weren't me. They didn't belong in my space. I didn't want them. Part of me realized in that moment that they weren't part of Deacon either. The darkness had been impressed upon him. The purest version of him was the man I saw loving on Casper. The man whose smile could light up a room. The man who made me feel like I *did* live in a fairyland when I was with him.

I'd seen the light in his eyes that only came from experiencing pure joy. Heard the sound of his laughter like a warm blanket wrapped around me. Felt the comfort of his embrace and how he came alive when those around him felt good.

The thread that ran between us from the first moment we met was illuminated again. Bright and blue and beautiful.

I had to believe this would work. That he just needed some time. Some separation to see things more clearly.

With one final look at the cabin, I backed out of the

driveway. Snow crunched under the tires as I turned the car around and headed to the main road.

The sky was cloudy again today. I missed the sun and the warmth it brought. I was tired of the cold and not being able to spend much time outdoors. I wanted to paint and sip on sweet tea and feel the sun's rays on my face as I listened to Deacon talk to Casper—telling him how much of a rascal he was.

My palms sweat as anxiety clawed up my spine. *Am I doing the right thing by leaving? By giving him space? Should I have just tried talking to him again?*

Ugh!

I was wound so tight, I felt like my brain was going to burst from the effort of thinking too much. I didn't know what to do.

So, I kept driving further into town.

About halfway there, my scar started to itch.

Damnit.

Lost in all the emotions of the day, I'd forgotten to put the salve on it this morning. Lifting my coat and sweater, I scratched at the edges, knowing it was just going to make it itch more, but the monetary relief was much needed.

My mind wandered to the first night Deacon saw my scar and how his eyes had turned molten at the sight. I knew he had traveled back in time, ridden with guilt for not getting me out of the building before the roof collapsed on us.

Another thing that hadn't been his fault, but he'd decided to carry the burden of it anyways.

Splaying my palm against the raised skin, I remembered what it felt like to have him rub the salve over my skin. How my breath caught, and my heart thundered in my chest.

I missed him.

His warmth.

His touch.

His laughter.

His *everything*.

All I wanted was for him to see that what we felt for each other was enough. That we could get through whatever trials came our way. I wanted him to see it so badly, my very bones ached with frustration.

Tears hazed my vision. Letting my sweater and jacket fall back over my ribcage, I wiped away at the water lining my eyes.

Then I felt it.

The car beneath me started to slide as I hit a slick spot on the road. "Oh my god," I breathed, my mind raced with terror.

I took my foot off the gas and remembered not to slam on the breaks, but I was already going fifty miles an hour on the state road. A scream ripped through my throat as the car jolted to the right. My hands shook as I tried to right the steering wheel, shifting it to the left.

Time slowed for an instant before the steering wheel

yanked to the right again, spinning the car—and me with it—around in fast circles. The entire world spun around me as I screamed. I was stuck in a kaleidoscope of white, gray and dark green.

It wouldn't stop.

IT WOULDN'T STOP!

"Oh my god! Oh my god! Oh my god!"

Some part of my brain made out the giant pine trees on the side of the road and how with each spin of the car, they came closer and closer until…CRASH!

The car must have hit one of the trees as an explosion of white smacked me hard in the face.

"Agh," I groaned as I brought my hand up to the side of my face. My fingers grazed something wet, but before I could look down at my fingertips, dizziness swarmed me.

Tinges of black edged my vision. The car was no longer spinning, but it still felt like *I* was as little stars danced across my eyes.

"No," I whispered to myself, trying to hold onto the thread of consciousness I had left. "No."

But my grip loosened, and everything went black.

Chapter 25

Deacon

Sweat dripped from my forehead as I kept hammering away at the distressed dresser. By now, the piece was beyond repair, the dents of my hammer looked more like giant craters and not at all the original inspiration I had in mind.

"Fuck!" I yelled as I tossed the hammer onto my work bench, scattering a carton of nails as it bounced right off and just missed my cheek. I would have deserved it. Maybe having the hammer smack me in the face would knock some sense into me.

I was ruining everything with Charlie, and I didn't know how to reel it back in. Much like the dresser before me, I'd ruined a perfectly good thing because I couldn't keep myself in check. I was lost. Like a ship without sails in the churning ocean—directionless and at the complete mercy of the sea.

Dropping onto my work stool, my head drooped low. I watched as the beads of sweat rolled from my face and onto the concrete floor, splattering.

All I could think about was her. It didn't matter how much hammering I did or how much I berated myself in my mind, Charlie broke through all of it. Her smile. Her cute as sin freckles. The way her lips felt against mine. And how she always seemed to hum a joyous note when I held her.

She was what I wanted.

And maybe I wanted her too badly. I was holding on so tight because I was afraid of what it might be like to lose her.

I thought I'd gotten over it. The images in my mind from the fire had started to decrease. I was finally letting someone in again. I was finally…happy.

Then, seeing that snow fall on top of her… My stomach coiled and I felt sick just thinking about it.

She said it wasn't my fault. But how could it not have been? *I* was the one who threw the snowball. It was because of my actions that she ended up with a giant bruise on her beautiful face. Just one more mark made by my stupidity.

She said it wasn't your fault, I told myself again trying to get the words to stick only to have them land flat on the fucking floor.

"What's wrong with me?" I sank my head into my hands and rubbed my palms into my eyes. "What the fuck is wrong with me?"

Tck, tck, tck.

There was a scratching sound at the door that led back into the house. Popping my head up, I listened a little closer.

Tck, tck, tck.

Cold air started to settle over my skin now that I was no

longer working. I rubbed the old hand towel from my work bench over my arms to get the sweat off before I headed for the door to see what was scraping against it.

When I opened the door, Casper meowed at me. Kneeling, I rubbed under his jaw and he jumped up, pawing at me.

"I know, little rascal. I've fucked up with your mom and I need to make it right."

He meowed louder this time, almost seeming distressed. That's when I realized there were no other sounds in the house. Not footsteps on the floor, or the clattering of dishes while Charlie made hot chocolate. There wasn't the faint sound of a brush striking canvas either.

My heart leapt as I picked Casper up and headed down the hallway back to the main part of the house.

"Charlie!" I called out.

No answer.

I could feel my heartbeat in my ears.

"Charlie!" I said again, this time louder.

Still, nothing.

Picking up my pace, I nearly jogged into the living room to find it empty. I scanned the area and found that her easel and paints were right where she left them.

A long breath left my lungs as I exhaled in relief. She was probably just out on the front porch. Now that the snow had mostly melted down, she was spending a lot more time outside. She'd told me a few nights ago that it was part of her creative process. Just being outside and observing the world before she sat down to paint.

"Let's go find her," I said to Casper who gave me a little

chirp in response. It was time for me to pull my head out of my ass and talk to her. Asshole didn't even begin to cover what I'd been to her the last twenty-four hours. She deserved better and if I had a chance in hell in making this work with her, I was going to have to let her in.

Fully.

No more walls.

No more barriers.

No more running away.

With Casper in tow, I headed for the front door but stopped when I passed the kitchen. Out of the corner of my eye, I noticed a piece of paper under the mug she'd been using all day.

Moving closer, I noticed there was writing on it. Breaking my own rule, I set Casper onto the counter and slipped the note from under the mug.

Deacon,

I'm starting to think that we've both been in this cabin for a little too long, so I'm going to head into town for a bit to get some fresh air...and a better perspective. After what happened yesterday, I know that you're hurting. Some part of you always has the need to protect. I think that's because you've lost so many people at such a young age. You've seen things that no one should have to witness. And because of that, there's a wall around your heart.

At first, I thought the wall was too thick. I'd never be able to get through to you. But since the first day I saw you, there's always been a tether between us—drawing us to one another. Maybe I'm just crazy and have had my parents instill too much woo-woo stuff in me, but I know in the deepest parts of my heart that I belong here with you. Once you showed me the true version of yourself, the one you keep hidden behind that wall, I knew you were it for me.

There is no one in this world I could feel the same for.

You're the one my heart yearns for. The one I want to hold me. ... To love me.

God, I hope I'm not crazy and you feel the same. But even if you don't, I can feel good knowing that you know exactly what you mean to me.

And if I'm not crazy and you do feel the same, I also want you to know I will be here. Right by your side, helping to chase away the darkness.

Love,

Charlie

P.S. - I really hope I'm not crazy. Xoxo.

My heart clamored in my chest as I looked out the window and noticed there were flurries of snowflakes in the air. The ground was still white with snow and her car wasn't next to my truck anymore.

Looking back to the note in my hands, I nearly crumpled the paper from frustration. I'd pushed her away and now she was gone. Out there. Where the roads were slick, and snow was starting to come down again.

Casper chirped at me and nuzzled his face into my hands.

"Don't worry, little guy. I'm going to go get our girl."

Snowflakes hit the windshield, creating a white cast that was difficult to see the road through. The pine trees lining both sides of the state road blurred past me as I sank my foot farther against the gas pedal.

"Come on," I murmured to myself, trying to be careful on the road but needing to go fast enough to find her in town. There was no way in hell I was going to let her drive back alone with the weather in this condition.

Pressing down a little more on the accelerator, my chest buzzed with energy when the back tires of my old pickup truck fishtailed along the road.

"Shit!" Taking my foot off the gas, I righted the steering wheel, and the tires found traction again.

It wasn't a good sign. If my truck's mud tires were having a difficult time keeping to the road, there was no way her tiny car was doing better.

"Come on, Sunshine. Please be safe." I sent a silent prayer out that I'd find her before she turned around. I'd already fucked up so much and this was my chance to make things right. The first step in the right direction.

In her letter, she'd written that I was the one she wanted. All I could think of was how I needed the chance to tell her the same thing. I was ready to let her in. To show her all the dark pieces of my past and how they've corrupted my entire sense of the world. And how her light showed me what could be possible if I just let myself be fucking happy for once.

"I promise, Charlie... I promise I'll do better," I whispered into the empty cabin of my truck, hoping she could feel my heart through the thread that had bound us together from the moment we met seven years ago.

She'd called it woo-woo stuff, but I knew it was real. Maybe part of me—in the beginning—had thought she was crazy. But I felt it pull me down the road toward her. The line was taut, like she was calling to me.

I just had to find her.

The truck nearly rocked side-to-side with how fast the windshield wipers were working. I was nearly to the edge of town when I saw smoke rising along the side of the road. Leaning forward in my seat, I squinted at where the smoke was coming from and noticed there was a white sedan lodged against a tree in the snow.

Panic rose in my chest as my stomach churned. It was Charlie's car. "Oh my god. No! No!" I yelled into the silence as I slammed my foot on the pedal, not caring about my own safety, just needing to get to her.

The car was about a quarter mile down the road and with each passing second, my heart beat faster in my chest. Like a wild animal, the pounding was relentless as bile coated the back of my throat.

If she's hurt... No! I wouldn't allow myself to think about it. She had to be okay. There was no other option.

Skidding to a halt next to her car, I threw the shifter into park and jumped out.

"Charlie!" I screamed her name as icy snow bit my cheeks.

Black smoke rose from the engine of her car and the whole area smelled like gas.

"Fuck."

As I rounded the trunk of her sedan, I noticed the entire front was smashed against a giant pine tree. My feet nearly fell from beneath me as I slipped on a patch of ice running toward the driver side of the car.

"Charlie!" I yelled again and didn't hear a response when I saw that her head was laid back against her seat, the airbag deployed in front of her.

"No. No! No!" Every muscle in my body shook as I saw the light of my existence sitting there—lifeless.

Yanking on the handle, I screamed her name again. She didn't move and that's when I noticed there was a giant gash on the right side of her face, blood matted her hair. She was hurt. And I couldn't get to her.

Images of Charlie wrapped up in that tiny damp towel as she tried to shield herself from the flames flickered to life in my mind. How her bright blue eyes were hopeful when she looked up at me. And the way her small arms clung to my neck as I walked us out of her apartment.

All of it came back to me in a rush that nearly knocked the air from my lungs. It felt like I was back there. Both of us surrounded by fire. Desperate to get away from the heat.

And just like that, the moment was gone and I was back in the cold snow, trying to work the door handle open to no avail.

"Fuck!" I screamed, raking my hands through my hair. That's when I noticed Charlie moved and her eyes fluttered open. My heart skipped a beat, then started racing again.

Bending over, I knocked gently on the window. Careful not to startle her. "Charlie," I said her name again.

Dazed, she took a moment to shift her gaze toward me. When she finally noticed me, she twisted toward the door, putting both hands on the glass window. A wince had her nose scrunching.

"Deacon." I saw her mouth move, but I could hardly hear her through the window.

"Can you get the door open, Sunshine?" My voice cracked as I took in the wound on her forehead. It was deeper than I originally thought. I needed to get her the fuck out of this car. I needed to have her in my arms.

Still slow to move, I watched patiently as she fiddled with the door handle then looked up panicked.

"It's okay," I said calmly, reverting to my decades of training. "Is it locked?"

Her blue eyes assessed the arm of the door where all the switches were, and she pressed the button to unlock it. Then she tried the door handle again and it still didn't work.

"I'm going to try the other doors, just hang on tight."

She nodded then I moved to the driver's rear door and jostled the handle. Nothing. Quickly jogging around, the doors on the passenger side wouldn't open either.

"Damnit!" I slammed the palm of my hand against the metal frame. That's when I heard the whip of flame ignite and felt the heat of my worst nightmare against my skin. The engine had caught fire. And Charlie was still stuck.

"Deacon!" I heard her scream this time and I looked through the passenger window to find her bright eyes alert with fear.

No. This isn't happening. This isn't fucking happening.

Frozen. I couldn't think or move. All I could see was the terror on her face. Ice moved through my veins keeping me stuck as my own horror took hold.

Think, Deacon. Do *something.*

There was a loud pop sound from the engine as another bright flame burst from the right side. It broke my haze, and I burst into action.

"Hold on!" I called out to her, and she nodded vigorously from shock.

Running as fast as my legs would take me, I headed for my truck and opened the toolbox in the bed. Grabbing the crowbar, I ran back to Charlie's car and told her to lean away from the door.

She did and I jammed the crowbar into the crack where the door met the frame. Metal scraped and cracked as I pushed the crowbar back against the frame. It was starting to work, but the fire was getting closer to the windshield, bright red flames bursting out through the seam of the hood.

"Deacon, hurry!" Charlie yelled as she pulled on her seatbelt. "I'm stuck!"

Time was running both at lightning speed and as slow as a snail as I jammed the crowbar back into the door seam again and again, pulling my way down the edge until I was able to get it nestled through the small opening near the lock.

The sharp smell of gasoline strengthened around me. If the fire got to the gas tank...

No.

Focus.

With one more stab of the crowbar, the door released, and I was in. Charlie let out a strangled whimper as she threw her arms around me. "Deacon," she gasped my name like it was the only thing keeping her together.

I nearly broke down right then, but we weren't out of the woods yet.

"Come on, Sunshine. We gotta get you out of this thing before the fire spreads."

"The seatbelt is stuck." She pulled at the gray belt across her chest with a panicked gesture.

With a snick, I slid my knife out of my pocket and flipped it open. Right before I put it to the belt, a loud groaning sound came from the front of the car.

"Deacon?" Charlie's voice wavered as we both looked forward to where flames were now consistently shooting out of the seams of the hood. The dashboard was radiating heat that was already starting to tinge my skin.

Looking Charlie straight in her eyes, I said, "We need to move now!"

She held the seat belt out for me as I moved my knife over the fabric, sawing it as quickly as I could. The fabric was thick though and with each saw of my knife, the fire spread quicker.

Charlie started gasping for air through sobs that wracked her body. The tears came for me too. I couldn't lose her. She was everything. She was *everything*!

Only a few threads left. Sweat spread over my forehead from the heat and anxiety.

Four threads.

Three.

Two.

Yes!

Throwing my knife somewhere behind me, I rushed to get Charlie out of the seat. I could tell she was feeling weak when I wrapped my arms around her waist and pulled, she could hardly keep her arms draped over my neck.

"Almost there, Sunshine. Stay with me. Please…stay with me."

The part of the belt that was over her lap snagged. There was no time. The fire was melting parts of the dashboard now. Rushed, I yanked the seat belt through the feed loop. Once. Twice. Finally, it released, and Charlie fell onto my chest as I landed backwards in the snow.

I held her close to me, burying my nose in her hair. The sweet scent of vanilla mixed with the tang of iron from the blood running down the side of her face hit my nostrils.

But she was safe. In my arms, where she belonged.

"Are you okay?" I asked, lifting her chin.

Her eyelids were starting to droop as she whispered, "I don't feel so good."

"Okay, Sunshine. Just stay with me a little longer. We need to get to my truck so we can get to the hospital."

"Okay," she groaned as I gingerly held her ribcage and maneuvered us up together.

Just as I got us both to stand, I saw the bright light emanate from behind her. Before I had a chance to tell her to run, Charlie's entire car burst into flames with an explosion that sent her flying into my chest.

Snow crunched beneath me. Pain shot up my spine from where I landed on my tailbone. It was all I could do to wrap my arms around Charlie and hold her tight against me, but when we both went down, I felt her slip from my grasp.

A sharp ring spliced my eardrums as I looked around, trying to get my bearings. When I turned to my right, I saw Charlie about two feet away from me. The wound over her brow was seeping blood again. Her eyes were closed, and her mouth was slightly ajar.

Blood rushed through my veins so loudly I could hear it in my ears as the ringing slowly faded and I started crawling over to her.

"Charlie!" My throat was thick from the adrenaline, her name coming out hushed.

She didn't respond. Not even a flinch of recognition of my voice.

I held her face in my hands, gently patting her cheeks to jumpstart her nervous system. "Come on, baby." I barely felt the hot tears rolling down my face.

"Charlie, come on. Wake up for me." I kissed her lips, the metallic taste of blood hitting my tongue.

"Come on!" I screamed. The silent, snowy earth swallowed the sound like neither one of us were here and my heart wasn't being ripped from my chest.

Placing my head on her chest, I heard the faint breath in her lungs and felt the subtle beat of her heart when I pressed my fingers to her wrist. She was with me. She was here. But if I didn't get her to a hospital quickly…

Using all the strength I had left in my shaking body; I carried her to my truck and laid her down in the back seat of the cab. Pressing a final kiss to her forehead, I whispered, "You're my sunshine, Charlie. Please don't leave me in the darkness."

Chapter 26

Charlie

Bright white light flooded my vision as I cracked my eyes open.

Everything hurt.

I thought I groaned, but I couldn't be sure because my ears felt like they were full of water.

I blinked again. Squinting my eyes tight enough so that the light didn't hurt too much, but wide enough for me to see that I was in a car.

Panic seized my chest as I realized what happened.

Crash.

Fire.

Explosion.

Deacon.

Tears came and there was no holding back the aching sob that wracked my body—making everything hurt worse.

"Deacon!" I tried to scream, but the tightness in my

throat strangled the effort I put in, making his name sound quiet and gargled.

"I'm here." Deacon's voice came through like he was far away, but then I felt his hand squeeze mine, realizing he'd been holding it the entire time.

"I've got you, Charlie. I've got you."

Something about the way he said it made me relax. Like there was nothing else I needed to worry about.

The heaviest fatigue I'd ever felt before settled so deep in my body, I could feel it in my bones. Flashes of light and darkness flickered through the window.

He has me. I'm safe.

I'm safe.

I'm safe.

The words replayed over and over again in my mind until I closed my eyes and let the darkness come again.

Chapter 27

Deacon

"Sarah!" I cried into the phone.

"Deacon, what's the matter?" Her voice was sharp with concern. "What's going on?"

"I…" With me back against the wall outside of Charlie's hospital room, I slid down until I hit the floor.

I can't do this. I can't lose her. I can't fucking lose her!

"There was an accident. Charlie…" Just saying her name out loud had my chest hurting so badly, I thought I was going to fucking die.

"Where are you, Deacon?" There was a rustling sound on the other end of the phone, like Sarah was getting out of bed or something.

"Hospital." The single word burned in my throat.

"We're on our way."

"Thank you, Sarah," I whispered into the phone. It was all I could muster before I broke down and let the weight of everything that happened consume me.

There was a slight lift in my chest when Sarah and Ranger rounded the corner of the nurses' station.

They came. I needed them…and they came.

It wasn't lost on me how this singular moment had already transformed my entire life. The walls I'd built so high around me had turned to ash on the ground the moment I saw Charlie's car on the side of the road. And those ashes scattered to the wind when I saw her hurt. There was nothing left of the man I was before. The only thing that mattered was getting her to come back to me.

"Deacon!" Sarah jogged toward me. I rose from where I'd made my permanent seat outside of Charlie's room. The doctors were still working on her. They'd threatened to call security and kick me out if I didn't leave her bedside. One of the nurses had walked me out and calmed me down right before I'd called Sarah.

I hugged Sarah fiercely when she crossed the final foot between us. Ranger came in right after and wrapped his arms around the both of us.

My friends.

My *family*.

Why had I closed myself off to them for so long?

Regret threatened my sanity, but I shoved it out. I was here now. I was *different* now. I could start over…I hoped.

The three of us held onto one another. I needed this. I

needed *them*. I'd been broken for so long that I'd forgotten to look up and see that there were people right in front of me who had my back. Who would show up when I called them. Who would help me when I needed them.

As we parted, Sarah slid her arm around Ranger's waist and she asked, "What happened, Deacon?"

Emotion clogged my throat again, making it difficult for me to speak. So, I took in a deep breath and tried to let my muscles loosen. It worked. Slightly.

"I fucked up, Sarah." Tears welled in my eyes again. "I fucked up really bad."

She reached for my hand and squeezed it.

Then, Ranger spoke. "You're a good guy, Deacon. So, whatever happened…we can fix this together."

He gave me a smile and it made me think that he might be right. No matter what happened, I could fix everything between Charlie and me.

Then, like I'd always done, my mind went to darker places. Worries of whether or not I would have the chance. If she would make it out of this nightmare okay. Or if I would be the cause of losing the most important person in my life.

I shook my head, trying to eradicate the thoughts from my mind. I had to hold onto hope.

"She's the one, isn't she?" Sarah asked, still holding my hand.

The question struck me like a blow to the gut.

I knew she wasn't just talking about the scar on my chest and that Charlie had a role in that story. She was saying that

Charlie was my person. The one I wanted to spend the rest of my days with.

Pausing, I thought about everything Charlie and I had been through together already. How deeply I'd always been affected by her. In the beginning, it wasn't just because she'd been a reminder of one of my greatest failures.

No.

When Charlie showed up on my front doorstep, I'd been stricken by her existence. Because she made me *feel*. Just her presence had broken through my barriers, and they were made of fucking steel. No one got past them. Except for Charlie.

Looking at Sarah I nodded, feeling the weight of that admission. For so long, I thought I was going to end up alone. That I *deserved* to be alone.

But that thread that had bound us together since the beginning had brought her to me weeks ago. I had to believe it would bring her back to me now.

"I think I knew it back then." I looked at Ranger and explained, "Seven years ago, when I was back in Charlotte, I saved Charlie from her apartment building when it caught on fire."

I thought back to that time and how even in the midst of a life-threatening situation, she had taken my breath away. With her crystal blue eyes and bright red hair. God. If I was honest with myself, some part of me had probably loved her even back then.

"She was the most beautiful woman I'd ever seen and she…terrified me. When we were both injured and wound up in the same hospital, I didn't visit her. She was on the oppo-site side of the floor. I knew exactly what room she was in, but I didn't visit her. I…couldn't."

Ranger gripped my shoulder and looked me straight in the eyes. "Sometimes the thing we want most in life scares the hell out of us. It's embarrassing to admit the number of times I wanted to talk to Sarah but didn't because I was scared of ruining it. Scared that I wasn't good enough for her."

"Yeah," I laughed, remembering the phone call Sarah and I shared when she realized she wanted Ranger. It took them a while to figure things out, but now they were as solid as stone. Unbreakable.

"It seemed like fate wanted me to be scared because of all the towns she could have ended up in, she chose Pebble Brook Falls."

"Does she know how you feel about her?" Sarah asked.

"I denied it at first. But then…I just couldn't. I thought I would be able to keep my distance and ignore my feelings, but I failed epically at that." They both looked at me like they completely understood what I was saying.

"After a pipe burst in the Badger Creek cabin, I offered for her to stay at my place for the night. The next morning, we woke up to being snowed in and I didn't have a buffer between me and her anymore. I couldn't hide it. She's…" I felt the tightening of my throat again as another pang of pure agony shot through my heart. "She's everything I never knew I needed. Fuck!" I raked my hand through my hair, tightening my grip on the strands so I didn't punch a hole in the damn wall.

"Hey, hey, hey," Sarah's soothing voice kept me grounded. I was losing it and without her and Ranger here…I didn't know what I'd be capable of.

"Have the doctor's given any updates?" Ranger asked, gripping my shoulder again to steady me.

I looked at him—at my friend. Ranger had his own past that I knew nearly kept him apart from Sarah. If there was anyone who understood what I was feeling right now, it was him.

Scraping a palm over my jaw, I tried to settle down. It was hard, when my raging heartbeat was a constant reminder of my distress. Every ounce of my soul wanted to be in there with her, making sure she was okay. Telling her how much I loved her and how fucking sorry I was for making her feel like she had to get away.

"They did a CT scan on her head to see if there was a brain injury. She was in and out of consciousness on our way here, but when we arrived, she wasn't alert."

Sarah raised her fingers to her mouth, trying to cover the shock.

"What happened?" she whispered.

I filled them in on the snowball fight and how my error led Charlie to being crushed beneath a pile of snow. Then how I freaked out and pushed her away, after I'd already let her in.

"I just couldn't face her. Every loss I've experienced has left a brutal fucking scar on me and I let those scars eat away at my sanity. After she got hurt in the snow, I thought she was better off without me. So, I shut her out. Today, she wrote me a letter telling me that I was her person and that she knew we needed some space for clarity. On her way to town…she must have hit an ice patch because I found her car totaled on the side of the road."

"Oh, Deacon," Sarah said at the same time Ranger whispered, "Shit."

"If I would have just let her in. If I would have just—" My voice cracked along with my heart.

"No." Sarah grasped my arms and dipped her head low, forcing me to look at her. "Don't you even say it, Deacon. This is not your fault. Accidents happen and there's no way you could have known. Don't do that to yourself."

"She's right, Deacon. The only way forward is to forgive yourself and move on. I'm sure Charlie wouldn't want you beating yourself up like this."

I thought about it. My sunshine. The light of my life… She was so kind, thoughtful and positive. Ranger spoke truthfully. There was no way Charlie would want me to carry the burden of guilt.

I could picture it now, if I told her the car accident was my fault. She'd put her dainty hand on her hip and glower at me, saying something like, *"You think you have control over every little thing in life?"*

She'd put me in my place.

Just like she'd done every time I'd shown her my ugly side.

"So, what do I do now?" I asked them right when the door to Charlie's room opened and the doctor stepped out.

My heart stopped beating. Then it jolted again, banging hard against my ribs.

He was a tall man. Looked to be about mid-fifties with dark as midnight eyes. There was a blankness to his face that I knew he'd probably mastered over the years from having to deliver difficult news. I saw it on the guys' I had served with when the losses started piling up.

"Are you Ms. Banks' family?"

"Yes." I didn't hesitate for a second.

Out of the corner of my eye, I saw Sarah and Ranger step closer to me. My jacket moved as Sarah placed her hand at my back.

The doctor nodded at us. "She's stable. For now."

"What do you mean for now?" The words were out before I even registered what I'd said. Sarah's palm flattened against my mid-back, rubbing up and down.

On a deep inhale, the doctor continued. "She had a pretty significant contusion on her forehead. It looks like she was struck by something during the accident."

"The windshield of her car was shattered in the middle." My voice sounded far away, like I was already starting to retreat inward. I focused on Sarah's hand at my back to keep me grounded.

"That makes sense then. It was likely a shard of glass that struck her on impact. Was there anything else that happened once you got to her? Any other signs of head injury?" the doctor asked me.

"The car was on fire when I pulled her out. Before I had a chance to get her to my truck, the fire reached the gas tank and exploded. We both fell a few feet backward."

He nodded, his dark eyes darting back and forth as he gazed at the floor like he was thinking.

"What is it?" I asked. This whole hanging on by a thread thing wasn't working for me. The woman of my dreams was in that room, and I needed to know what the fuck was going on.

He looked back at me and with a steady voice that severed my nerves, he said, "While her CT scan was clean, she hasn't regained consciousness yet."

Time stopped. The world caved in on me. The weight of his words was unbearable. I just stared at him. "She's not awake yet?"

"I'm afraid not."

Some distant part of me felt Sarah wrap her arms around me. I stopped breathing. I couldn't see through the haze of tears. Couldn't think through the swarm of fear in my mind.

"What does that mean?" I felt my lips move but barely heard the words that came from my own mouth.

"It means we wait and hope her brain heals."

The fate of my life shifted in an instant. The light my woman brought into this world was snuffed out like the blow of breath to a candle's flame.

Darkness descended and I knew I was never going to be the same ever again.

Chapter 28

Deacon

"Sir."

There was a jostling of my right arm that woke me from a deep sleep. Blinking my eyes slowly, I looked up at the person whose hand was still over my forearm.

A woman in blue scrubs, but not the same woman from last night.

"Sir, why don't you go home and get some better rest?"

Sitting up straight, I felt the ache in my back from being hunched over the edge of Charlie's hospital bed all night. Her hand still rested in mine, but when I looked at her beautiful face, her eyes were still closed.

My heart sank. She wasn't awake yet.

"Have there been any changes?" My voice was froggy from sleep. I ran my hand over my face and wiped at my eyes, trying to get them to focus better.

The nurse's face was solemn. "Not yet. But I promise

you, she's in good hands. Dr. Schneider has been checking on her case every hour."

"Okay. That's good."

"Why don't you go home for a little while. Get a shower, rest a little. If anything changes, I'll make sure to call you right away."

I sat there. My body turning to stone. The thought of leaving her all alone in this hospital bed made my stomach coil. What if she woke up and I wasn't here? What if she thought I'd left her? What if…

"No." I shook my head. "I can't leave her."

The nurse knelt beside me and patted my arm. "In order to take care of the ones we love; we need to take care of ourselves. I don't mean to offend, but you look worse for wear. It'll do you both some good if you go home for a little while and take care of yourself."

Love.

Yes.

I did love Charlie. It was unquestionable. But it was the first time I'd had a moment for it to really sink in.

I'd never loved a woman before. Not really. The feeling was overwhelming.

I looked back at her. She seemed so peaceful. Her long auburn lashes fanned out over her freckled cheeks. I reached up to touch the silken strands of her hair. She looked just like she did every morning when we woke up next to one another.

Peaceful.

Angelic.

"I can't," I whispered, drawing my hand up to cup the side of her cheek.

"Okay." The nurse patted my arm again. "Is there anything you need to take care of there? Anything you might want to call and ask a friend to help with? I've found people often forget important things during a time like this."

As I stroked Charlie's hand with my thumb, the nurse's words hit hard. "Casper! Shit!"

Panic rose along my spine as I remembered the little rascal had been without us for nearly twenty-four hours.

"Who's Casper, dear?" the nurse asked.

"He's our cat." I looked at the older woman and she smiled at me.

"Is there someone you can call to have them check on him?"

I knew Sarah and Ranger would be more than willing to check on him, but I wasn't sure how he would react around strangers. Charlie had mentioned that I was the first person besides her who he really connected with. He'd been skittish around everyone else.

Charlie would kill me if something happened to him. The last thing we needed was for him to get scared and dart out of the house if Sarah and Ranger checked on him.

"No, I need to be the one to check on him."

The nurse moved to the side to let me out of the corner of the room where my chair was, but I stayed put. "She's stable? Nothing will happen to her while I'm gone?" I'd gone through years of medical training in the military and even more after that when I became a firefighter paramedic. I knew Charlie's status and everything it meant, but I needed reassurance. Needed someone else to tell me that the woman I loved would be okay if I left.

"Yes, she's stable. Just think of it as her taking an extra-long nap to give her brain some rest. Like I said, I'll call you if anything changes."

I looked back at Charlie and felt my chest cave in a little more. I didn't want to leave her. But I also knew that Casper had held her together when she'd lost all her friends. He was the most important thing in her life aside from her parents. She had trusted me with him, and I needed to make sure he was okay.

Slowly rising from the chair, I straightened my back and did a few side stretches to even out the kinks. Then, I leaned forward and pressed a kiss to Charlie's forehead.

"I'll be back soon, Sunshine. You just keep resting."

There was no response. Not that I expected there to be one, but the silence was still deafening.

Turning toward the nurse, I said, "Let me give you my cell phone number." She took it down and after one final look at Charlie, I headed home.

By the time I got home, fatigue had almost taken me out from the adrenaline dump that still had my hands shaking on the steering wheel. I didn't sleep at all last night as I sat by Charlie's side and watched her rest. All I could think about was all the moments we hadn't shared together yet. How badly I wanted to take her in my truck and ride through my property at sunset–seeing the glimmering light over the rolling hills. To see how her red hair would look in the summer sun. What her freckled skin might feel like against mine when I showed her the nearby lake, and we went swimming together.

There were countless experiences I wanted to share with her. But most of all, I just wanted to hear her laughter. I wanted to hear the sound of my name passing her lips. I wanted to *talk* to her.

Still sitting in my truck, I stared at the front door. I knew what I would find inside.

Quiet emptiness.

Charlie had brought such life to my house—she'd made it a home. Without her, I didn't want to be in it. I didn't want to know what life might feel like without her.

I slammed my hand against the edge of the steering wheel. "Fuckkkk!" I screamed—the strain of not having used my voice much today sliced into my throat.

What lesson was hidden in this torment? And why did Charlie have to be the one to suffer for it? Why did this have to happen?

Climbing out of my truck, I had to put my shit aside and make sure Casper was okay. My footsteps were heavy as I trudged through the remaining bits of snow and up the steps to the porch. My shaking hand hovered above the doorknob. I didn't want to go in there alone. I didn't want to hear the silence knowing that Charlie might never come back to me—

even when she did wake up. She might choose to stay far, far away.

It was the consequence of my actions. A fate I would have to deal with if she wanted it. Still, I couldn't bear the thought of it.

Letting loose a long exhale, I finally opened the door and stepped inside.

Casper's little feet ticked across the floor as he bounded toward me. Heat assaulted my eyes when I saw him and his sweet little face. He let out a long meow in greeting as he stood and placed his front paws on my pant leg.

Kneeling, I scooped him up. "Hey, little rascal." He bumped his head into my chin and started purring. "I know, I know, I missed you too."

His little white face pulled away and he looked over my shoulder. I knew exactly who he was looking for. It made my chest burn. "She's okay, buddy. She's just resting right now, but I promise she'll be back soon." I hoped it was a promise that wouldn't fall flat. I hoped with all of the broken pieces of my heart that her brain would heal, and she'd make her way back to us.

Holding him close, I inhaled deeply. There was a faint scent of Charlie's signature vanilla on his coat from when she'd cuddled him yesterday morning. It made me long for her warmth even more.

Setting him down, he followed me into the kitchen where his food and water bowl was under the island. He still had plenty of water, but the food was empty. Grabbing the bag from the pantry, I filled it to the brim, and he went to town.

"That's it." I stroked his back. "Make sure you eat it all and I'll give you some more." His head popped up for just a moment as he blinked slowly at me. Then, he dove his face back into the food.

I had to wait until he was done before heading back to the hospital, so I could give him some more to have for dinner. Walking into the living room, I stopped at the back of the couch. Images of all the nights we'd shared together in front of the fireplace whirled through my mind.

Her laughter had brought so much life to the space. And her touch had brought so much life to *me*. I wanted her back in my arms. Fuck. I *needed* to feel her again. Needed to know that she would still want me after everything that happened. That I hadn't ruined the only good thing in my life.

Letting my head drop low, I closed my eyes. I was so damn tired from the adrenaline surge and my mind unwilling to stop thinking. But I knew sleep would evade me, even if I tried. The only way I could get some shut eye was back at the hospital by her side.

Glancing over my shoulder, Casper was still mowing down on his food. When I looked forward again, my gaze settled on the door leading to the garage. I walked over to it and opened it, the woodsy smell of sawdust and raw wood creeped into my nostrils.

More images of Charlie enter my mind. Mostly of how excited she'd been to see my work and all the questions she'd asked, wanting to know the story behind each piece.

I moved through the space, feeling the void in my chest

in her absence. It had taken the threat of her being taken away for me to realize just how badly I needed her.

I hated that.

I hated that it took her being in a near-fatal accident for me to let my walls fall. To know that by having her by my side, I could face my past and everything that came with it.

I wished I could turn back time and make things right, but I couldn't.

All I had was the future and I was damn sure going to make the best of it.

Heading toward the back of the garage, I saw the half-finished bench she'd fallen in love with. There was no part of me that saw a point in finishing it, knowing I was going to be alone for the rest of my life. But when she came in here and I saw her bright blue eyes glow with excitement, I knew some part of me had made that bench for her—for *us*.

It was just waiting. For her to come along and turn my world upside down. To show me everything I'd been missing.

After running a hand over the seat of the bench, I smacked it against my pant leg. Dust flew everywhere, but there was a thread of hope that blossomed in my chest as I took in the vine and orchid details I'd carved into the back well over a year ago.

It was Charlie's favorite piece, and I had all the energy to burn. When she woke up—and I knew she would—I wanted her to have something to come home to. A gift to show her how much she meant to me.

And most of all, to tell her that I'd finally found someone to sit on the bench with me.

She was my woman. The one I wanted to spend the rest of my life with…if she'd have me.

Grabbing my whittling tools off the work bench, I made sure my phone was turned all the way up and then got to work.

Chapter 29

Deacon

The heart monitor beeped consistently next to Charlie's bed. Two more days had passed since the accident, and I knew I was going to have to call her parents tomorrow if she didn't wake up by then. I'd been putting it off, not wanting the first time I talked to them to include delivering the news that their daughter was officially in a coma.

They'd hate me.

And I couldn't start out our relationship like that.

Maybe it was selfish. Not wanting them to know quite yet… It was more so not having the strength to tell them that I'd chased off their daughter with my fears of losing her, only to have that fear become my near reality.

Maybe I should have called them already, but I just couldn't do it yet.

I'd give myself one more day.

I just needed her to wake up before then.

During the morning and evening breaks I'd spent

checking on Casper, I'd finished the rest of Charlie's bench. After a coat of stain and sealant, I'd placed it on the front porch. Right where she wanted it. I couldn't wait to see her face when I finally got to bring her home and show her the work I'd done on it.

I couldn't wait to hear her voice. For her laughter to fill up the space in the living room. To hold her beneath the blankets in front of the fireplace.

A knot lodged in my throat as I lifted her hand to my lips.

She'd asked me to open up for her. To let her in. It was about time I tried.

"I told you about the friend I lost overseas. The one who loved doing puzzles. But what I didn't tell you is that there were three more guys after him. My closest friends. Guys I'd known since basic training, and we all got lucky enough to go all the way together.

"Bryant was the funniest fucker you'd ever meet. It didn't matter if we were stuck on a mountain side being shot at, he'd always have a joke that took the edge off the situation. He was the one who kept us all grounded. To this day, I don't think I've ever laughed as hard as I did with him.

"And Michael"—I rubbed at my eyes with the back of my hand—"was so damn smart, none of us understood how he didn't get assigned to intelligence or move up the ranks faster. Looking back now, I realize how he hid how smart he was from everyone else. I don't think he wanted the responsibility of making decisions for other people. He just wanted to serve his country and make his father proud. He didn't care about getting awarded with higher positions. He was just a good fucking guy." My voice cracked as emotion lodged in my throat. But there was a lightness taking hold in my heart. Like telling Charlie these things somehow made them easier to carry. It felt like I could finally remember my fallen brothers for the amazing men they were and not have to forget about them because the pain was too much to bear.

I could do this—I realized—with her by my side, I could do this.

With a smile on my face, I sniffed and wiped another stray tear off my face. "Jackson…oh, Sunshine, you would have loved him. He was so quick-witted and a complete smart-ass. He got us in trouble more times than I can count but seeing him get under our sergeants' skin was worth every fucking push-up. Honestly, he would have been the one to tell me I'd been a jackass about you. That I should have gotten my shit together and found you in your hospital room after that fire and told you how I'd felt right then and there."

I snorted, thinking back to how stupid I was. How much time fear had robbed me. "He would have told me to get on one knee and beg you to marry me or he'd do it himself. He…" Fresh tears welled in my eyes, clouding my vision. Squeezing my eyes shut, I felt them move down my cheeks.

When I opened my eyes, I said, "He was my best friend, Charlie. We'd been through hell and back together. Four deployments. Shit with his parents. I can't even tell you how many bar fights he had my back in." I laughed.

Then the sorrow of the loss took hold again. Threatening to draw me back to my old ways of silence and indifference.

It would be so easy to go back there. To let myself become numb and angry. To start building that wall again.

But I looked at Charlie's beautiful face and knew I couldn't be that version of myself anymore. It was time to be brave. It was time to move forward.

"I wish they were with me right now," I whispered. "And maybe in a way they are. Giving me the strength I need to be the man you deserve. To be the man I should have been all along."

I swept a strand of hair from the side of her face then kissed her knuckles. "Come back to me, Sunshine." This time I didn't wipe the tears away. "Come share your light with me."

CHARLIE

A distant roar of rushing water surrounded me as the perpetual darkness faded to a light glow. Squinting my eyes to see, I looked around.

Tall pine trees.

A wooden dock.

Crunchy snow beneath my feet.

…the cabin.

Thick mist clouded everything around me, still making it incredibly difficult to see. But I was there—at the place where inspiration struck, and I was able to reconnect with myself. It was my home. The one I'd made for myself. A part of the one I'd made with *him*.

A deep ache settled into the bones of my ribs at the thought of Deacon.

Where is he?

I moved toward the dock, freshly nailed boards remained sturdy beneath my feet. A smile crept over my lips as I remembered him taking hours to rebuild the dock because he kept looking up at me while I was painting. Not that I'd ever admit to him that I saw him doing that, but it was nice knowing that I had an effect on him, even back then.

I looked over my shoulder, back at the cabin that was now shrouded in the hazy moisture hanging in the air. The small back patio was empty. No sign of Deacon anywhere.

I sat in one of the chairs on the dock, knowing that he'd make his way to me eventually. We were bound to one another. Wherever one went, the other would follow. Closing my eyes, I let the sounds of the water below me soothe the pain of his absence. I hated when he wasn't with me.

For a few moments, I concentrated on the rushing rapids until there was a distant voice that called to me.

"...loved doing puzzles."

Deacon.

My heart stampeded in my chest. I'd know his voice anywhere.

Whipping my head around, I looked to see where he was but couldn't make much of anything out through the fog.

"Deacon!" I called to him, my voice coming out like a

strangled whisper. I yelled his name again, but it didn't go far.

"Looking back now, he hid how smart..." There he was again. Talking to me. He was trying to tell me something.

Straining my ears, I moved off the dock and away from the loud river.

"Where are you?" My words echoed this time, moving through the trees like rustling wind.

"Jackson...oh, Sunshine, you would have loved him. He was so quick-witted and a complete smart-ass. He got us in trouble more times than I can count, but seeing him get under our sergeants' skin was worth every fucking push-up..."

My mind whirled as I spun around, trying to figure out where he was. Because... Because I knew exactly what he was doing.

Emotion swelled in my chest.

He was letting me in.

He was telling me about the friends he lost and the life they'd shared together. He was... Bringing my fingers to my trembling lips, I laughed out a cry. Not one of pain, but of happiness.

He was letting me in!

"Where are you, baby?" I started moving around the backyard of the tiny cabin, peering through the thick brush of the trees to the left and right. Then I ran up the steps to the back porch and jostled the door handle.

It was locked.

I peeked through the windows but couldn't see through them.

That's when I heard his voice again—bright as day. "Come back to me, Sunshine. Come share your light with me."

The mist around me started to clear and I could feel the warmth of a beautiful blue light surrounding me—it was *our* light.

The thread that had bonded Deacon and I together from the start. The calling of our souls, forging us as one.

Slowly turning around, I gasped when I saw him. Radiating the purest light I'd ever seen, Deacon smiled at me. His lips pulled wide—completely unabandoned. The fullest version of himself was a sight to behold. Heavenly. Happy. With no more room for the sorrow that had haunted him for so long.

He was…*magnificent*.

One step forward. Two. I walked toward him until his chest nearly brushed mine.

The most piercing green eyes I'd ever seen gazed at me like I was the most precious thing in the world. His fingers moved to brush a strand of hair from my face.

So warm.

So gentle.

His touch felt like…

"It's time to come home." His deep voice was a soft blanket over my fragile nerves.

"You found me."

His head tilted to the side slightly. "I'll always find you, Sunshine. Always."

He cradled my cheek in his palm. "Are you ready?"

I looked up into his devastatingly beautiful eyes. The green reminding me of the pine trees surrounding his home —or was it *our* home now? It definitely felt like it.

"Yes, I'm ready." I smiled at him.

When he stepped closer, he brought his lips to mine and that bright light pulsed around us filling me with warmth and peace.

Blinking my eyes open, I had to squint against the harsh white light. It took me a moment to realize I was lying down and that every part of my body ached.

"Ah," I gasped, when the sharp pain in my skull ran through my head like a hot iron.

"Charlie!" Deacon's gruff voice sounded next to me.

I looked to my right and saw him, but he was different from just a few seconds ago. Now, he looked exhausted with blue circles under his eyes, his dark hair was disheveled. Even his normally close shaven beard had grown out, like he'd completely forgotten it was there.

"Deacon," I croaked, my throat suddenly very dry. The moment I said his name, my head felt like it was splitting again. I brought my hand up toward it, but Deacon grasped my hand gently and brought it to his lips.

"You have a bandage around your head, Sunshine. Do you remember what happened?"

Scrunching my brows at him, I leaned forward despite the pain and touched the side of his cheek. "I heard you."

His head pulled back slightly as his jaw went slack. "You heard me?"

I nodded, then instantly regretted it as another bolt of pain shot through my head.

"When I was asleep, I heard you tell me about your friends. The ones you served with in the military."

"You heard me," he repeated, shock written all over his face.

"You brought me back, Deacon. I was lost in that place for so long—just wandering around. I didn't think I'd ever see the light again, but then you were there. I heard your voice."

Tears gathered in his eyes as he cusped my hand and kissed it over and over.

I felt my own eyes well with moisture as I said, "I felt that thread between us pull taut. It was so beautiful," I whispered. "Like a bright blue light and when I turned around, you were there. Telling me it was time to come home."

"You came back to me," he husked, opening my hand and placing my palm against his cheek. "You came back."

"For you. Always for you." Tugging on his hand, I brought him closer to me. With gentle hands, he scooped me into a hug and ran his fingers up and down my spine.

To be in his arms again…that's when I let the dam of emotions break loose. My shoulders shuddered as I cried into his chest. Not caring that my head was still splitting because nothing else mattered except for this. Being with him again. Knowing that his walls had finally come down and he was mine. Just as I had always been his.

We stayed like that until my body ached too badly for me to sit up anymore. As he carefully leaned me back against the bed, he pressed the alert button for the nurse to come in.

When he settled into his chair again, his fingers intertwined with mine.

To our left, the door swung open and two people in scrubs walked in. "Look who's awake!" The woman in purple scrubs smiled widely at me.

"Sherry is one of your nurses," Deacon whispered to me, giving my hand a squeeze.

"And I'm Dr. Schneider." The man in the long white coat raised a hand in greeting. "It's good to meet you, Ms. Banks."

"Thank you," I said as he moved closer to the bed and Sherry took a look at the monitors on my IV machine.

"Did Mr. Calhoun fill you in on everything that's happened?"

I looked to Deacon and flashes of the accident flooded my mind. I winced when I remembered the car exploding, then being in the back of Deacon's truck.

"I was in a car accident. Deacon saved me." I shifted my gaze back to Dr. Schneider. "How long have I been out?"

Dr. Schneider glanced at Deacon, then his dark eyes settled on me. "Five days total."

"Five days?!" I gasped, feeling that dagger-like pain to my head again as I whipped my neck to the side, facing Deacon. "Casper?"

He chuckled. "I admit, it was Sherry who prompted me to remember the little rascal was at home. I was so lost in my worry over you. But he's just fine. I've been checking on him every morning and night."

"You've been here with me the whole time?"

"You didn't think there was a chance in hell I wasn't going to be by your side through this, did you?"

My heart stuttered at his admission, but then again, I'd known all along that Deacon was my safe haven. "No, actually," I laughed.

"That's my girl."

Dr. Schneider cleared his throat and Deacon and I looked at him. "Now that you're awake, there's some more testing I want to do before I send you home."

Home.

Yes. That's exactly where I wanted to be.

And in a lot of ways, I already knew I was home because Deacon was right by my side.

Chapter 30

Charlie

"Charlie! What do you mean you were in a car accident? Are you alright, honey? What happened?" My mother's shrill voice sang down the line as Deacon drove us home.

"Mom, calm down. I'm fine."

"Fine?! How can you be fine if you were just released from the hospital?"

I looked at Deacon who gave me a sympathetic shrug of his shoulders. When I'd woken up, he'd told me that his plan was to give me one more day to wake up before he called my parents. He said he didn't know how to tell them about the accident and hoped he wouldn't have to explain that I was officially in a coma.

One day shy. That's how close it had been.

Any longer and my brain injury would have been classified as a coma.

I couldn't shake the shiver that ran down my spine. Especially when my mind wandered to what might have happened if Deacon wouldn't have found me in my car when he did.

"They wouldn't have released me from the hospital if I wasn't fine, Mom."

There was a momentary pause like that fact made her think. "Just tell us what happened, sweetheart," my dad chimed in—always the calmer voice of reason when my mom was freaking out.

So, I spent nearly the rest of the ride home explaining the accident and telling them how Deacon pulled me from the car right before it exploded.

"He saved you?" My mother's voice was barely a whisper. "Again?"

I rolled my eyes as Deacon chuckled.

"Mom, you don't need to give him a bigger head than he already has."

When Deacon rose an eyebrow at me, I knew his thoughts had strayed to the gutter. I punched him in the arm, and he feigned pain.

"It sounds like you've found quite the catch, sweetheart."

A smile split my lips. "I think so too, dad."

"Well, I'm not so sure," my mom said. "Why didn't he call us as soon as you were in the hospital?"

"Do you want to answer that one?" I bit my lip trying not to laugh as I brought the phone closer to Deacon.

His hands gripped firmer on the steering wheel as he adjusted himself in the seat. A blush crept up his neck.

He was nervous.

My big tough, grumpy as hell, man was *nervous*.

I giggled and his eyes narrowed on me again.

"It won't happen again, ma'am. I can assure you that," he finally said. I could tell he was holding his breath, waiting for my mother's response.

The line was quiet, and I knew she was just letting time go by to make him sweat. Dad had always been the softy while my mother was the over-protective dragon who would roar at anyone she thought did wrong by me.

"Let's just hope there won't be a next time," she finally said, and Deacon's shoulders sagged with relief.

"Agreed." He nodded even though she couldn't see him.

"Alright you two, we're pulling up the Deacon's place now. I'll give you a call a little later, okay?"

"Okay, honey! We love you!"

"Love you, sweetheart!"

"Love you too," I said before tapping the red button on the screen to end the call.

"Well, that went better than I expected." I let a whoosh of breath out as I gingerly shifted in my seat to face Deacon as he pulled down the gravel driveway. There wasn't a muscle in my body that didn't still feel tender, and my head had a dull ache to it, but I was thankful that I got away with moderate injuries. It could have been much, much worse.

"You're telling me. I thought they were going to get in their car and come steal you away from me."

I snorted. "It was a smart move not to call them while I was unconscious. I wouldn't have wanted them to worry for no reason."

Deacon's green eyes slid over to me. "No reason? I hardly call seven stitches to the forehead and a major concussion, no reason."

"Awe, don't go all over-protective alpha man on me now. I'm totally fine." His tires hit a pothole in the road, making my body jostle against the seat belt. "Agh," I winced as the belt tightened against my ribs.

Deacon slowed down to a snail's pace, then eyed me again. "Totally fine. Right." His lips pursed.

I rubbed his forearm and winked at him. "Just a little sore. That's all."

"Mmhmm," he grumbled.

My heart lifted when his house finally came into view. Even though the doctor only made me stay one more night after coming to, I'd missed this place. I couldn't wait to get inside and see Casper and spend the night snuggled on the sofa in front of a warm fire.

"Stay here," Deacon said as he put the truck in park. "Let me get the door."

"Deacon, I can get my own door." It was my turn to grumble.

"As long as you ride with me, no, you can't." Leaning in, he placed a kiss on my temple then got out and headed toward my side. He hadn't kissed me—truly kissed me— since I'd woken up. I was damn near starving for the man, but I knew we had some things to discuss first.

I just hoped we could get it over quickly so I could jump his bones.

He opened my door and helped me out of the truck.

"Are you okay?" he asked once my feet were firmly on the ground.

He still held onto my forearm though, to steady me. "Yes, thank you." I looked into his face and wanted so badly to run my lips along his jaw and my fingers through his hair. I just wanted *him*.

We walked slowly to the front porch and that's when I noticed something was different. "Oh my gosh!" I gasped. "Deacon, you finished the bench!"

To the right of the door was the wooden bench I'd fallen in love with, but the vine and orchid detailing along the back was complete and the entire piece had been stained. It was the most beautiful piece of woodwork I'd ever seen.

As I moved closer toward it to take in all the fine details, Deacon said, "I know how much you liked it. I wanted you to have something nice to come home to."

Come home to.

My stomach tightened as I turned around to face him. *Home.* I wondered if he understood the impact his words were having on me. The weight they carried in my heart.

"You did this for me?" I swallowed the knot in my throat. He stepped so close, I had to tilt my head back to look up at him.

My eyes fluttered closed when his knuckles ran down my cheek and his thumb brushed along the edge of my jaw. I could live a thousand lifetimes, and it would mean nothing if I never got to feel his touch again.

When I opened my eyes, I saw something shift in his

gaze. Recognition, perhaps, of exactly what his touch did to me.

"Seeing you in that hospital bed wrecked me, Sunshine. I… I almost lost it. Finishing the bench was for you, yes, but I think I needed something to put my energy into. I thought that if I had something waiting for you… I don't know. It sounds stupid now, but I thought it might help bring you back to me."

Rising to my tip toes, I kissed his cheek. "I think it worked, Grumps."

He huffed a breath before sliding his arms around my waist, pulling me close. "Can we get a new nickname for me?"

"Mmm," I hummed, then shook my head. "No."

He scoffed. "No? When we start going out and seeing people in town, I don't want them to think I'm some asshole."

Stepping out of his embrace, my hand slid down his arm until I reached his hand. Our fingers intertwined and I led him to the front door. "No one will think you're an asshole just because I call you Grumps. You've been in Pebble Brook Falls for a long time, Deacon. I'm pretty sure everyone already knows the kind of man you are."

He tugged on my hand, whirling me around in a circle until I landed against his chest. There was nothing but pure affection in his eyes as he gripped my chin between his thumb and forefinger. "And what kind of man am I?"

"Fishing for compliments?"

"Only from the woman I love."

I stopped moving. My heartbeat soared to an unimaginable rate as my gaze danced back and forth between those pine green eyes that were now sparkling with joy.

"You love me?"

"I know that we still have a lot to figure out together, Charlie, but…" He exhaled a long breath, and I knew his thoughts had strayed to the accident. A shiver ran down my spine as a fiery image watered my vision. "I didn't want to wait another second without you knowing how I feel about you."

His face came into full view, and I was wrecked. Completely and totally destroyed by the beauty of him. Yes, he was the most handsome man I'd ever seen with his strong jaw, inky black hair and irises so green they reminded me of the warmth of summer in the dead of winter.

But there was more. Lingering beneath the surface. Deacon had spent his entire adult life sacrificing himself—his own safety—for others. He'd saved my life, on more than one occasion now. While there was darkness in his past, I knew he was trying. He was trying for *me*.

Rising onto my tip toes, I ran my hands over the top of his head until my forearms draped over his shoulders. Then, I looked into those unworldly eyes and said, "I love you too."

His entire body shuddered against mine, like he was shedding his demons right before my eyes. And when he brought his lips to mine there was no more reservation. No more uncertainty simmering beneath the surface. He was mine. Completely mine.

The kiss was gentle—achingly tender. Like we had all the time in the world to explore one another.

"Say it again." His words were a whisper over my mouth.

I smiled. "I love you."

The moan that escaped him as he brought me closer had my toes curling in my boots.

"I love you," I said again before claiming his lips with mine.

His hands dove into my hair as I ran my tongue along the edge of his bottom lip. I wanted to taste every single part of him. Not leaving a single stone unturned. When his tongue met mine, I hummed into his mouth. He was so warm and tasted so good.

"I want you, Deacon. Right now."

Tck, tck, tck.

We both looked behind me and saw Casper's furry little face peeking out through the blinds next to Deacon's front door.

"Having me might have to wait a little longer, Sunshine."

"Casper!" I whirled around to look at Deacon again. Not a single edge of shadows haunted his face. He beamed at me, in all his glory.

"Come on, let's go see the little rascal." Deacon led me inside where Casper was meowing louder than I'd ever heard him meow before.

Kneeling to the floor, tears filled my eyes as he hopped into my lap and started giving me head bumps.

"Hi, buddy. I missed you so much!" He sounded like a

little motorboat when I brought him into my arms and snuggled him close.

"We had a pretty good time together," Deacon said as he knelt beside us. "But there's nothing quite like having you back home."

There was that word again. *Home.*

He said it like I wasn't supposed to move back into the tiny cabin. He said it like I was meant to be here, in his house with him. Forever.

It made my heart stumble as I looked at him. There were so many things we needed to discuss. But they could all wait. I'd made it back safely and I had both of my boys by my side.

Deacon got a fire going in the hearth. It still amazed me how much I loved sitting by a crackling fireplace after having nearly died *twice* by fire.

I guessed there was just something different about my brain. Something that allowed me to move on quickly and I was thankful for that because this was exactly where I wanted to be. Snuggled up close to Deacon on the couch with Casper by our feet. The flames cast shadowed light over the dark living room, and it was perfect.

But I was about to ruin it.

"Are you ready to talk about it?" I curled a little closer to

Deacon. His gaze shifted from the hearth to me, and he nodded.

Swallowing the lump in my throat, I hesitated. Not wanting to disturb the peace we'd found together. But I also knew this was something we needed to talk about so we could leave it behind us.

He looked at me expectantly. I could tell he wanted me to start us off.

"I could hear you. When I was asleep. Not everything came through clearly, but I knew that you were telling me about your fallen brothers. I could...*feel* your words like a warm light dancing along my skin."

Deacon's Adam's apple bobbed, and he sat up a little straighter. "I'd heard about it once. How talking to people while they're unconscious can help stimulate their brains. Much like playing music or talking to a baby in the womb. When I saw you in that hospital bed, I knew the only way I could bring you back to me was to let my walls down. I needed to change everything I was before. I needed to be better for you."

I placed my hand over his and rubbed my thumb along his skin.

"You're the first person I've ever told about them."

My heart swelled with his admission. This was a huge step for Deacon. I knew that. And somehow, it felt like a step we were always meant to take together. Sharing the darkest parts of ourselves. The worries and fears that gripped us so strongly, we had to pull away for them to let go of us.

"I want you to know that I will always walk by your side,

Deacon. No matter what darkness you face, I will be right there with you."

He brought his forehead to mine. "I know that now. For so long I thought I had to carry the burden by myself. But you've shown me that it's okay to ask for help. It's okay to let someone in."

Tears welled in my eyes. I grazed his lips with mine in a feather-light kiss. "I'm so glad you let me in. This"—I placed my hand over his heart—"is where I want to be. Always."

Reaching up, he placed his hand over mine then threaded his fingers through my hair and pulled me into a kiss that had my entire body tingling. His tongue moved over the seam of my lips. I let him in, relishing in the warmth that flooded my lower stomach.

"You saved me, Charlie," he whispered.

I looked into those mesmerizing eyes, knowing a lifetime of gazing into them wouldn't be enough. "We saved each other."

Epilogue

One Month Later

DEACON

"You know I can just keep my eyes closed right?" I asked Charlie as she stood on her tiptoes, giving her best attempt of covering my eyes with her hands.

"I know you'll peek."

I raised a brow, and I felt the tiny hairs brush against her open palm. "I'm no surprise ruiner."

"Mmhmm," she hummed. "Says the man I could barely keep away from this place all month!"

"I was only trying to break in because I missed you." It was the truth. Aside from the flooring renovations I'd had done after the burst pipe was fixed, Charlie had spent count-less hours painting away in the tiny cabin. We'd decided together that her moving back in wasn't the right play. We both wanted the other close and given how quickly things were progressing between us, her and Casper staying with me made the most sense.

That didn't stop her from wanting to turn Badger Creek Cabin into a little getaway space for us and anyone else who needed it.

Her giggle broke through my thoughts as she started to lead me through the front door. "I missed you too! But this had to be done. It was calling to me and I can't wait for you to see it."

"Me too, Sunshine."

Having her maneuver me through the small space was a clusterfuck to say the least. But by the end, she got me to the edge of the kitchen counter where I could stop tripping over her tiny feet.

"Ready?" she squealed with excitement.

"Let's see this thing," I responded.

"Okay! Open your eyes!"

It took a few blinks for my eyes to adjust to the space, but once they did my jaw went slack in awe of what Charlie had created. Months ago, she'd started on the far wall, turning it into a misty scene of the cabin's backyard.

Now, the entire interior space made me feel like I was outside.

She'd continued the scene of pine trees on the back wall, bringing it along the space next to the bed. Then the painting transitioned to a field of tall grass with hazy gray skies over rolling hills, just like the ones throughout my property. It was a perfect replica and somehow it looked even better than the real thing. Whimsical, like I was in a dreamland that seemed overwhelmingly perfect. As I continued turning, the sky she'd painted started to brighten until I looked back at the front door we'd come through and saw the view of a sunrise. Soft hues of purple, red and orange melded together in such a way that I found myself losing my breath at the sight.

"Charlie," I whispered, bringing her in close. "This is magnificent."

"You like it?" She sounded unsure.

I looked down at her, grasped her chin between my fingers then kissed her lips. "It's the second most beautiful thing I've ever seen in my life."

"What's the first?" She batted her long auburn lashes at me while a hint of a smirk danced at the corner of her mouth.

"I think we both know the answer to that question."

She rolled her eyes at me. "Yeah, but I want to hear you say it, Grumps."

I lifted her onto the kitchen counter and groaned as she wrapped her legs around my waist. "What did we talk about? Grumps is out. I need a new nickname."

She leaned forward and tugged at my bottom lip with her teeth. The sensation had my cock flexing against my jeans. "I might be persuaded with some kisses."

I chuckled. "Is that right?"

"Mmhmm!" She nodded, biting her own bottom lip.

"What about here?" I dipped my head low and kissed the crook between her neck and shoulder. Goosebumps rose along her skin and some feral part of me loved watching her come undone from my touch.

"Nope." Her lips popped on the p.

"Hmm." Narrowing my eyes on her, I reached for her hand and lifted her wrist to my mouth, pressing my lips just over her pulse. "Here?"

Lust filled her gaze as she shook her head.

"I think we need to go lower then." Kneeling in front of her, I lifted the pale pink sweater she wore revealing the edges of her scar. I kissed the raised skin, no longer feeling the heavy weight of guilt bear down on me at the sight of it.

"What about now?"

She leaned back on her hands and said, "Just a little lower handsome and you've got a deal."

I huffed a breath. "Oh, I think I can manage that. Lift your hips for me, beautiful." She did as she was told, and I made quick work of her jeans button and zipper before sliding her pants down to her ankles.

A lace baby blue thong was the only thing standing between me and her sweetness. "Always wearing the prettiest things for me." I ran my thumbs along the edge of the lace.

Her legs' grip on my waist tightened. "Stop teasing me, Grumps and give me what I want."

"Feeling feisty, are we?" I cocked a brow at her.

"Only when my man denies me pleasure."

I nipped at the sensitive flesh of her inner thigh, and she yelped. "Oh, there's no denying here, Sunshine. You might want to hold tight onto the edge of the counter."

I watched as she laid all the way down on the counter and

raised her arms above her head so she could grip the edge behind her.

"That's my girl," I whispered against the tiny triangle of fabric covering her sex. Hooking my finger into the side, I ran the fabric back and forth over her clit. As her head tilted back and she released a moan, I knew the friction was just enough to get her riled up.

"I love seeing you come undone for me, baby girl. Love watching your pretty little lips part so I can hear your breathy moans. Fuck. It makes my cock so damn hard."

"Never mind," she breathed. "No kisses. Just you."

"Already begging for it." I leaned over the counter and sucked her bottom lip into my mouth, then released it. "You know what that does to me."

The blue of her eyes were glassy with lust. "Please, Deacon. I want you to fuck me."

Leaning my head back until the ceiling came into view, I damn near came in my pants just from the sound of her sultry plea.

Straightening, I unclasped my belt buckle and had my pants undone faster than ever before. My cock felt heavy as I released it from my boxers, and I saw Charlie glancing down at me.

Her tongue darted between her lips. It demolished the last thread of control I had. I wanted to bury myself so deep inside of her until the only thing I could feel was her body surrounding mine.

I slipped her thong down her legs, letting them fall to the floor. Running my thumb over her pink clit, I said, "I'm going to make you come so hard. I want to hear you scream my fucking name. Do you understand?"

The corners of her mouth tilted upward as she nodded. Taking my length in my hand, I slapped the tip against her pussy.

"Tell me you want it."

"I want your cock. I want you to fuck me hard, baby."

It was all I needed to hear as I lined myself up at her entrance, then slid my hands over her breasts and slammed into her.

She cried out. Her lips forming that perfect little o that I loved so damn much.

"Hold on," I coaxed, seeing that her hands had slipped from the counter.

Once she had the edge gripped again, I pulled all the way out, teasing her entrance with the head of my cock. Then I pushed into her, nearly making myself see stars as she contracted against me.

"Deacon!"

"I know, baby girl. It's. So. Fucking. Good."

Her breasts bounced as I rolled my hips against her over and over again. There was no controlling my thrusts as wild lust took hold, consuming every part of me. It was a frenzy, chasing after the blissful sensation that only *she* could give me, but not wanting to go too fast and have it be over.

But then, I realized, she was *mine*. And I could have her any time I pleased. Never having to think again of what it might be like to watch her leave. That thread between us pulsed as I buried myself deep inside of her, leaning forward again to cover her chest with mine.

I rolled my hips forward, meeting the apex of her thighs again. "Kiss me, baby girl," I whispered, hovering my lips just above hers. I wanted her to claim me. To take everything she needed. To come completely undone beneath me.

Letting go of the counter edge, she wrapped her arms around me, threading her fingers through my hair as she sealed her mouth to mine. Her tongue was warm, and the sweet smell of vanilla wafted around me as she started moving her hips in tandem with my thrusts.

"So needy for my cock. So fucking ready for it. Always."

"You feel so good," she murmured. "I love you." She placed a hand over my heart. "I love *this*."

Emotion swelled in my chest, making my entire body tingle as I slowed my pace. I was nearing dangerously close to the edge and wasn't ready to tip over. I wanted her to fall with me.

"I love you, Sunshine. I love you with every broken piece of me." I pulled out, then pushed slowly into her again.

"Not broken." She grasped the sides of my face and kissed along the edge of my jaw. "Not anymore."

I buried my face into the crook of her shoulder, sliding my hands beneath her head, holding her as close as I could. Her grip around my shoulders tightened as I moved inside of her, rolling my hips forward again.

My legs shook with how good it felt to be this close to her. It was other-worldly. Like falling into one of her paintings. The most beautiful moments of my life had been with her, and I knew there was a lifetime to go. Of her shedding her light everywhere, we ventured together.

I could see it all.

That whatever darkness came our way, I'd be okay with her by my side.

"Deacon, I'm…"

"I've got you, baby." Keeping her close, I picked up the pace, making sure to press myself against her clit to give her the friction she needed. "I've got you."

I felt her tighten around my cock, sending me spiraling toward my climax. Holding her tight to my chest, I ran my teeth along her shoulder, nipping and suckling on the sensitive curve of her skin.

Her back arched and her body quivered as she screamed my name. Just in time for me to find my own release. Sinking deeper into her with one final thrust, I roared my love for her before collapsing forward.

Our breaths were heavy, her chest pushing into mine with each inhale as we just laid still together. After a few moments passed, I rose to my forearms, hovering just above her.

"You're incredible." I pressed a kiss to each one of her cheeks and she smiled.

"Get used to it, handsome. I'm sticking around for a while."

My eyes darted back and forth between hers, as I tried to imprint every shade of blue of her irises into my memory.

"How about forever?" My voice was thick, but I stayed focused on her.

A lock of hair fell into her face as she tilted her head to the side, her smile growing wider. "Forever's a pretty long time. You sure you're up for that?"

I rubbed my nose against her chin then gave her a chaste kiss.

"Forever won't be long enough," I said, meaning every single word.

She wrapped her arms around me again, pulling me in close until her breath tickled the cuff of my ear. "Forever won't be long enough."

CHARLIE

There was a touch of warmth to the breeze this morning. Not that it stopped me from making more hot chocolate.

Steam rolled over the edge of the mug as I tucked my legs under myself, resting my elbow on the armrest of the bench Deacon had finished for us.

The front door to our home creaked open, Casper's white fur caught my eye as he darted out with Deacon following right behind him.

Stopping in front of me, he leaned down and pressed a kiss to my lips. "Feeling inspired today?" he asked.

I looked out over the tall pine trees, seeing the tops wave

back and forth in the wind. I nodded as he sat down next to me, placing an arm over the back of the bench.

"I think we both are from all the ruckus I heard coming from the garage. How's the armoire coming?"

He stole my mug of hot cocoa and took a sip. "It's going to be a pain in the ass to move to the gallery, but I'm really proud of it. The oak tree carvings are turning out pretty great."

I settled into his side. Being close to him would never get old.

"So, you're really on board for this thing?" I peeked up at him. "Opening the gallery with me."

He settled his stunning green eyes on me. My heart skipped a beat as that thread between us pulled taut.

"It'll be our next great adventure, Sunshine."

I smiled.

Because it certainly was.

Bonus Epilogue

Five Months Later

CHARLIE

Sunshine & Co was written in large swirling letters above the barn-like structure that Deacon and I found just a few minutes from downtown Pebble Brook Falls right at the end of winter. Renovating the space had become our pet project. It had consumed us most days, but now that it was finally complete and we were about to cut the ribbon for the grand opening, I felt nostalgic.

I missed the days when we had the space to ourselves, and we got to create something together. *Sunshine & Co* had been our love child, bringing us even closer together. Originally, Deacon thought it would be a great investment for me to have a gallery we owned together to display my artwork. But I'd convinced him that it was time he shared his own art with the world.

"What's going on in that pretty head of yours?" Deacon's arms slipped around my waist from behind me. Closing my eyes, I let myself settle into his firm body. He always felt like home. With him here, my spirits were immediately lifted.

I laid my head back on his chest and looked up at the space. "Just wishing we had a little more time before the grand opening."

His lips tickled the cuff of my ear. "Sunshine, the grand opening is in an hour. It's a little too late to go back now."

Twisting in his arms, I looked up into those pine green eyes. They were so bright and lovely; I couldn't help but smile. "I know. I just miss building it all with you. Now that it's over…I don't know. I find myself wanting to do it all over again."

"It was a special time." His hand moved up and down my back.

I nodded.

"This opening will be just as special. All our friends are coming to celebrate us and what we've built together. And once we've settled into it for a little while, we can start talking about our next big adventure."

I raised my eyebrows. "Really?!"

His laughter sent goosebumps down my arms. He laughed so often these days. But I still didn't take it for granted.

"Yes." He kissed my cheek and pulled me close to him. "But right now, we should soak in this moment. You've worked hard for it."

"We both have," I whispered against his chest.

"Why don't we go inside and check it out one last time before everyone gets here."

"Okay."

Deacon interlaced his fingers with mine and opened the large oak door. As we strode inside, pride swelled in my chest at what we'd accomplished together. The large space had giant industrial windows that framed all four walls. Thick beams of oak wood lined the ceiling, giving it that rustic outdoor feel that was vital to the artwork Deacon and I would showcase. At the center of the room, there were four manufactured squares. All of them were a pristine white with art lights to display each one of my pieces.

I could still feel the ache in my palms and fingers from painting so much over the past several weeks. Once Deacon and I had decided to lease the space, a flurry of inspiration had struck both of us. When we weren't snuggled on the couch together or hanging out with our friends, we'd spend countless hours creating.

It was the life I'd always wanted. Parts of it illuminating things I didn't even know were possible. Like having a partner who shared in my passion of creating and how important it was to have someone who understood me in that way.

Sliding my hand into the back pocket of Deacon's jeans, I leaned into him. "I still can't believe we did all of this in four months."

"I know. I'm pretty sure I slept more when I was deployed than I have since we leased this place."

I peeked up at him, in complete awe of how much he'd come out of his shell since the accident.

We didn't talk about his demons often. Doing so didn't feel as necessary as it had before because he'd come into the light on his own. But when he did share little things with me, like he just did, it meant a lot. Understanding the weight of his past was something I'd had to grow into as well. Knowing when to push and ask more questions and when he just needed me to listen or give him his space.

"What?" he asked when he realized I was staring at him.

I shrugged. "Just thinking about how beautiful you are."

He whirled me into a spin before hugging me close to his chest. "Beautiful huh?"

"Yup," I snickered.

"Hm. Well, just don't go telling the guys that you think I'm beautiful. They'll give me hell for days."

"But it's the truth." I curled my fingers through his dark hair.

"Can't we go with ruggedly handsome? Or hot and smoldering?"

My chest bumped his as I laughed. "Smoldering? Isn't that just the Rock's thing? You know, from the new *Jumanji* movies."

"Never seen them. But he doesn't get to claim it all for himself. I can smolder too."

"Is that right?" I pulled back, putting my hands on my hips. "Let's see it then."

"Okay." Deacon took a few steps back and rounded his

shoulders. Twisting his neck, he turned his head away from me so I couldn't see what face he was making.

Clapping my hands, I did a little count down for him. "Three! Two! One!"

With another twist of his neck, he swung his face toward me. His eyes were narrowed into slits, with his right eyebrow arched high. But what had me bursting out laughing was the way he pushed his lips out, giving old school influencer duck lips vibes.

"Oh my god!" I bent over, hands on my knees, barely able to catch my breath from the laughter. "Never make that face again."

He threw his hands in the air. "Was it not smoldering enough for you?!"

Straightening, I placed a hand on my aching belly as I gasped for a breath. "Let me just say that if you ever do that in front of the guys, they will disown you. Honestly…if you ever do that again, I might disown you too."

"You would never," he husked as he strode toward me.

I squealed as he caught me in his arms and leaned back until my feet were off the ground. "You love me too much."

I chuckled. "That might be true."

Setting my feet back on the ground, his hand wove into my hair. A frenzy of butterflies swarmed my stomach as his thumb grazed over my bottom lip. "Your laughter is still my favorite sound in the world."

"And yours is mine," I breathed against his lips before he kissed me. Sparks jutted through my body all the way down to my toes. The kiss was tender and sweet, a reminder of the love we shared.

It was just one version of us though.

I knew what happened behind closed doors. Just the thought of it had my toes curling in my boots. We were an ombré of colors on a canvas. The bright white light of love that transcended into a beautifully sensual darkness. With *him* I got to be everything I needed to be.

As our lips parted the alarm on my cell phone rang. Taking it out of my back pocket, I showed the reminder on the screen to Deacon.

"Only thirty minutes until everyone arrives. EEK! I'm so nervous now!"

Deacon smiled at me without abandon. The look of him had me feeling dizzy. "No need to be nervous, sunshine. Everyone's going to love it."

"Oh my gosh! Charlie! This is incredible!" Willow exclaimed as she took me into her arms and squeezed me tight.

"Thank you so much!" I said as she rubbed her hand up and down my back in greeting before we pulled apart.

About a month after the accident, Deacon had finally let me out of our love bubble to meet up with his friends.

Willow and her new husband, Johnny, had just made it back into town from their extended honeymoon and we'd become fast friends. We both connected over art as she was a fashion designer and created a lot of her own pieces.

"I still can't believe it's real. I never would have imagined myself being the kind of girl who did spontaneous things on the regular, but after finishing the gallery, I honestly can't wait for Deacon and I's next project."

"I don't blame you!" She looked around with wonderment shining in her blue eyes. "It must have felt so good seeing your vision come to life."

"It definitely did."

Bark! Bark!

Willow and Johnny's dog Asher came barreling through the door as Johnny strode in behind him. Kneeling, Asher almost knocked me off my heels as he dove his head into my stomach in search of scratches.

"That's such a good boy, Asher! Such a good boy!" I scratched him behind his ears and along his spine until his body shook.

"Careful now. You don't want Casper to think you've betrayed him," Johnny said as he wrapped his arm around Willow's waist.

I didn't have to look behind me to know that Deacon had walked up. "Oh, he will most certainly feel betrayed."

"Don't say that." I turned around and pouted at him. "You're going to make me feel bad."

Warmth seeped into me as he tugged me into his side and

whispered, "I'll give him extra cuddles to make up for your indiscretion. Don't worry."

I elbowed him in the ribs. "*OOF*," he grunted, making me giggle.

"Y'ALL! This is amazing!" Sarah's high-pitched squeal permeated the space as she darted through the door Ranger held open for her. We collided into a tight hug and warmth spread through my chest as we tilted each other side-to-side.

"I'm so glad you're here!" I said to her as we pulled back and looked at one another. Her dark eyes were crinkled along the sides from her wide smile.

"Hey, brother, it's good to see you." Ranger clasped Deacon's hand before pulling him into a bro hug.

"You too, I'm glad you two were able to make it out."

"Are you kidding me? We wouldn't miss this for the world." Sarah gave Deacon a side hug.

"You want to give us a tour?" Johnny asked.

"Yeah, let's start over here."

I hung back for a moment, watching as Deacon led our friends to the right side of the space where my first art installation held the painting I'd made of *Badger Creek Cabin's* backyard. It hadn't taken very long for Deacon's friends to adopt me into their group. Now, I spoke to Sarah and Willow on a daily basis, and it felt *amazing* to have such wonderful people surrounding me.

In the weeks after my accident, I thought a lot about the time I was in the hospital after the fire and how difficult it had been to be abandoned by my friends. Honestly, it hurt worse than I let on.

But this moment—right here—healed my heart in such a profound way. When I'd left Charlotte, I knew I was in search of something. A place where I felt like I belonged. Watching the man of my dreams lead our friends around the space we'd created together, I knew this was where I was meant to be all along.

DEACON

"Where are you taking me?" Charlie asked as she slipped her hand into mine before we headed out the door. My truck bed was already filled with all the necessities we'd need for the little trip I had planned.

"Can't a man have his secrets?" I joked.

Charlie stopped in her tracks, forcing me to stop with her. Bees buzzed around my stomach when I turned to find her glowering at me. She was so damn feisty, my sunshine. Never letting me get away with anything.

"Not *that* kind of secret." I tucked her under my arm. "Geez, what kind of man do you take me for?"

"The kind of man who makes his woman suffer by not telling her what we're doing."

I chuckled. "I like to call that intrigue. Or keeping things spicy."

"Oh!" She perked right up. "So, this is a sexy time surprise."

She followed me down the steps of our front porch and when she moved in front of me, I gave her perfectly round peach a smack. "Only if you're a good girl."

She spun around, her fire red hair whipping across her shoulders as she said, "I'm always a good girl." Then she winked at me before sashaying her hips all the way to the fucking truck.

Tilting my head back, I got a sobering look at the summer sky and moaned. "She's going to be the end of me."

"Come on, grumps! This door isn't going to open itself." When I looked over at her, she had a hand on her hip as she eyed me with a mischievous glint. My woman was independent as all get out, but she knew I loved opening doors for her. It was the small gestures, showing her acts of service that made me feel good.

Striding over to her, I pressed a kiss to her temple before opening the door. When she hopped in, I rounded the hood of my truck and sat in the driver's seat next to her.

"You ready?" I asked.

She nodded enthusiastically.

"Good, because I've been wanting to do this for a long time."

"I still can't believe you own all this property. I mean, I knew you owned it, but seeing all of it is just incredible." The awe in Charlie's voice had my chest swelling with pride. She'd come to Pebble Brook Falls in search of a sanctuary. She'd wanted to get away from the concrete jungle and find a place that called to her soul. The fact that *I* was able to provide that place for her…it was the greatest accomplishment of my life.

"I'm glad you like it, Sunshine."

She snuggled up to my side as I crested the top of a hill on our drive back to the house. "I love it."

Turning the steering wheel, I positioned the truck until the bed was facing west. Right where I wanted it.

"What're you doing?"

I looked down at Charlie, her crystalline blue eyes shining with wonder. "Getting your surprise ready."

"I thought showing me all of the property was my surprise."

"It is, but you haven't seen the best part yet."

"EEK!" She clapped her hands together and I laughed. "Okay, now I'm excited."

Leaning over, I gave her a peck on the lips and said, "Stay here."

"Don't take too long!" she called out to me as I shut the door.

My heartbeat kicked up. This moment was finally happening, and she had no idea. Which, honestly, boggled my mind because the woman was damn near clairvoyant when it came to what I was thinking.

Unfolding the air mattress, I used the portable pump to blow it up before spreading the blanket and pillows over top of it. Rubbing my hands together, I patted my jeans pocket to make sure the ring was still there. It was, much to my relief.

"Okay, it's go time," I whispered to myself. Then, I rounded the back of the truck and opened Charlie's door.

She placed her hand in my extended one and hopped out. As soon as she looked over the bed of the truck, her face glowed with excitement.

"Deacon! This is so cute!"

I swallowed the knot in my throat. "I'm glad you like it. Let's get you settled in."

Placing my hands under her arms, I lifted her onto the tailgate of the truck before I hopped up myself and we both crawled onto the air mattress.

"This is what I wanted you to see." I pointed ahead of us where the sun was skimming the top of the tree line, hues of orange, red and purple painting the sky like one of Charlie's art pieces.

"Wow," Charlie whispered, breathlessly. "It's incredible."

"When I first moved here, I'd spend almost every night doing this. Finding random hills on my property to see which one had the best view of the sunset. It took a while, but this one…it's my favorite spot."

She settled her head on my chest. "I can see why. I don't think I've ever seen anything like this before."

"Well, I was hoping you'd spend your nights coming here with me… Forever…if you want to."

Charlie sat up and maybe it was the sunset or the fact that

I was about to ask her the most important question of my entire life, but she looked like an angel. The glow of the evening light haloed around her face, making her adorable freckles darken and her blue eyes shine. The sun gleamed in her hair, showing off all the shades of auburn and red. She was the most beautiful thing I'd ever seen in my life.

"Forever's an awfully long time, Grumps. Are you sure you're in for that?"

My hands were shaking like a leaf on a tree as I fumbled for the ring in my pocket. When I finally grasped it, I pulled it out and showed it to her. Those rosy lips that I loved so much popped open right before she covered them with her hands.

"Deacon," she breathed.

I willed my voice to be steady as I said, "Charlie, before you came into my life, I was a shell of a man. I was so haunted by my past that I had stopped living. All I wanted to do was be alone." I took her left hand in mine and stroked the top of it with my thumb.

"The moment I saw you, I couldn't breathe. Couldn't think. All I knew was that you were the most beautiful thing I'd ever laid my eyes on and if it took sacrificing my own life to get you out of that fire, I would have."

"Deacon—" Her eyes shuddered as she grasped my hand.

"I would have, Charlie. Because I love you. More than life itself, I love you. You brought me out of the darkness. You taught me how to laugh and smile again. You showed me that no matter what comes my way, I can survive it with you by my side."

Palming the side of her face, I brought my forehead to hers. "You saved me, Charlie. And it would be my greatest honor to have you as my wife. Will you marry me?"

Tears tipped over the rims of her eyes as she nodded. "Yes! Yes, I'll marry you!"

Blissful rays of light burst through my heart as her words sank in.

She was mine.

She was truly *mine*.

Forever.

I hugged her tight to my chest, the warm smell of vanilla wafting around me as I settled my face into the crook of her neck. Happiness flooded every cell in my body, it felt like I was fucking floating.

I was *so damn happy*. I thought my heart might burst from my chest.

"I love you!" Charlie exclaimed as she pulled back and captured my face in her hands. "I love you so much!"

I looked down and reached for her hand so I could make it official. Spreading her fingers wide, she watched as I slipped the ring onto her finger.

"Holy shit, Deacon! It's so pretty. Oh my god!"

"You like it?"

Her glassy eyes met mine. "It's perfect."

"Phew! I had Willow and Sarah help me pick it out because I didn't know what the hell I was doing."

We both laughed and when she smiled at me, the sunset as our background, I knew my brothers were here with me. Each one of them surrounding us with their light. Reminding me that, even in the darkest of times, there is always hope for a better day.

Be sure to check out the rest of the Pebble Brook Falls love stories! Hang out with Johnny + Willow in *If I Asked You to Stay* and Ranger + Sarah in *If You Loved Me.*

Also by Brianna Remus

Falling for You Trilogy

Dare to Fall

Dare to Need

Dare to Love

Pebble Brook Falls Series

If I Asked You to Stay

If You Loved Me

When You Saved Me

Stay in the Know!

With the ever changing landscape of social media, the best way to stay in the know about my upcoming releases is to subscribe to my newsletter. Becoming part of the subscriber family also gets you exclusive access to bonus scenes from my books that will never be released anywhere else!

Subscribe at www.briannaremus.com

About the Author

Brianna Remus is a Florida-based author who lives with her husband, three pups and terrorizing cat. A true romantic at heart, you can find her gazing at the stars, floating in the ocean, or reading a good HEA romance!

facebook.com/AuthorBriannaRemus

instagram.com/authorbriannaremus

bookbub.com/profile/brianna-remus

tiktok.com/@authorbriannaremus